DURHAM
TOLL HOUSE

By: Kev Fletcher

INTRODUCTION

The terror, which never truly ended, began as far back as 1798, with the building of the Toll House. Was the place evil? Probably. But when Victor Schafer arrived, with his band of gypsy nomads, it sunk into the depths of the abyss.

Schafer had a problem with Freemasons. Nothing personal, he just didn't like them. But he had an even bigger dislike of the Roman Catholic church. His main prey were high ranking priests, and given the opportunity, he would string them up on a gallows pole. But he wasn't happy with that. He would then hang their carcases in small cramped cages on North Road, where they rotted in full view of the city. A reminder to everyone that the Roman Catholic church was 'evil.'

He had his own disciples. But, in the end, they took their '30 pieces of silver' and did the same to him. Well, not quite the same. They strung him from the gallows, but kept him barely alive, then hung him up in one of their contraptions for all to see. He was kept him from death's door, fed on scraps of rotting meat and they doused him in water every morning ... just for the fun of it.

After three months, someone cut him down. Many people lay claim to having seen him dead, but his body disappeared soon after. Was that the end of Victor Schafer?

Perhaps those 'many people' told lies.

THANKS TO:-

Jan Yarrow for help and understanding in this venture. Taking me to Altea for research, and being the wonderful person she is.

Christine Hutchins for her knowledge of the English language and her encouragement throughout my writing. Often saying "I can't wait to find out what happens at the end," at a time when I didn't know myself.

Phil Woods for having climbed up the Obelisk (when drunk) and showing me how he did it (when sober).

Allison Brook and Anne Harrison for helping me with my research in Durham Library. I appreciate the time and effort you both put in helping me produce this book.

As always, my novels are about the north-east of England. My home, my heritage. I hope I do it justice.

COPYRIGHT

CHAPTER ONE

"WE ALL HAVE A STORY WE WILL NEVER TELL"

Seeing the Toll House for the first time was a bewildering surprise to me, as it appeared out of the semi-darkness, looking every inch as though it didn't want to be found. I was told it was little more than bricks and rubble, but there was far more to it than that. It was in ruin, and well beyond any form of renovation, but it still had a majesty that kept it alive … barely.

It hadn't been desecrated with graffiti, which was a 'positive', but it didn't really matter anyway because I was at that spot to issue the last rights. It was going to be demolished … whatever condition it was in.

The official line was that it had 'collapsed inwardly on itself', the roof crumbling along with it, and the whole structure was a 'death trap'. According to the notes I had been given, it had been uninhabited, and abandoned when the owner passed away back in the 1950's. But if it was classified as a danger, shouldn't someone have taken responsibility for it long before I was given the job?

Tucked away in the middle of a little copse of woodland, I assumed it remained anonymous for decades, until someone made a bid for the five acres of land it was stood on. It was at that moment there just happened to be a problem to be solved.

There I stood, the crows scalding me from up above, determined to chase me away from their colony of nests up high in the oak trees. And that building, or what was left of it, stood like a testament to a lost era. It gave me a spooky feeling, even in daylight, and that was rather sad because it was a home (rather than a state-run business) for most of its existence.

I noticed it had been visited recently as the long grass leading up to the door was trampled. Small footprints, obviously made by the local children who probably dared each other to go there in the twilight to search for ghosts. Who knows … perhaps they found them.

The main body of the house was rectangle in shape, with a turret 20 yards away that must have been linked to the property where horses and carriages had passed under. There were curved portions on the main building that looked like they once held ornamental towers, like a miniature castle.

The inside of the structure was covered in tiles, some of them stripped away in places to expose the wooden skeleton beneath. They must have been added to the house at a later date because they seemed so out of place with the original construction. None of the remaining windows were boarded up, but no glass survived, in the frame or on the ground. Yet for some reason the sun remained outside, seemingly refusing its invitation to peep inside, making it all the more mysterious.

The entire building looked as though it had been caught up in a severe storm where it had been lifted up off its foundations and then dropped from a great height. If there ever were happy times in that place, their memories were long gone. All I could sense was heartache and fear. It had history, in abundance, but I didn't sense any joyous vibe or blissful ambulance. I knew right from the start that building was a malignant scar that refused to heal.

Let me introduce myself - I am John Hampson. Property developer, of sorts, but better known in the trade for being a 'dog's body' to multi-millionaire business tycoon James Lawrence. And that is very much the truth, of it. I don't dislike the guy, far from it. I would only be half the man I am now if it was not for him. He dug me out of a hole when times were tough and self-esteem was low, and no-one should ever forget those with the courage and strength to change a person's life.

His words will always stay with me: "Confidence is not constantly asking yourself: 'Will they like me?' Confidence is saying: 'I couldn't care less if they don't!'"

Durham city is my home ... making money for Mr Lawrence is my life. It's that simple. There are very few rules to follow, and I don't think the guy is bothered if I make money or not, as long as I look as though I am, keep moving, and don't chalk up a loss!

One sunny day in May, we made a business transaction to buy a plot of land located at the north of the city of Durham, close to Wharton Park, which would be the perfect acreage for five lavish dwellings that would pull in 'top dollar'.

Influential businessmen from Japan were looking to buying properties close to the centre of the city, and Mr Lawrence saw the prospect of getting the buildings constructed within the year; slapping a couple of million price tag on each holding; and watch as his bank balance grew. Plus, he would have the benefit of having his most important clients sat right in his lap, in the city of 'The Prince Bishops'.

We couldn't believe our luck. The interest from the Japanese money men was intense, due mainly to the links with the Teikyo University which has its campus in the city. Such was the significance of our venture, the commerce sector were virtually forming a queue to put the money on the table … and the foundations for the buildings hadn't even been laid.

Even though the deal had been finalised and the ink was dry on the contract, I checked out the land for my own curiosity. A business meeting was called to tie up all the loose ends regarding removal of the structures and debris that needed to be disposed of, so we could clear the area ready for the builders to move in.

"It's prime property so why hasn't this land been snapped up before?" I asked.

"Well it's not really prime property as such," said Bill McCracken, our business advisor. "The location is perfect, it couldn't be better. But we have dug down and the top soil is sat on an old gravel pit, with a 90% chance there could also be coal-mine shafts below that. Probably thirty feet down. That isn't particularly worrying because we can fill in the holes, but half the acreage is wooded land built on a bog, and that will take some sorting. However, the main obstacle is a 90ft Grade II listed monument that sits on the edge of North Road."

"Yeah I saw that," I replied. "A Cleopatra's Needle-type structure. Where the hell did that come from? What's it supposed to signify?"

"As tall as it is, I don't think anyone knows it's there!" Bill replied. "Apart from standing right in front of it and actually touching the structure, it is completely hidden. It's not even located on half of the maps of the city. I think we could move it brick by brick and nobody would know it was gone."

"So why don't we do that?" James asked, seeing it as the most logical answer to the problem.

"Oh, don't think we haven't thought about it, James," said McCracken. "I put that plan to the council, suggesting we take it to Beamish Museum, but they insist it stays where it is. But it took the bastards three days to find out it truly existed! They thought I was winding them up. It wasn't on their council map so I had to show them photos to prove it wasn't a joke."

The company had experienced many shortcomings with Durham County Council, who were notorious for blocking any planning proposals, and anything else that needed approval. James believed it was a power struggle, implying the council did it simply because they could!

"They do it every time," James barked. "This is the council that spent two million pounds of tax payers money to move a bronze statue of a guy on a horse from Durham market place a mere twenty yards. Then, after moving it, the police told them they had blocked the access road to Silver Street, so they had to move it back! Two million pounds flushed down the pot! That doesn't include the cost of moving it back to where it originally came from. They don't have a brain cell amongst them."

I had looked at the land and although it was difficult terrain, apart from a drainage problem with the bog, there was nothing that a JCB couldn't handle. Cleopatra's Needle, or whatever it was, could very easily be moved, so long as we had authorization.

I explained the logistics of the site and the approach to the plot: "There is access from Albert Street at the rear, so we won't need to get permission to close North Road to move in the big machinery. It should be plain sailing," I said, circling the entrance in bold pen on the already ink-stained map.

"What about the Toll House?" said James, "Can someone check it out? The church, who we bought the land off, want it to remain. They cannot actually slap a preservation order on it, but they can go to people who can. But, for the sake of common sense, we need it levelled."

"I've been, James," I replied. "I went this morning. It's a ruin, and it won't take much effort to remove it. But its about 70 yards from the road, strategically out of place. I thought the whole point of a tollgate was to take taxes from people as they passed through on the main road. It's the right shape, built for it's purpose, but not in the right place."

"They must have moved the road, then. Obviously!" chipped in Bill in his usual dramatic manner. Always a man to get my hackles up without him even trying. Ex-army, he thinks the country owes him a pat on the back, when the closest he got to a tour of duty was two weeks manoeuvres in the Cyprus hills with the Territorial Army. He was a pen-pusher in the T.A., doing what he does best, letting others do the dirty work. I never liked the man, and that sentiment crept out on occasions.

"It's still standing, but only just," I said. "More rubble than actual structure. But if it's a listed building, where do we stand on that?" I asked, thinking it was a perfectly reasonable question.

"You can't officially 'list' a pile of bricks, can you? For God's sake, man," said the gentleman pushing the pen.

Perhaps it wasn't as reasonable a question as I thought.

"OK, if it's only rubble, what is there to check out?" I asked. "Let's just move it!"

James interrupted our argument: "The church claims it could be a significant historical building. Mine shafts were not logged or mapped in early Victorian times and the mining companies dug willy-nilly for coal wherever they felt it may lie. Some records suggest the miners came across a tunnel linking the Toll House to various locations in the city, including Durham Cathedral. There was no 100% guarantee that they ever existed, because rumours of secret exit tunnels from the Cathedral were common place throughout the centuries, yet none were ever found. Certainly none that got beyond 100 yards. The Toll House is the other side of the city, two miles away! Exit tunnels may have been built in day's of conflict but they must have been filled in. But this theory from the church that there could be one will be a disaster if the council find out. Any business opportunity and the council will jump on it. Next they will be organizing day trips down tunnels and grant McDonald's permission to build a 24 hour drive-in. I want to know, what lies beneath the Toll House? Get a digger in, John, and see what you can find. If there IS a tunnel … get it filled in … with discretion."

Calling into a pub for "a couple" of beers on the way home from work was a habit, and to be honest, it was one I was trying to break. In days gone by, when I had a job without fulfilment or appreciation, it was a way to kill the previous ten hours of boredom. And it ruined my life. These days I look for an excuse for a pint. I am not an alcoholic anymore. Trust me … I honestly mean that. It was a dilemma caused by the stresses of work, but I don't struggle with that anymore.

I've been married twice, divorced the same number, and there comes a time when you 'pay the piper' because the reality was as plain as day … those ladies were far better human beings than I was. Two beautiful caring women, and they both called time on me because they couldn't get me out of the pub.

I have a beautiful 18-year old daughter, called Kimberley, who is my 'rock'. She never saw me out of control, as far as I am aware, because I was never a violent alcoholic. But she knew the reason why she lost her father. Kids know more than we give them credit for. Although I truly believe I did right by her, I would say those words, wouldn't I?

Without the alcohol I didn't think I had a personality. It took a long time to realise I didn't have a personality with it, either! But an alcoholic doesn't listen to advice, and they don't tell the truth, either.

"Oh it's under control doctor. I used to drink ten pints a night but now it's down to two."

And sometimes I was so convincing I even believed it myself … until I got to the pub. In denial. But you can't deny the anxiety attacks; the sweating and the tremors; the vomiting and hallucinations.

When Kimberley was nine, I came across my old school pal, James Lawrence, who I hadn't seen for at least a decade. No longer the snotty little kid with holes in his jumpers and rips in the arse of his pants. How things had changed for him. He had ambition from an early age, we all knew that, but his family held him back. Abusive mother, and God only knows what his perverted father got up to. Although we went through our entire school years together, I don't think anyone really knew what went on in that house. I don't think any of us wanted to!

James often had cigarette burns on his arms, the occasional black eye, and we kids all knew how hard he suffered. Our mothers did too. They probably fed him more often than his own parents. I remember seeing him hoarding food at a kid's birthday party when he was about eight years old, wrapping it in paper to take home. He saw out his troubles, almost accepted it with a brave little face, but what got to him most was his poor hygiene. We saw him often in the school toilets trying pitifully to wash his clothes with soap and water, constantly asking us, "Do I smell?". We gave him t-shirts, the ones we didn't like ourselves, given to us as presents from a Gran or an Aunt. Perhaps we didn't like the colour or the style, but he was most gracious with his thanks. I don't think his mother ever asked where he got them from, because I don't think she cared.

Social workers? Oh we didn't have those at our school in those days. We had the nit-nurse and the occasional doctor, but whatever happened out of school hours was never questioned. Not like schooling today.

But, despite the hardship, James survived. He had vision when everyone of us were wearing blinkers. He spent a lot of time in the library to keep away from his home life, and he had talents that were never picked up by the teachers, probably because he was the poor kid who kept himself to himself.

When we left school he grew up quicker than any one of us in our gang. He left home at 16, started a job as a car mechanic, and rented a little flat. I never saw him depressed, not that I'm suggesting he never was. But, whereas, as in my teenage years I couldn't handle loneliness, he was so comfortable in his own skin. He was certainly more streetwise than any of us, but he didn't have much to learn I suppose.

It wasn't until a couple of years after we left school that I found out he was the father of a child. A holiday romance in Blackpool that ended up biting him on the arse. The girl broke the news to him about their little girl (who she called Kelly) during a phone conversation, but then said she never wanted him to see the child. Sadly, that was how it worked out. They lived 250 miles apart so any relationship was probably doomed right from the start. She didn't want a romance, but he did. So a part of him probably died when he said goodbye.

One New Year's Eve we were sat in a park after a party we had gatecrashed. Someone gave us a cheap bottle of plonk each, then sent us on our merry way. About two o'clock in the morning we were sat under the stars as drunk as skunks. It was times when he was 'wasted' that he opened up, and on that occasion he told me: "When you die, all you leave behind of yourself are photographs. My daughter won't be in any one of mine."

He was stating the obvious, but that touched me greatly. He really wanted to raise that kid.

James has been married since, to a lady with two sons from a previous marriage, but he never fathered another child. He was on the rubbish tip aged 15 ... but, by a smidgen of luck and 99% effort and hard work ... he was a self-made millionaire by the time he was 30.

He presented me with a job offer, and how could I refuse? It was a hand out, and I knew it, I'm no fool. But so what? I was given the incentive to put my life back together and I intended to repay him for putting his faith in me. He said he didn't want to see me offer him gratitude - he wanted to see a fighter.

I learnt from him. He was thrown to the wolves - but he returned leading the pack. You go into the ring believing. Occasionally some fighters die; some get hurt; but you must always have the mindset that it will NEVER happen to you. He told me: "It is better to fight for something, than live for nothing."

A story with a happy ending? Well ... not quite ... we found the Toll House!

CHAPTER TWO

"ME AND MRS JONES ... WE'VE GOT A THING GOING ON"

James wanted research done on the monument to see how much objection we would face in our quest to get it moved 'lock, stock and barrel' to a nearby museum. We hadn't actually asked Beamish Museum if they wanted it at that time, we were just throwing ideas around. But, they were experts at translocating listed buildings. So why not this one?

The council had already given us a point blank "No, it stays where it is", but we weren't ruling anything out, because officially it was the property of the land-owner. The council had 'donated' it to the church in the 1990's, so did they really have a say now that we owned the land ... and the monument?

Stranger things have happened.

"Why 'list' a building if it cannot be seen?" asked Bill, and Cleopatra's 'pin cushion' (as he insisted on calling it) was lost to view. The only place it could be viewed was from the loftiest point of Durham train station, where about 20ft of the peak was visible. Even on North Road, which is a mere 30 yards from the actual structure itself, the trees bury it in foliage.

Bill believed the open air museum would jump at our offer, particularly as they specialise in Victorian or Edwardian architecture. "I think it would be a huge coop for the museum," he said proudly. "We may even get them to do the donkey work and actually pay us for it. We will just give it to them." He gave a contented smile, genuinely believing he was onto something.

Alan Ravenhall, the final devotee in our quartet of JL Property & Developments team, smiled too, but for different reasons. The company's financial advisor, he was no fool, and he replied: "It is ours – officially – to maintain and keep in reasonable order, but not to sell, move, dismantle or give to bloody charity! It's laughable. I'm sure Beamish Museum would like Durham Cathedral, too, but there are laws stopping them from having it. A listing tells you that the 'said building' is of special architectural and historic interest and is being saved from people like us, who want to pull the bugger down."

"It is ours, Alan," Bill insisted. "The council handed it over to the church, and we bought it … and the land it stands on … from the church."

Alan was a little different to the rest of us. Schooled at Trinity College, Cambridge, he used his wit for satire. His comments always clever and insightful. And I am not the only one to have a problem with Mr McCracken. Alan and Bill could trade insult for insult, but there is only ever one winner. Witty intellect is a powerful tool that can pack a mighty punch, and Bill rarely produces an answer to carry on the fight.

Trying to gather information on Cleopatra's 'pin cushion' was quite extraordinary, considering it's supposed 'importance' to the city. There was no information in the Durham library whatsoever, which I found staggering, but the nearby school did inform me it was built by William Lloyd Wharton who owned most of Durham during Victoria's reign. The facts were a bit sketchy, as one schoolteacher believed the monument to be in alignment with something … but she didn't know what it was in alignment with. Which was more a hindrance than a help.

Finally I got to the bottom of it. I bumped into a friend of mine, Phil Woods, who claimed he had actually been inside it and at one point climbed to the top.

"It's called the Obelisk, and we used to try and climb it on our way home from the pub," he proclaimed most proudly. Fuelled by beer, a lot can be achieved. "It happened most Saturday evenings, and I'm amazed how easy it was to get inside, and how high we got up it. It's blocked off now, so no-one can get inside."

Gradually I built a picture, thanks to the internet, and it came to light that it was built in 1850 as a gift to the University of Durham as a North Meridian Mark for its nearby observatory. The University lit up the sandstone tower as a beacon to determine due north during its studies of astronomy. But, after a few years, the University switched from looking at the sky and making astronomical observations, to being a meteorological station. Changing from the sky at night to weather in the morning, it was no longer needed.

The entrance was bricked up in 2008 to stop vagrants trying to make it a home. The council 'pulled a fast one', and gave it to the church, meaning the tax payers were no longer responsible for its upkeep.

Such an incredible structure hidden away amongst trees and over-grown bushes, only glimpsed ghost-like through the undergrowth. Perhaps James and Bill were right suggesting it would be better off at Beamish. The museum gets three-quarters of a million visitors annually. Instead, this mighty, incredible, structure was seen by no-one.

I returned to the Toll House that same day to nose around its foundations and see if I could find any entrance to a tunnel. It was a beautiful day and the sun shone brightly through the oak branches, forming exquisite patterns across the ravaged brickwork. What was left of this once fabulous building, stood in desperation. The wood beams didn't have much of a roof to hold up. But they hung on for grim life, refusing to give up their day job.

The rooms were filled with a sense of the past, as if they fought to hold its secrets. It was sad. Having avoided modern man's destructive touch up until now, I didn't want to be the Grim Reaper dealing the final blow.

I found small pieces of broken porcelain under one of the windows. A dainty figure of a lady in a ballet pose. Part of a music box perhaps, or a decoration for a fancy dressing table. Next to it, protruding out of the soil and glinting in the sunlight, was a tiny watch face with the words H.Moser & Cie. It was old, a sort of rectangular shape that looked very 1920's in style, obviously part of a ladies dress watch.

The fire-place was black with coal dust. It seemed to be the original, as I couldn't see any modifications. I knew some of the Victorian models were designed with a ledge on the inside that many people used to hide valuables, and indeed this one had the same. But I felt my way along the ridge and all I came across was coal-dust inches thick. There could have beeen more ledges, but I couldn't reach up high enough to find out.

The floor was made of wood beams that had stood the test of time remarkably well. However, if there was a cellar (and I genuinely believed there was one), there was no visible way of getting down to it. That would be something I planned to investigate before the bulldozes move in.

I looked around for any other traits of habitation, such as hatch doors or holes in the ground. Then I noticed a small dog peeping though the undergrowth, watching my every move. I remember seeing it the first time I went to the house, stood in exactly the same place. Inquisitive but always keeping its distance. It didn't bark, it didn't make any sudden movements, it simply stood and stared. I walked towards it but as I stumbled through the thick undergrowth I looked up and it was gone, as though it had simply vanished into thin air. There is a quaint cottage about 50 yards or so towards Fieldhouse Lane and I assumed it had bolted towards there. Perhaps it was stray, or maybe belonged to someone close by.

I got to the cottage and noticed a lady was soaking up the sun in her beautiful garden, dressed in shorts with a striking pink off-the-shoulder blouse. Apple trees lined up in perfect order around the pristine lawn, and in the centre there was a large pond with budding lily pads and an ornamental quaint wooden bridge that crossed the middle. The flower beds were a riot of spring colour with the regal spikes of Lupin popping up in every flowerbed.

I tried to attract the lady's attention without startling her, but I didn't do it very well.

"Errrr … excuse me," I said, rather timidly, but she didn't hear me.

Then I spoke louder and she stepped up from her deckchair, turned in my direction and examined me like a victim looking for the criminal at an identity parade. The way she stared, I think she found him!

"What the devil are you doing there?" she cried out, rearranging her blouse for fear of showing too much cleavage. "This is private land!" she proclaimed, waving her hand in a shoo-ing fashion.

"I'm sorry to disturb you. I really am very sorry, I didn't want to shock you."

"You do realise you are trespassing, don't you?" she said, laying down the law as she stormed forward.

I gazed at her wondering what she was going to do next. At close quarters I'd say she was nearing fifty, but the way she moved suggested she was a lot younger. She looked me full in the eyes with menace, saying: "You must have climbed over the fence. Didn't you see the signs? This whole area is private land." Then climbed down from her high horse and calmly enquired, "Why are you covered in soot?"

"Oh, I didn't realise," I said, looking down at my dirty hands. "I've been rummaging around the fireplace in the old Toll House in the wood." I tried to dust down my grubby shirt but only made it ten times worse.

"It's all over your face, too," she said, pointing to my nose. "You look like a child."

"I'm John Hampson, and I'm part of the company that has bought this land."

"Please to meet you Mr Hampson, I'm Fay Jones. My husband used to tend to that land when it was owned by the Catholic church many years ago."

"So he will be able to tell me about the history of the Toll House and the Obelisk."

"He certainly would Mr Hampson," she replied, turning to me smiling, "If you can find him! I've been trying to catch up with him for two years. He scarpered with my life savings, every single penny, and he was last spotted living it up on the Costa Brava with a Spanish red-head."

"Oh dear, a bit of a sore point," I said trying to keep it together without showing any emotion because I didn't know what she would do next.

"If you find him," she replied, "please tell him I would like my money back … and a divorce."

"Yes, I will. What's his name again?"

"It's Arsehole with a capital 'A'!"

"Oh I know a few of them," I laughed, and she did too. She had a delightful smile when it eventually broke through the darkness.

"You need a wash," she smiled. "You have no idea how ridiculous you look."

I shrugged my shoulders, as though there wasn't much I could do about it, or I didn't really care.

"Do you have a dog, Mrs Jones?" I asked.

"A dog? No. Why do you ask?"

"I've just realised, that's a song isn't it? 'Me and Mrs Jones, we have a thing going on'. Billy Paul sang it. One of my favourites. You know, I like the sound of Mrs Jones."

"Well I don't think we have a 'thing going on', Mr Hampson," she laughed. "You don't wear a wedding ring, I see. If you like the sound of my name, perhaps you might like the sound of my telephone number?"

Have you ever got into a conversation and suddenly thought to yourself 'What the hell have I just said'? There comes a five second silence that you can cut with a knife, and both parties don't want to look at each other. That was the very moment.

"Errrr about the dog, Mrs Jones," I mumbled.

"Please call me Fay. As I told you, I don't have a dog."

"Oh I saw a dog run this way and I thought perhaps ..."

"Do you mean the little fox terrier?" she said, gesticulating with her hands to show how big the dog was.

"I would imagine so," I said, trying to picture what a fox terrier looks like. "Wire-haired thing, with a tufty beard."

"Yes, that's it," she smiled, nodding her head. "So you have the 'gift'? I thought so. You look the type."

"What gift is that?"

"You can see the dog. Not many can."

"I don't follow," I replied, fearing we were about to get all spiritual.

Then she opened the gate and invited me into the garden for coffee, at which point the conversation headed in another direction. To the roses that were blooming either side of the garden path.

"I never get sick of seeing flowers. I never tire of their sweet fragrance," she said, bending down to cup a yellow rose in her hand. "Do you like flowers Mr Hampson?"

"Call me John," I said, but before I had time to answer her question she added: "Their petals are delicate works of art."

"Yes I like flowers," I replied. "I miss a garden. My ex-wife took the house in the divorce settlement. I rent a property but it only has a yard unfortunately. It's not quite the same is it?"

She blanked my reply, which was extremely annoying. She seemed a very amiable lady, obviously confident on her own patch of land, if a little bit eccentric. She looked like a remnant hippy, one of the stragglers from a flower power generation.

"What are you going to do with the land?" she asked, as she disappeared into the house to boil the kettle.

Was she expecting me to follow her into the kitchen or was it another 'throw-away' question she couldn't be bothered to listen to the answer? It was so frustrating. I didn't answer, and it didn't seem as though she expected one. So I sat in the garden basking in the sun waiting for her return.

I didn't get a cup of coffee, even that idea didn't last long in her head, she came back clutching a bottle of gin and two glasses.

"Will you be building houses on the plot of land?" She asked, pouring the gin into a glass, having handed me the other one.

"I don't drink during the day, if you don't mind, Fay. I'm officially on the job."

"Please yourself," she said, shrugging her shoulders. "You don't mind if I have a glass to indulge myself, do you?"

"It's your garden, it's your gin," I replied as I placed the glass on the beautifully decorated garden table.

"It is indeed. You don't begrudge a lady her one vice, do you Mr Hampson?" she laughed.

"Please call me me John," I said, once again, hoping she would at least listen this time.

"So John, what are you going to build on your new estate? Let me guess, a care home for the elderly? A retreat away from the maddening crowd? A brothel perhaps?"

"A brothel? That took me by surprise. What sort of man do you think I am?"

"The Toll House has been used as a brothel before, or so I believe. Check it out."

"When was it a brothel?" I asked. She had my full attention. The problem was I couldn't keep her on the same subject long enough?

"Was it during your time here?" I asked.

"No," she said, twirling her index finger along the top of her gin glass. "In the 1930s or there abouts. That house has seen it all."

"What other things has it seen?" I asked, edging my chair closer to her, not wanting to miss a word. And once again she reacted as though I hadn't asked a question.

"You do understand you cannot clear that plot of land, don't you?" she said, talking like a teacher to a child, wagging her finger in my direction.

She continued: "Look at the deeds. Look at the contract you signed. You cannot remove the Toll House; or dismantle it; or build on the land where it stands. It remains ... as it is in its current state ... until Hell freezes over."

"I didn't actually sign the contract," I said, "And I didn't know that, either."

"Well, whoever did, will know that," she said before taking a huge gulp of gin. "They know it! You bought this plot of land here," she said pointing over her garden hedge, "But the plot where the house stands, may as well be another country as far as you and your friends are concerned, because it isn't yours!"

"Who owns it?" I asked.

"That is debatable," she said, putting her glass on the table. "Officially it is the property of the Roman Catholic Church. But over the years I have heard many stories. Some say the Freemasons, and one cockamamie story suggested that it is owned by the Vatican!" She laughed out loud. "Now that would be a story. People love a bit of romance or gossip around these parts. What they don't know, they make up!"

Then she became studious. I could see intent in her eyes: "If the Pope is involved … I think he made a pact with the Devil."

"That's a bold statement," I said.

"Not really. Why has nobody bought that land before? Why has it stood there all these years decaying, decomposing? It's Holy land but the church know what its all about. Gallows used to stand here. Oh, the history books say hanging took place on the land where the University hospital currently stands, just up the road from here. It did, for the gypsies and the lawbreakers. But the evil and the heinous were saved for here. The most vile of the unholy met their death just yards from here, and were strung up on the road to rot and decay in front of all who visited this fair city. The viaduct blocks the view now, but in its day this place was visible from every point of Durham. Hanging them up wasn't meant to discourage, as you would think, it was to show the city people that evil was amongst us."

This woman certainly knew how to tell a story. She had me on the edge of my seat. I didn't want her to stop.

"Who told you all this?" I asked.

"My husband. He knew the old priests. They employed him. I know it happened because some nights you can hear the gallows dropping and the cries of the victims."

"You are suggesting it still happens now? You are starting to worry me, Fay," I whispered. "Or do you mean ghosts?"

"No not ghosts, because ghosts can't harm you. But there is something there," she said.

"Something that CAN harm you?" I asked. "How do you know they can harm you?"

Once again she deflected the question as though her attention span was similar to that of a goldfish … three seconds.

Then she turned towards me, saying: "How much did you pay for the land?"

So I deflected her question. It became very difficult for both of us to hold a two-way conversation. "How do you know those people can harm?"

She eased back on the deckchair, putting her hands behind her head, taking a lifetime to reply.

"We summoned them one night."

"Who summoned them? You and your husband?" I asked, "How did you do that?"

"With an Ouija board," she said, giving a curious look of remorse, like a child who had disobeyed mother's orders.

"Why did you do that?" I asked.

"You don't know who will come to the table," she said, "It's not something you have control over. You can't pluck an apparition out of thin air just by saying its name."

I didn't know how Ouija boards worked, I just assumed they were a tool for con artists.

"So you and your husband were contacted by someone from the past?" I asked.

"I don't want to talk about it," she said, and she meant it. "You don't believe in that sort of thing, so it's irrelevant."

"I hope this is not one of those – you have to believe it before you can see it – kind of stories," I said with a disparaging tone that she obviously disproved of.

"I couldn't care less if you believe it or not," she bawled back. "You asked the question – why should I be bothered if you don't like the answer? It's not up for debate, John."

"So," I said, trying to figure out what she was saying, "These people can harm humans? Do you believe you have opened up a doorway? Are you saying the Ouija board released a monster?"

"Monsters, as you call them, have been here longer than I have. Occasionally at night you can hear the last rites being read out to people on the other side of the Holy order who believe the Eucharist is evil. Then you can hear the blood-curdling screams. 'May God pardon thee whatever sins though hast committed by evil use of sight'. I am not a religious person but I can quote you the Last Rites word for word in English or Latin. I've heard it often enough."

"You said ghosts can't hurt you," I replied. "What are they if they aren't ghosts?"

"Who knows?" she answered. "Come here one night and ask them? Pitch a tent in the garden. See how long you last before you are legging it down North Road."

No matter how bizarre it may seem, I actually considered it.

"How can I learn more?" I quizzed. "Who do I go to? What about your husband?"

"Benjamin, my ex-husband? Good luck with that," she said, taking another sip of her gin.

"Do you have a contact number for him?" Which I soon realised was a stupid question considering she was trying to track him down.

"If I had his number I would be straight onto the police, wouldn't I?" Then she looked at me for a few seconds, and leant forward saying she really wanted to help me: "Try Durham library. Ask them for information on the Polish Count who was involved with the building of the Toll House. He was buried in the Cathedral, so that makes him rather extraordinary, don't you think?"

"He is the guy I should be afraid of? The one you summoned?" I asked.

"No, he is the good guy. He was exploited, along with many other people, but he names the bad guy in his book. Take it from there. That's all I know."

She knew a lot more than she was willing to reveal. I left her to make the most of the sun … and the gin. We exchanged phone numbers and I knew I would be back … very soon.

CHAPTER THREE

"HIDDEN TRUTHS ARE UNSPOKEN LIES"

Bill McCracken rarely shows emotion beyond resentment. He doesn't even show a civil interest in his own wife or kids, let alone his work companions. So I ask myself … why do I bite?

But Alan Ravenhall had Bill in his pocket. Carefully spoken, he engaged without drama, but his words packed a powerful punch.

They always had an air of finality to them. It wasn't as though he was always right, but you knew you would have to put forward a water-tight defence to prove him wrong.

I had a lot to learn from Alan, because Bill always got the better of me.

The land where the Toll House stood was a concern, and I wanted to know where we stood before I issued notice for its clearance. I knocked on Bill's office door then walked in to find him in conference with James.

"Sorry guys," I said, "Am I interrupting anything important? Shall I come back later?"

"Na, it's OK," said James.

"I've been talking with one of the residents up on Western Hill, James. I'm concerned about the restrictions we have on that land. If we build on land we don't own, you don't need me to tell you the consequences."

James looked at Bill for an answer, and it took quite a while for the telepathic thoughts to work before he came up with one. Bill threw the ball back in my court: "What are you suggesting?"

"I'm suggesting that the building that I'm supposed to get removed has a court order on it. To the extent that it is not our building in the first place! We don't own it! You admitted that, so do you seriously want to take the risk of seeing a ten million pound project go tits up?"

James was quick on the uptake: "Are you proposing that we leave it as an eye-sore and build around it? This is going to be a Beverley Hills-type complex that Durham has not seen the like of before. Does a prospective buyer want to look out of his front window and see ten tons of rubble and debris smack bang where his garden should be?"

"Well perhaps I'm backing the wrong horse here, James," I replied, "But I think I'm onto a winner when I say that we are going to reap the whirlwind if we go against the church."

A deep intake of breath and finally Bill spoke: "It's small print. It doesn't matter a jot. It's a ruin. The Toll House is not listed, but it is 'officially' on private land. But who gives a shit? It's had its time, and we move on. As for the tower, Grade II listing says the building has to be 'preserved' and not 'altered'. The tower has already been altered because the council have bricked it up to stop tramps making a home out of it. That is not preserving. And then they gave it to the church, who just happened to give it to us. Nobody can get onto the land to view the bloody thing, so it is not available to the public. Give me one good reason why either can't be moved?"

James was happy enough with the reply: "I can go with that, John. Sounds a business plan to me."

"If the truth was known, they want rid of the Toll House," said Bill in his habitual patronizing voice.

"If they want rid of it they would sell it!" I barked back. "Have you tried to buy it?"

No reply.

"So obviously you have," I said in an equally condescending tone, "And obviously they have refused. What more proof do you want?"

"Oh grow up John," Bill said, just about waving a red flag to a bull. "There are times when we turn a blind eye and go with our gut instinct. You don't become a millionaire by following the rules. If you suffer from heat stroke – get out of the kitchen!"

"Are you happy with this, James?" I asked, hoping for some common sense. But I didn't get it.

"I am, yes. Go ahead as planned. I'd like to see that plot of land cleared. Do the safety checks then send the men in."

I was under instructions and there was nothing I could do about it. Yeah, I was a bit deflated the fact nobody would listen to reason, but who was I to argue? Perhaps they were right.

The staff at Durham Library were very helpful and gave me a wealth of information on the Polish Count, but very little was known about the Toll House. They had maps of the period and it showed up for the first time in 1798 in plain old black and white.

"How many tollgates were there at that time leading into the city?" I asked, wondering if the Toll House was one of many under construction during that period.

"There was a toll 'booth' in Durham market place," said the librarian, "And tollgates on the three roads leading to the city centre at Framwellgate, Crossgate and Gilesgate. But your Toll House was the only one commissioned during that era."

"Was that unusual?" I asked.

"It was unusual where it was built," she said, confirming what I thought right from the beginning. "It's nowhere near the road. Perhaps it was a 'fiddle' to build someone a house. That sort of thing did happen in those days. Each road into town had a tollgate. Framwellgate covered that area at the top of the street, so I suspect the Toll House was built for someone of importance. Probably for a member of parliament or law official"

"What about the Polish Count?"

She thought for a second: "Jozef lived with the Cathedral organist and his wife when he first arrived in Durham. That is well documented in books and in his autobiography. Then he moved into a dwelling he eventually called the 'Count's House' which was about 100yds from Durham Cathedral. It doesn't exist anymore. Part of the walls are still there but the house is long gone. He certainly had the power and prestige to get the Toll House built. You have to remember that Durham hierarchy paid him to live in the city. But I don't think there is any record of him living there."

The kind lady produced a journal from the archives, which must be the oldest book I have ever touched.

"This was published in 1790 and shows you the charges at tollgates," she said, scattering dust as she opened the time-worn pages. "It says here the charge was six pence for a full wagon, and four pence when it returned empty. The toll was charged for every 'coach, chariot, landau, berlin, caravan, chaife, calath or hearfe drawn by horse or any other beasts of draught.'"

"If visitors were charged when they arrived - when they left - and when they were inside the city, that must have been an expensive day out," I joked. "I'm surprised anyone went in at all!"

So having established a date for the building, I asked if they knew about the Count. The flood gates opened.

"The dwarf musician?" asked one of the ladies. "Oh there are many books on him. You should go to the Town Hall, they have paintings and his actual clothes."

"Dwarf?" I asked.

"He was a huge celebrity in his day," she replied. "We have a copy of his book, too. You can borrow it."

She put me in touch with a local historian called William J Woodhouse, who had written many books on the city. A well educated gentleman, he also used to manage the work that was done on the restoration of Durham Cathedral.

From the library we phoned Mr Woodhouse to ask him if he could help with my research, and he seemed rather enthusiastic about meeting me. We arranged a little get-together for the following day. Meanwhile, I decided to walk the 50 yards from the library to the Town Hall to come face to face with the Count himself.

Once again I was astounded at the people who were willing to help me in my pursuit of knowledge. The information centre went over and beyond the call of duty. They bypassed the daily sight-seeing tour and gave my own personal guide.

The lady referred to the larger of the rooms as the Guildhall, and she took me immediately to a painting of Count Jozef Boruwlaski. The lady informed me: "He was a celebrated musician who toured Europe for decades, performing at major venues in London, Vienna and Paris. He met many kings and queens."

There was a glass case exhibiting his clothes, hats, personal items and his violin. Everything in perfect detail, but in miniature. The paintings were exquisite. They showed him looking noble in a fine black suit, stood next to a full-sized table that was almost as tall as he was. Not only could I look into his eyes, but I could almost feel his personality.

———————————————

I read Boruwlaski's book in one evening. It was an enchanting read that set the mood of the period eloquently. From cover to cover the reader is always made aware of his disability and how he coped with it. Sometimes he didn't cope at all, and many times he struggled physically and emotionally.

Was he really an extraordinary musician and dancer? Was his act that good? Or was it a one-man variation of the Freak Shows that were so popular in music-halls in that era? His diminutive size appeared to be his principal selling point.

The man never grew taller than 3ft 3ins, and seeing his tiny, but beautiful, evening suit in the Town Hall showed he was a man of high society and culture. A man-about-town who looked the high life. He was born in Poland, one of six children, three of whom were dwarfs.

He was a pituitary dwarf, which means his body (including his torso and head) was in proportion and he looked like a child that refused to grow up. That made him popular in Eastern Europe amongst royalty, because (amazing though it may seem) most royal households employed a resident dwarf for novelty value! I kid you not.

He was taken in by Countess Humiecka and he took up residence on her massive estate. It was there that he took the name 'Count,' but he wasn't really a count at all. Image was very important to him, and he used quite a lot of 'artistic licence' in his book. He claimed (in his autobiography) that he was given a diamond ring by Marie Antoinette, who later became queen of France, but history claims she was elsewhere at the time of his visit. But, to his credit, that was an easy mistake to make considering the future queen had ten sisters and every one was called Marie.

All was going very well for him until the countess fell pregnant. Superstition in the late 1700's was a very serious matter. They were still burning witches at that time. And as well as throwing spilt salt over the left shoulder and keeping rosemary by the garden gate, any woman who saw a dwarf during pregnancy could (in all probability) give birth to a dwarf herself. The well mannered Boruwlaski accepted the circumstances and moved on, residing with the ex-king of Poland. But he recounts: "I aroused the jealousy of the court dwarf called Bebe, who threw me onto the fire."

Obviously Bebe was not a dwarf to mess with, and Jozef was soon legging it down the road … patting out the flames.

After a long successful career as a musician, he retired to Durham where he lived for many years before he died aged 97.

I returned the book to the library the following day, and one of the librarians (who had done some research on my behalf) found a mention of the Toll House and Count Boruwlaski in a Freemason's book called 'The 33rd Degree', dated 1799.

I was becoming wiser by the minute.

Jozef was a Freemason of "high esteem," who was very well regarded in the fraternity. He was, indeed, the brains and the brawn behind the Toll House, and the book confirmed it was built specifically to be used for Freemason initiation ceremonies. 'The 33rd

Degree' was written in Freemason code. To suggest it was 'heavy reading' was an understatement, certainly not an interesting bedside read. Words, and there were many, came and went without making much sense. It was written for those who had a story to tell, but only the privileged would find out what it was. The Toll House was mentioned frequently but, without the code, it was impossible to work out why.

My phone buzzed. A missed call, but being in the library, it wasn't etiquette to answer it. I didn't take much notice of it because I didn't recognise the number, but I later saw there was a voicemail.

"Hello, John. Fay here," announced the voice recording. "You said you were interested in talking to my ex-husband about the land you bought. I thought I'd ring to tell you that the police have just called to say they have tracked him down in Spain. They haven't made contact with him yet, but they know where he is living and where he is working. Give me a call if it is of any interest to you."

My heart gave a little flutter at the sound of her voice, but I wasn't really sure why.

CHAPTER FOUR

"ONCE YOU BECOME FEARLESS … THE WORLD BECOMES LIMITLESS"

Local historian William J Woodhouse lived less than a mile from my own home, in a countryside setting that had a picture-postcard landscape. I didn't know him personally, but I passed his wonderful Victorian house every day on my way to work. An ornamental wishing well held centre stage in the lawn, surrounded by red and yellow bedding plants. If it seems as though this reads like the cover to a Beatrix Potter book, I have done my job well, because maybe it was.

Before I had chance to knock, I heard the noise of the key in the lock, obviously the old guy had seen me walking up the path. The oak door swung open, revealing the gentleman with a welcoming smile, as though I was his first visitor for months.

"Hello, Mr Woodhouse, I'm John Hampson. I phoned you earlier."

"So you did young man, come in," he said, ushering me into his wonderful home.

He had a wizened face, probably whipped and forged by the four seasons of British weather for decades. No-one can hold back the sands of time, even though many have tried, but his eyes shone bright with life. This man had stories to tell, but he gave me the impression he had a whole lot more to experience. Sadly, as I was soon to find out, his wife didn't share my optimism.

As we walked in through the enchanting entrance, there was a door cast ajar and I noticed children's toys scattered on the carpet.

"I hope those aren't yours," I laughed.

"The grand children,"he said, leaning across me to close the door. "We get them Saturdays and Wednesdays. It's nice that we are still wanted. They keep us young. Do you have children?"

"Yes. One daughter."

"They can be a joy," he replied, and that pricked my conscience. I made a mental note to phone Kimberley as soon as I was done.

He introduced me to Rose, his wife, then we walked into a large room that was his office, but seemed to be his 'man cave' too.

"You have some top of the range equipment in here, Mr Woodford," I said, looking at his iMac computer and varied musical keyboards on stands. They were all wired for sound, so he clearly used them.

"Yes, I'm quite up to date with technology, thanks to my son," he laughed, "But that computer is capable of far more than I tend to get out of it. I guess I only use 2% of its capability for documents and spreadsheets."

"I see you play piano," I said, pointing to an upright that was next to the window.

"Yes, I have played all my life," he replied. "I used to be the organist in St Nicholas' Church in Durham city for 18 years."

"And a synthesizer," I said, pointing to a Roland keyboard. "Welcome to the modern world."

"If you can play piano you can play all the other fancy stuff, it's the same configuration of chords," he said, playing a couple of notes. "That Roland cost me almost two thousand pound, but we don't talk about that anymore," he laughed, keeping his voice down fearing his wife was listening. "The wife thinks I got it for a couple of quid at a car boot sale. I didn't tell her a lie, I just knocked a few noughts off the price I paid. My biggest fear is that she sells it for a fiver when I go, thinking she's made a profit."

That really tickled me.

"So then, how can I help you?" he asked, slumping himself down in a massive couch that almost devoured him.

"I hope you can get back out of there," I said, offering him a hand.

"I'm fine," he laughed with genuine gusto. "We can face that obstacle later."

I sat down on the window ledge, and we started our discussion.

"I'm currently working on a building project opposite Wharton Park, and I've come across a building. Well, more a 'ruin' than an actual building, and I was told you may know about its history."

I could see him picture the area in his mind, closing his eyes in concentration.

"Which one?" he asked, "The old coach house?"

"No, it's not on the main road, it's set back behind North Road."

"Western Hill?"

"Yes," I said, and I had become very aware that he knew the building I was referring to.

"Ruin, you say?"

"Well, sort of. It's a building but it's hanging by a thread," I answered.

"We are clearly talking about the Toll House," he replied, nodding his head in satisfaction, as though he had just won first prize on Who Wants To Be A Millionaire.

"Yes. What do you know about it? I have discovered it was built in 1798, and that's about all anyone seems to know about its early years."

Although his hands and fingers looked like worn leather, his mind was very much alert, and he pointed to a bookshelf. His shaking fingers made me question how good he was as a musician. Surely his best days of 'tinkling the ivories' were well behind him.

"The second shelf down," he told me, "There is a book with a black cover and gold binding. It's called 'Durham's Darkest Mysteries', written by myself. Take a look at it."

I took it from the shelf and turned to hand it to him but he waved me away saying: "No, take it. I'm not suggesting you read it now, but there is a chapter in there about the Toll House. It will interest you.

That building has a very strange past. It was never built as a tollgate."

"That was what confused me when I first saw it," I said.

"It was built before North Road was constructed," he said, "With the full intention that it would be conveniently tucked out of the way. The house was officially financed by the local government, but it was a con. The council already had the plans for the construction of the huge viaduct for the train line. The viaduct, as I'm sure you know, still stands today. It was built by Thomas Elliot Harrison with local government money. So, those with the purse strings were fully aware that the new North Road would be constructed to pass under the viaduct. But someone, who was connected to the Masons, passed the plans for the Toll House."

"So it was a 'white elephant'?" I asked.

"Not at all," he replied. "It was built for the purpose of the Freemasons with the sole intention of being a very special Masonic Lodge. The Masons were developing into a powerhouse in the late 1700's and there were many Lodges in, and around, Durham city. Every town and village had at least one Masonic hall. Durham city had eight at that time. But none like the Toll House."

"What did the Masons stand for in Durham?" I asked.

I had the general idea, as my father had been a Mason when I was a child, but I never got to know what he actually did. He insisted "once a Mason you will never face hardship", believing everybody helped each other. Yet we faced hardship many times as a family, having to sell our house more than once. Whatever it stood for, it never came to our rescue.

Mr Woodhouse continued: "You have to understand, Mr Hampson, in 1798 the city was … how can I put it ... experiencing difficult times. The rich were getting richer and the poor either starved or were 'encouraged' to move away. The city was under control, almost to the point of being a fascist state. Previously, the Wharton family had moved in from Westmorland and took over every inch of available land, almost without exception. Robert Wharton became mayor, and others in the family took up office as MPs. They literally owned every nut and bolt the city was built with. They imposed their name on anything - anywhere. Even to this day you see Wharton's name peppered everywhere. But the toll charges, imposed in 1790, changed the way the city worked."

Mrs Woodhouse appeared with coffee, and William went to look for history books in drawers and cabinets in various rooms. I looked out of the window and made small talk with Rose.

"Your garden is most impressive, Mrs Woodhouse. Do you get involved yourself or do you have a gardener?"

"Both, really," she said, placing a tin of biscuit on the table. "There is only so much we can do at our age. We have a gardener who comes weekly."

"How old is William?" I asked.

"82 next September."

"He is remarkably sharp for his age," I replied.

She gave a look of concern, "He is ill, Mr Hampson. Yes he is as sharp as a tack, but the doctors know how ill he is. I worry about him. He needs stimulation. His brain needs inspiring, and I can't help him with that because we don't share the same interests. You have no idea how excited he was when you phoned him. Two like-minded people. That's good for him. You have walked into his life when the world seems to have walked out!"

Every illness is about losing control. I understood that. I went through similar feelings getting over my illness. Alcoholism is a cruel mistress. I became over-sensitive to everything because of alcohol. And when it takes hold of you it makes you love deeply, and hate even deeper. I was living by extremes because my emotion detector was wrecked.

"There is very little I can do," said Rose. "Sometimes he doesn't have enough to fight with."

"I'm sorry, Rose," I said, sensing every emotion she was going through.

She left and I had to admire the way she was watching over him. They had a bond, and after all those years together, that connection was probably the one thing keeping them functioning. I got the feeling, the way they looked at each other, that if one passed away, the other wouldn't be long in following. I had never experienced love like that, and I admire people with the ability to devote everything to someone else.

My host returned and immediately he went to forage about in the bookcase.

"Back to the Toll House, Mr Woodhouse" I said as he searched frantically for something that didn't want to be found, "Who ran it?"

"That's the million dollar question. History seems to suggest it was the head-quarters of all the Masonic Lodges in the region. They proposed a Grand Master, and he ran the show, but I dispute that. I think that they had that intention, but it didn't work out that way." he replied. "It was meant to be democratic, but it wasn't."

Then I thought I'd throw something else into the mix: "I was told about a dwarf who was supposed to have lived there, but that was blown out of the water this afternoon. The lady in the Town Hall says he lived down by the river near Prebends Bridge."

"Count Jozef Boruwlaski!" he cried out, startling the life out of me. "Oh yes, he was involved with the Toll House. I'm looking for his autobiography right now. He names the Grand Master."

"I read it last night," I replied. "An interesting read."

"Oh, you have read it. Very good."

After a few minutes he almost jumped with glee and raised the book above his head. He seemed to know the book from cover to cover, thumbing his way through the dusty pages looking for one specific chapter.

"This is the second edition, published around the time the Toll House was built. Boruwlaski talks about the Masons throughout this volume, saying *'I may be allowed to say that there is nothing in the world (that) can be compared to the sublime law of Masonry. However its members may differ in their religious professions, there is no dispute, no jealousy among them; all are tolerated, and everything governed with the greatest harmony and love. Upon such a basis of reason stands the noble law of Free-Masonry. Further information on the subject it would be improper to give; and those who pretend to publish our concerns, must not be relied on, for certainly those authors never professed Masonry.'"

"He values the secrecy of the Masons," I said. "Even more so in the book 'The 33rd Degree'."

"How did you get hold of that?" he asked.

"They have a copy at the library. I couldn't understand a word of it."

"I think that was the purpose of it," said Mr Woodhouse, "So nobody, apart from themselves, could understand it. God knows what they got up to. In the third edition of the Count's book he names the 'benefactres' who ply him with money, and they cover half of European royalty! The king of Poland and the Duke of Gloucester (brother to King George III), sent him money, as did various Members of Parliament. Lets not forget he was paid by Durham City just to live there and be part of the cream of their society. He was a major 'player' in the city guild of fellowship, particularly the Granby Lodge of the Masons."

"Is this where the Toll House comes into it?" I asked.

"Yes. The Count names a gentleman called 'Smelt' as the Grand Master. That was the name he went under in this country but his real name was Victor Schafer. He was a foreigner, we know that, but nobody could pin-point his origin. Prussian most probably. He was already making a name for himself long before he arrived in Durham. He turned up out of the blue in London in 1794, accompanied by a number of foreign aliens from a Hamburg Masonic-type cult. They were a mixture of many races and creeds. They tried to join a Lodge in Wood Green, understandably nobody wanted them, probably because of their 'exotic' nationalities. They were classed as gypsies, but I think that simplifies what they really were. They ranged from nomadic Mongols, Slavic Russians, to Turkish Muslims. How do you get such a cultural mix as that in Hamburg in the 1790's? They can't have just bumped into each other in a Hamburg coffee shop."

"According to the text you read out, Boruwlaski joined the Freemasons because they did not have a religious divide," I said.

"That was what the Masons wanted us - the outsiders - to believe," he replied. "Boruwlaski wrote in his book of his hatred for Turkish Muslims, calling them 'maggots in cheese.' But was that impression formed prior to him meeting this band of gypsies … or after?"

"So why did they go to London?" I asked.

He was quick to give me my answer: "France was at war with Prussia and Austria, so it was probably as good a reason as any for them to move on because this group of vagrants didn't have any allegiance to anyone other than themselves. They went to London and formed their own Society simply called '108', which was obviously a meaningful number to them, but no-one knows why they chose it."

I was astounded by his knowledge, but I was so delighted by his enthusiasm. The euphoric way he told the tale.

"They caused quite a stir while they were in London, and their Lodge was burnt to the ground soon after they had taken it over. Nobody was charged with any criminal activity, yet 23 people died. Ironically none of the deceased were part of '108'. So that asks the question – who were those people? Then records show that Schafer, or 'Smelt' as he was known, turns up in Durham soon after that atrocity. He then befriends Count Boruwlaski and mingles with Durham society for a matter of months, before setting up home in the newly built Toll House. Somehow, in a very short space of time, Schafer was running Durham."

Another piece in my extraordinary jigsaw.

"So you are suggesting the Count was being used?" I asked.

"Without a doubt," he replied. "The Count was a good guy. You have to understand how he lived his life. He, himself, had 'manipulation' down to an art-form. You have to admire the man for getting through his disability the way he did. But he took advantage of it, particularly across Europe. I'm sure he was a decent musician, however his size was his greatest asset. He attracted curiosity – and money - from far and wide, and Schafer took advantage of him."

"Did Jozef ever live in the Toll House?" I asked.

"I doubt it, then again, I wouldn't rule it out" was his answer. "He severed all association with Schafer very soon after he - and his mob - infiltrated the Toll House. Jozef would have been alive for almost forty years of the Toll House's existence. I'd be surprised if he was involved with it for more than a year."

At that point I was dying to read the chapter that William wrote in his book.

"Do you mention Schafer in your book?" I asked.

"Not by name," he replied. "But you should return to the library and ask to read his book. They have a copy, probably the only copy left in existence. It was produced around 1805 and banned soon afterwards. It's called 'The Satanic Temple' and it will give you some insight as to what went on in the Toll House at that time. He was a repulsive individual who got his comeuppance. After hanging his 'victims', he hung their carcases in a small cramped cage on North Road where they rotted in full view of the city."

"Who were the victims?" I asked. "Who was he at war with? The Freemasons?"

"He got the Toll House on the strength of being a Freemason. His main prey were high ranking members of the Catholic church. He had his own disciples. But, in the end, his 'disciples' did the same to him. But they put him in the contraption when he was alive! They kept him from death's door for three months, feeding him scraps of rotting meat and dousing him in water every morning."

"Oh my God!" I replied. "Where was he buried? Is there a grave?"

"Many people lay claim to having seen him dead, but his body disappeared soon after. Someone cut him down, either one of his disciples or someone who wanted to make double sure he had departed from this world. There was no marked grave that we know of, but his disciples – and they were many in number – claim he was laid to rest. Perhaps they told a lie. That wasn't the end of Victor Schafer."

CHAPTER FIVE

"YOU HAVE ONLY SEEN THE VERY LEAST OF WHAT I CAN DO"

Oh how I wish I could live my life in a TV commercial. Or is it just me? Am I the only miserable whinger, complaining when everyone else is smiling, living their perfect lives in their imaculate uncluttered homes? I suppose everyone has a flash car on their pot-hole-free drive, living in surburbian perfection. They shower each other with gifts because "they're worth it," and show love by spending money on exotic presents that nobody (in my world) can really afford.

My existence, up 'til then, was never like that. But my life was changing. Not so much my life, as my attitude towards it.

The tale of Victor Schafer made a mark on me like a disfigured piece of flesh or faulty tattoo. I couldn't wash him away or get the harrowing picture of him - and that cage - out of my mind. The most horrifying death imaginable. Adults, and children, must have walked that route daily, asking themselves if that 'human being' was going to be alive that very morning.

What could the conversation have been as they looked up at that creature clinging onto life?

"Good morning Mr Schafer, I hope you are feeling well today."

In this day and age, to think of hanging a human carcass to rot is inconceivable, but it happened often on that very road, and not just on Western Hill. They did it 100 yards up the road at Dryburn, too. That puts Death Row into another perspective.

The actions on Western Hill were often supervised and instigated by Schafer himself. Which is probably why 'they' – whoever they were – made him suffer the consequences. You 'reap what you sow' in this world, they tell us, and he had three months to ponder what he had scattered.

It had me re-evaluating my own life. Whatever we do wrong, no matter how harmful and wicked it may be, nobody ends their life suspended above a busy road praying for God to end it.

I thought of my daughter, my mother, my father, and selfishly … myself. Perhaps that was the whole point of the exercise – the reason why they did it - to make people think, and repent.

The tinkle of glass on glass as Fay mixed a cocktail, and although I declined her kind offer, I wondered how dependant on drink she really was. So I asked her.

Her pretty dress hung loosely from her sunburn shoulders, touching her body only occasionally. She raised her 'made-up' eyes to look at me, giving away signs she had prepared for my visit, which was rather flattering, I thought. I met her gaze with a smile.

"I don't think I'm dependant on anything," she said, having taken a long time to reply.

"Are you suggesting I drink too much?" she added, swirling the colourful drink around in her glass.

"It's none of my business," I replied.

"So why ask?" she barked back.

Why indeed.

"So now you know where your husband is," I said. "Does that mean the police will arrest him?"

"I don't know. He is living in a coastal town on the Med called Altea on the Alicante coast. He's a landscaper by trade but the police say he is working as a self-employed gardener. You said you were interested in meeting him."

"I may get the opportunity if he is extradited. But seriously, can you see that happening? It's impudent to ask, but how much money did he steal from you?"

"Almost a quarter of a million. It was money from a house my father sold. Benjamin and I were on the verge of divorce, so my father tucked it away in a separate joint account prior to any court proceedings. Ben hacked into the bank account under my name, drew out the money and did a runner."

"Can the police extradite him?" I asked, as I had no idea how the law worked abroad.

"The police say they can. He has broken the law in this country and they want to charge him. It's not as though he is just a suspect, they have a cast-iron case against him. As long as the Spanish police are in agreement, they can arrest him and file charges in England. As always, there will be a lot of paperwork involved, so it could take months."

Fay picked up some papers from a table.

"I found these," she said, handing them to me. "Ben found these in a tunnel close to the Toll House."

"So there is a tunnel!" I remarked rather loudly.

"There are quite a few," she said, "All linked. But only one entrance on the land you bought. I only know bits and pieces of the story, but Benjamin is the man you should talk to. He knows all about the tunnels."

There were three pieces of aged, brown, parchment, each illustrating diagrams and maps displaying a compass pointer showing north, with 'X' as the starting point. They showed an elaborate spiders web of passageways and tunnels, and I assume each of the three maps were at different levels suggesting a subway system of amazing complexity.

"Are they what you are looking for?" asked Fay.

"They are amazing!" I replied. "I am spellbound. Do you know if any of these lead to the Cathedral?"

"I think they spread out across the entire city," she answered, and if that was the case we had ourselves a piece of Durham city history beyond compare, and a conundrum for our building surveyors before the project even started. I could just picture McCracken's face when I broke the news. How would he get around this? Would he feed his inner demons and feign any responsibility and say "build on it"; or feed his inner angels and actually show an interest in what historical impact we could make to the city?

I already knew his answer: "Which one of those demons or angels is going to pay the most?"

Although the maps were complex and arguably as good as any method of logging depth and distance that they had at the time, the one glaring omission was where 'X' marked the spot. The most essential data on any guide is the starting point that says "You are here!"

"You said there is a tunnel close to the Toll House?" I asked Fay, hoping she knew the exact spot, but something inside me suggested Benjamin had kept that little piece of knowledge to himself.

"I knew you would ask me that," she retorted, pulling a face that indicated my worst fears. "It's on your land somewhere, well hidden."

"Is there a cellar in the Toll House?" I asked.

"There is a cellar, but it is not part of the tunnel system."

"What's in the cellar?" I asked.

"Human bones ... according to Benjamin."

"Human bones? What the Hell?" I said, wondering if she was serious. "Actual human bones? From dead people?"

Fay laughed, virtually to the point of having hysterics: "Yes! From dead people. They would hardly be from living people, now would they?"

"You know what, Fay, I wouldn't be in the least bit surprised! The more stories I hear, the more I think I need a lie down!"

"I don't tell you 'stories', that makes it sound as though everything I tell you is fabricated. I tell you what I know, answers to the questions you ask. Apparently there are bones down there, and, once again, the person you need to talk to is Benjamin. They are not from recent times, but bones non-the-less."

Not only could the council be on our case, but the prospect of a police enquiry into 'dead people' was very much a possibility. Life was certainly a box of chocolates with this little lady.

We clambered over Fay's garden fence like a couple of geriatrics, neither of us being much use to the other. But once on firm ground, on the other side, we made ourselves presentable and headed towards the Toll House.

"The entrance to the tunnel could be anywhere," I said, and as the land was overgrown and choked with brambles and weeds, we literally could have been stood on the very spot without knowing.

Fay hit the nail on the head when she said: "We don't even know what we are looking for, do we? Is the entrance a wooden hatch or do we have to move a large boulder? What would Indiana Jones do in this situation?"

"Did Benjamin go down the tunnel?" I asked.

"Yes. He went down once, but he said he would never do it again."

"Why?"

"He said it was a gateway to Hell!" she said in a matter-of-fact sort of way, as though she didn't understand what all the fuss was about. "He said the tunnels lead into old tombs and burial crypts, each one linked to another. That was enough for me. I told him never to talk to me about it again. I've got to live here. There have been times I have seen, and heard, things no-one should experience. I don't understand why it happens, and I think it is probably better that it stays that way."

She knew what all the fuss was about, alright. She just blanked it out. Walking became extremely difficult the nearer we got to the bog land. Brown decaying water seeped into our shoes, and it started to suck us in like quick-sand. We weren't dressed for the mess.

"Come on, Fay, let's head back. There's nothing we can accomplish today. We need a digger on this land."

She agreed and we went back to the garden, climbed back over the fence, then sat by the ornamental pond and continued our little chat. I took off my soaking socks and hung them on the fence to dry.

"Do you think the police have Benjamin's phone number?" I inquired.

"I don't know. They don't want me to contact him so they wouldn't give it to me even if I asked. I've told you where he is – on the Costa Blanca – and that's where he can stay as far as I am concerned."

"But you want your money back?" I said, almost in jest, which I nearly apologised for.

"Of course I do! Wouldn't you? It's a quarter of a million pounds, for God's sake."

I thought about Fay's doomed relationship as she squirmed at the very mention of Benjamin's name. That was deep-rooted hatred, if ever I had seen it. Her voice was filled with revulsion every time I mentioned him. She gave me her side of the story in such a descriptive way that she had me in her 'team' from the outset. A woman scorned, without doubt. But I really wanted to meet that guy. And you know what, I could see it happening.

"Tell me about your ex-husband, Fay," I said, with a smirk on my face knowing full well her reply.

"He is a bastard! That's all you need to know. Why are you smiling?"

"I would like to talk to him," I said.

"I know you would."

"Well then, can I put forward a proposition?"

"I don't know where you are going with this, John, but I'm sure I'm going to say 'No!'"

"Would you like a holiday in the sun? Altea perhaps? A three day break."

"Are you on drugs?" she snapped back. "You want ME to go to Spain to meet the guy who took all of my money, humiliated me, and walked out on our daughter? Get a life, John. I don't even KNOW you!"

"So that's a 'no' then?" I laughed. She didn't.

I hoped I hadn't over-stepped the mark, but a heavy silence settled over the garden. I even felt the birds had stopped chirping, which wasn't as absurd as it may seem, because it really seemed as though time had stopped still. And when it returned to normality ... it was time for me to go.

I felt awkward as I left. I apologized for being so presumptuous and pushy, and she tried to make me feel more at ease by saying she was sorry for her pert reply. But the damage was done. I should have thought it through first. And perhaps I should have done more thinking before my next offer - two minutes later - when I phoned my daughter: "Hi Kimberley, dad here. Now that you have finished your exams … do you fancy a little holiday in Spain?"

But before I left, Fay handed me a photo of Benjamin, saying: "All I know is that he is a gardener in Altea. That is all the police told me. But he is a drinker and is sure to frequent the bars on an evening. He is not dangerous or threatening, but he will know the English police are after him, so be careful. He will value his freedom, for sure."

"He looks a character," I replied, holding her hand because I knew it was very difficult for her to share her memories.

"That's the only photograph I kept. The party after our Sarah's wedding day. I binned the rest in a moment of rage. That's the thing about photos. I used to be afraid that one day they would become worn or damaged and my memories would fade with them. But even though they are gone, I can still describe every single one of them."

"My boss told me something similar when we were younger," I said. "We had a drunken moment in the park over the road from here one New Year's Eve. Photos meant a lot to him too. And it was the ones he didn't have that meant the most."

I left her with her thoughts, and only when I got inside the car did I analyse what I was holding. It wasn't the best photograph. Benjamin looked as long-haired and shaggy-faced as an unshorn sheep. There was hair, and plenty of it, hiding most of his features. A beard is a beard, as uniform as a growth of hair can be. What if he was bald and clean shaven? I wouldn't be able to pick him out of a football team, never mind a holiday crowd. That photo give me very little to go on, and assuming he changed his name for obvious reasons, I may as well fly to Spain with a photo of 'Cousin It'.

A couple of days passed, and more trouble landed at James' feet, with threats from the local council (and counter threats from business advisor Bill McCracken) about a preservation order on some of the trees on the land. That was not a piece of paper Bill could simply push under the carpet and pretend didn't arrive. Some individuals were starting to take a lot of interest in what was going on with the proposed plans for Western Hill, so the clearance work was put on hold, once again.

"Who signed the letter," I asked.

"Furnell," said McCracken, sitting back in his black office chair, putting his hands behind his head, while looking up at the ceiling. "Same old – same old."

"What's his problem?" asked James.

"Jobsworth," said McCracken. "He sees himself as a guardian of the people. A comic book super hero."

"We must have known about the preservation order when the property was purchased," I replied, feeling I was banging my head against a brick wall.

"Why can't we just stick to the rules and do what the council ask?" I added.

"We ARE John," McCracken replied. "Furnell put a block on the clearance work to nose around to see what our intentions are. If he can hold up the job … he will. Being an arsehole is part of the job description."

Jim Furnell and James were old sparring partners when it came to property development. Furnell went bust in a real estate deal that cleaned out his company and left him on the arse of his pants. James was involved in the bankruptcy, more as a silent partner than in confrontation, but Furnell never forgot it. Like an elephant with a long memory, he was always happy to probe his trunk into our affairs. And with dead bodies in the cellar, something I was keeping to myself at this stage, life was just about to get very interesting.

CHAPTER SIX

"EVEN WHEN A CLOCK DOES NOT WORK - IT IS RIGHT TWICE A DAY"

Being on the first flight out of Newcastle airport at six in the morning had Kimberley on the ropes. Not an early riser at the best of times, getting up and preparing for the flight three hours before take-off was never going to be easy. 3am was a number on the clock that was seen but never witnessed by her. To my darling daughter – it was a catastrophe!

Irritated and tired, it was difficult to work out if her moaning was aimed at me; the large screen displaying the departure times; or the huge case she dragged along that looked as though it was full of house bricks.

"You do realise that we are only going for three days, don't you?" I asked the girl sporting the look of a zombie with its brain blown out. "Not three weeks!"

She didn't reply, and I don't think she was capable. But even a clock that stops working is right twice a day, so all she needed was a bit of motivation.

With an early flight there is less chance of a flight delay, but I was surprised at how many passengers were circulating the concourse. A never ending sea of faces battling against an invisible current. Everybody wanting to get somewhere but most of them unsure where in the airport they wanted to be. Is there such a thing as 'organised confusion'? We are all issued with a seat number, and we are all going to get to it eventually. So why the madness?

"What sort of plane is it Dad?" asked my darling daughter in between yawning.

"Why? What difference does it make? Are you up on planes?"

"Well, is it a type that has a record of crashing?"

Was the question worth answering?

"I'm sure, whatever type it is, Kimberley, this one has never crashed before."

That irritation thing I have just spoke about … I think it was catching … and I caught it.

The flight was a major success in that Kimberley slept throughout and the agitation from tired screaming children was minimal. Arriving on time was a bonus, and thankfully the Spanish airport staff were regimental in retrieving my daughter's case. Unfortunately, as I dragged it off the carousel, it still weighed the same in Spain as it did back in Newcastle. I'd have gladly paid the Spanish staff over the odds for them to 'lose' half of it.

The transfer was more complex. We could have booked a taxi direct to Altea for the hefty sum of £110 but we went by coach to Benidorm, then a taxi from there to our hotel 10km away, at an economical cost of £34. I would call that a bargain. But once

Kimberley had seen Benidorm there was a flood of questions asking why we were not staying there.

"I'm officially on business, we can get a taxi there tomorrow if you want to."

Our hotel in Altea was the Cap Negret, a stunning complex right on the beach front, and not even my daughter could complain about that. Four star hotel; stunning pool; two bars; sea-view; spacious rooms. We booked in, change of clothes and off out into the scorching sun to head to the beach. We had arrived!

The beach was disappointing – there wasn't one – it was stones rather than sand. But let's call it a 'beach', anyway, because it sounds better than a 'quarry'. So we hired a couple of sun-beds and settled ourselves down for some relaxation. I must admit, I had never seen a sea as blue.

"Do you remember the last time you took me on holiday abroad?" Kimberley asked.

"Yeah, Majorca two years ago. Why?"

"Did you think you would get back with Mam?"

"Your Mam wasn't there."

"Yeah, but you never stopped talking about her."

I started to wonder where this was going.

"I was just wondering how she was coping, nothing more," I replied.

"Do you miss her?" she asked, as she rubbed sun lotion on her arms, looking out to sea.

"I miss the company. I miss you! But life isn't that easy, is it? Your mother has Steve now, and you are an adult. You don't always act like one, but you are grown up. I'm proud of you."

"She doesn't love Steve, you know."

"How do you know that? That's just stupid talk."

"You can tell when someone loves someone, Dad. And when someone doesn't."

"I'm not going there, Kimberley. They seem happy enough to me. And I don't think your mother would like you telling me this."

I was uncomfortable with tales being told out of school, and we change the conversation to anything we shared an interest in. We covered her university prospects (briefly), the contents of her case (even more briefly) and why we were really on this trip, although I had put her in the picture even before we booked the holiday.

"This guy you are chasing," said Kimberley. "Does he know you are after him?"

"No, he has no idea who I am."

"All you have is a photograph. You have no idea where he lives or works, you just hope to bump into him?"

"That's about the bottom line, yeah."

"If you find him," she said with a sense of mischief on her cheeky face, "How will you confront him? Full on, face-to-face, handcuffs, wrestle him to the ground? Aren't you a bit old for that, Dad? It won't be embarrassing, will it?"

I had to laugh.

I spent an hour with her before taking a walk.

"You will be OK here, won't you?" I asked.

"Yeah, fine. I will phone you if I need you."

We arranged for me to return to that spot on the beach in a couple of hours and then go for lunch. I had my map of the town, a bottle of water, and a head full of brightly coloured snooker balls. She was right … what chance did I have of finding the stranger? Just because he worked in Altea (occasionally) there was no guarantee he lived there. But he did work for a local church, and I had done my research. There were three of them – Iglesia Nueva Vida de Altea: the Church of Altea: and The Virgin of the Consol. The first two, as impressive as they were, didn't have a garden of any shape or form. So I decided the third, The Virgin of the Consol, must be the one.

I wandered the cobbled streets and I could see why the resort appeals to the sun-worshippers who like a touch of culture in their lives. Typically Spanish with its pretty, narrow cobbled streets with whitewashed houses boasting flowerbeds bursting with Mediterranean colour. But how 'typically Spanish' can a tourist resort be? At a rough guess I would say the foreigners outnumber the locals by about 10-to-1, and I would assume it only reclaimed its nationality when the holiday season ended.

There is plenty to inspire someone with a creative eye, particularly with the magnificent sea and mountain views from the old town, but the steep climb certainly knocked the wind out of me. It was the sight of the impressive 500-year old ancient walls and gateways that made the climb bearable in the scorching sun. But it was the striking blue-and-white tiled church dome, peeking out from the houses, that made it a goal to aim for. That was The Virgin of the Consol, the only one of the three churches that could possible have a need for a gardener. All of my eggs were in that basket.

I'm not a religious person, but the place over-awed me. Old sandstone and stained glass, built on a hill overlooking the Med. That was a picture postcard I'd happily send home, showing all its majesty, pomp and circumstance wrapped up with a bow. As I walked through the main door the bells just happened to strike a chorus to add to its magnificence. Bang on cue, as though just for my pleasure.

"What do I do now?" I thought. I'd researched getting there, but finding the guy was always going to be hit and miss.

I phoned Kimberley to say I had arrived: "What do you think? Shall I approach a priest?" I asked her.

"Is there on there?"

"There just happens to be one five yards away offering help and advice to tourists. He seems friendly enough. But what if he cannot speak English?"

"Dad, he's a priest! They are meant to be friendly. That's their job. If he's talking to tourists, chances are, he will be talking in English."

"Yeah, you're right. Perhaps it would be better if he didn't. I'm going to tell him a pack of lies, so it won't sound so bad in broken English."

"Best of luck Dad."

Oh, what the Hell … I decided to take the plunge.

"Hello, sir, do you speak English?"

"A little. Enough, I think."

That was reassuring. I showed him the photograph and asked if he recognised the gentleman. There was an immediate connection.

"Sergio!" he said, pointing and laughing. "Jardinero."

Sergio? He couldn't be the same guy.

"Jardinero?" I asked.

"Jardinero means gardener. Errrr … he works in the garden. But he does not have hair like that anymore. That is funny."

"That's right," I replied, "It was taken a long time ago. Sergio is part of my family."

"Oh, very good," he said, "Are you Segarra, too?"

That had me at a loss, I was confused. I tried to gesticulate 'confused' in a sort of made up sign language, but he understood.

"Sergio Segarra. Are you Segarra?"

The penny finally dropped: "No, no, I am not Segarra, he married into my family. When does he work here?"

"Monday, Wednesday and Friday. He will be here tomorrow … Friday."

The 'Sergio' thing did concern me. Was it the right guy? But I did expect him to hide his identity when he fled England.

I explained I wanted to make our meeting a surprise and asked him not to tell 'Sergio' he was going to have a family visitor. He said he was happy to keep it a secret, and explained the gardener would have a two hour lunch break at 12 midday, so I should be at the church for then.

I had been in town less than three hours and already I had a plan, a motive, and a rendezvous. Sometimes it pays just to fly by the arse of your pants.

"I thought it was Benjamin you were looking for?" asked Kimberley. "Who is Sergio? And you actually told lies to a priest?"

"Sort of, but it was in broken-English," I replied, "And that doesn't count as a lie. It says so in the bible, somewhere near the back."

I tried to joke my way out of that one.

We moved to a restaurant overlooking the beach, and Kimberley looked out to sea as the waiter arrived to take our order. She held her gaze seaward as she told him what she wanted, as though she was only half giving him her attention. He stared at her for a while, he seamed transfixed, yet she never looked at him once.

When the waiter left I told her: "You are so like your mother. Everything in your own time."

"I never trust foreign waiters. So full of themselves."

"He's only doing his job."

"I cannot believe you ordered egg and chips, Dad" she laughed. "Here we are in Spain, and you order egg and chips."

"What's wrong with that? You ordered pizza. Pizza isn't Spanish. It's Italian!"

Then she turned back the clock once again: "Do you remember that place we went to in Greece when I was young, and Mam ended up with sunstroke and collapsed in the street?"

"Yeah. Mykonos. What about it?"

"You were really in love with her then, weren't you?"

I took a deep breath before answering. Once again, I didn't know where this 'love talk' was going.

"She collapsed and I was very worried about her. It could have been anything … heart attack, epileptic seizure, anxiety. She was stressed on that holiday. And 'yes', I did love her."

"Would you like her to be here now, with us?" she added.

"She's not just gonna appear around the corner, is she? For God's sake, Kimberley. Please say she isn't here. I've seen you texting. Are you texting her?"

She cried out in fit of laughter, "No, I'm not texting her. Relax Dad. She isn't here, don't worry."

I was very uncomfortable with that family talk. Even sharing family memories with my own daughter had me on edge, and that cannot be right. Guilt, on my part, had played a major role in suppressing our father-daughter relationship in those times. And I regret it deeply. What did she really think about me? You know what? I was too scared to ask her.

Perhaps I didn't need to ask.

"You hurt yourself too much, Dad. You never give me excuses. You don't try and justify why you left. But it stays with you and I think you should get rid of it. You can't undo the past. Don't you think it's time you stopped destroying yourself? Whatever makes you feel guilty the most, you seem to embrace it."

"That's very intellectual coming from an eighteen-year-old," I said. "I am impressed."

"I didn't make it up myself. I'm just quoting Mam."

We had a quiet evening, visited two tranquil (but pleasant) beach bars before returning to the hotel to retire. Next morning Kimberley joined me for breakfast in the hotel restaurant, half an hour late and just five minutes before it closed. But she had a good excuse … she was on holiday. She seemed to have the mentality that time-keeping is an option you can take or leave. I actually think she had just got out of bed, grabbed what she was wearing from the night before, and headed straight for the lift.

"I feel as fresh as a daisy this morning, but enough of me ... how are you?" I joked.

No reply.

"Dear me girl, have you been in the drinks cabinet during the night? You look dreadful!"

"I think my drink was spiked last night," she muttered, turning her nose up at the offer of "tea or coffee" from the waitress.

"Rubbish!" I replied, "You never left my side. Nobody did anything to your drink."

We had originally made plans to travel to Benidorm that particular morning, but the scenario had changed. I had to go to the church before noon.

"It's almost 11 now, Kimberley, so let's say you stick by the pool this morning and I will meet you when I get back and we can take a taxi to Benidorm from here. I shouldn't be any later than one o'clock, depending on the circumstances. But don't drift away. Stay here."

I set off immediately and I made it to the old town by 11.30, giving me an opportunity to catch Benjamin at work. I went to the rear of the church but there was no-one in the garden. I could feel my heart pump ... every single pound was like a jack-hammer. I waited ten minutes, then I thought I was about to catch sight of him. I heard footsteps heading in my direction from behind an old marble wall. The anticipation grew like a nervous kind of energy, tingling through me like an electric spark. Then the footsteps stopped. I waited. No-one appeared. I steadily walked towards the wall, then peered around the corner. An old lady was stood there, peacefully trying to unfold her map the right way up. Having disturbed her quiet moment, I think she was as startled as I was.

"Sorry," she said, adjusting her wide-brimmed straw hat. "I think I'm lost."

We both found our 'bearings' and headed into the church by a side door.

I feared Benjamin must have left by the front door of the church so I headed in that direction. Then the priest I saw the previous day just happened to be heading towards me.

He recognised me immediately and raised his hand to attract my attention. I shook his hand then he started to tell me that Benjamin had arrived at work as normal, but was ill and had to return home.

"I told him a family person wanted to see him at 12 o'clock," he said, going against everything I had told him! So much for truth in Catholicism. What about the 8th commandment that condemns lying and God being the author of all truth? I was incensed.

"It was supposed to be a surprise," I replied, finding it very difficult to hide my frustration. "I told you not to tell him I was here."

"I don't think he wants to meet with you," he said in a tone that seemed half apologetic and half curious.

"Why does he not want to meet me?"

"I don't know for sure. I told him about the photograph with the funny long hair and he didn't want to stay."

I thanked the priest but I don't know why. Deep inside I was about to explode. I obviously appreciated the time I was having with my daughter, but I had travelled a long way to catch up with that man, and that was snatched away so abruptly. But at least it confirmed (beyond reasonable doubt) that he was Benjamin, and I had the alias he was working under. But I had let him slip the net when I thought I had him in my grasp.

Before walking away I thought I would try my luck at attempting to get some information from the priest, but he gave me nothing. I asked for 'Sergio's' home address or phone number, but the request was knocked back. That was probably understandable under the circumstances, but worth a shot. The guy didn't want to meet me, so what was the priest to do?

"Can you give me a specific area where I could look?" I asked. That too fell on deaf ears.

"Does he live over there?" I said pointing to the north bay. But he wouldn't answer.

"Sir, this is very important to me," I said, making one last ditch effort. "I have flown here from England. I am not the police, I am not here to cause Sergio any harm or hardship, all I want is information about some land I have bought. It will help me very much. I return home on Sunday. If I leave you my phone number and the address of the hotel I am staying at, could you pass it to him? Tell him I can help him greatly, because the English police are closing in on him."

"English police?"

"Oh dear," I thought. "Get out of that one!"

"It's nothing important, trust me, but he will understand."

He agreed to do that. I wrote a short note explaining I wanted to ask him about Victor Schafer and the entrance to a tunnel leading to Durham Cathedral. I also said I was now in possession of the three maps of the tunnel that he once owned. The priest could probably sense the anxiety in my tone of voice, and he seemed genuine when he took the letter from me and said he would pass it on.

If desperate times call for desperate measures, I felt I was free to act as desperately as I wished.

CHAPTER SEVEN

"EVERY VILLAIN IS A HERO – IN HIS OWN MIND"

Kimberley wasn't a kid any more, although it did seem as if she was hanging onto her mother's words (rather than her apron strings). But then again, she always did. I think we had a very strong father-daughter bond, but Susan's words resonated more. When her mother spoke – Kimberley listened. So did I, come to think of it.

The similarities between mother and daughter were remarkable, from intellect right down to fashion sense. Same hair style; same bone structure; identical body shape.

Kimberley still had traces of child in her smile, and she could play on it. She knew how to act naive to get what she wanted, and it never failed her. But that talk about her mother seemed pre-planned, even stage-managed, as though the pair had talked it over. That bothered me.

———————————————

Benidorm by day is just as frantic and ferocious as it is by night. Forget New York ... Benidorm is the town that never sleeps ... period! For years it has had to suffer the "cheap and tacky" tag that never goes away, but these days I don't think anyone (who lives there) cares anymore. Even if it is 'cheap and tacky' ... Kimberley took one look ... and fell in love with it!

The town was a maze of streets filled with 'fun.' The colours reminded me of children's toys from when I was a kid. Brilliant cherry scarlet to shocking amber gold. Colours flashed in every direction like fireworks.

I find it difficult to explain to people the attraction of Benidorm. It is a good time, for sure, but it's more than that. The beach and mountain scenery is comparable with anywhere in the Mediterranean, and we sampled the delights and everything the place had to offer. A memorable day.

On our way back to Altea, I received a text from an unknown number asking if I was available that evening. It could have been anyone, so I tried to phone the individual but they didn't answer the call. I texted back, saying I was in Spain and if the caller was someone back home, a meeting would be rather difficult. Only then did Benjamin (aka Sergio) reveal himself.

The man on the run was about to make an appearance.

He text, still refusing to answer his phone, but a meeting was struck for 8pm at the Red Lion pub, which he said we could find "down a side street just off the Boulevard dels Music main drag." That meant little to me, but I would find it.

"I'm going, as well," insisted Kimberley, but I wasn't too enthusiastic about taking her into a strange environment.

"I'm not so sure," I replied.

"Of course I am," she demanded. "It's compulsory, part of the deal. What's your alternative, Dad, lock me in my room? No way! I'm on holiday and this could be the best bit!"

She right, she was on holiday, I would just have to live with it.

The text changed my mood to 'serious', but not for my daughter, she was buzzing! And that became infectious. I started to feel excited, rather than nervous, and pleased that we were meeting this guy. What was the worst that could happen? He was willing to talk, and that could only be a good thing. We now had a ball game going.

Kimberley dressed as though she was going 'clubbing', showing a little bit too much leg and cleavage for a father's liking, but that was her perogative. I wasn't going to make an issue of it. She was keen to attend this 'meeting of minds', she was happy, and that was all I could ask for.

We arrived early and I assume Benjamin chose the location because it was his regular haunt and he had friends there. I didn't know for certain, just presumed it would be a safe haven for him, so I didn't think he would be alone.

"An English pub on the Spanish Costa Blanca?" I said as we approached the joint. "I've read about these places. The bank robbing fraternity who fled from England. A meeting place where they all gather. Or am I running ahead of myself?"

The pub was quaint enough, full of tourists rather than crooks (I assume), and I didn't get robbed when I got my wallet out at the bar. Always a good sign. Kimberley was turning heads, and just like her mother, she didn't know that she was. Two Spanish kids, who were just out of their teens, were homing in. I suspect they were saying to each other: "She cannot possibly be going out with that old bloke!" … or the Spanish equivalent.

"Eat your heart out boys," I mumbled under my breath. "You aren't going to get anywhere near!"

We sat away from the bar and I watched the door constantly, waiting for the guy in the black and white photograph to appear in colour, and end the mystery.

Eight o-clock, on the dot, he walked in. His hair was short but he still had a beard (well … sort of), and I recognised him immediately. He didn't know me, and that was to his disadvantage. He headed straight to the bar without even looking around. Small, stocky, well tanned, he actually looked Spanish.

I waited until he had a drink in his hand then I walked over to introduce myself.

"Hello sir, I'm John Hampson."

He looked me up and down, I offered my hand, and he shook it.

"I know your wife, and I'm here as a friend to ask for your help," I said, trying to reassure him that I was a genuine guy. "Please let me introduce you to my daughter."

The very fact my daughter was there must have eased his nerves, because he was putting a lot on the line meeting up with me. I could have been anyone - police, immigration control – and as far as he was concerned, all that charade could have been a set up.

He shook Kimberley's hand and gave her a smile and a friendly nod of the head. But despite being introduced to us both, he still hadn't spoken a word.

"Shall we sit over there in the corner?" I asked, pointing to a table out of the way of the crowd, and he obliged.

We took our places, but as I glanced to my left I caught sight of two men gazing in our direction. They appeared from nowhere. When I looked back at our table, out of the corner of my eye, I swear I saw Benjamin give one of then a wink. At this point I wanted to keep one step ahead of them. Was the wink to suggest everyone was in position? Benjamin could see them – they could see us – but I was stuck in no-man's-land in the middle with my back to our unknown guests. Kimberley could see everyone and I wanted her to watch my back. It did briefly cross my mind to tell her, but what was I gaining? It would only stress her.

Someone had to talk, so why not me?

"I work for a company that bought the land on Western Hill. You know the area very well, I believe. I met your ex-wife a couple of weeks ago, in a chance meeting, and she told me you know the history of the Toll House."

He thought, he shuffled about a bit, and finally we got a few words from him.

"How did you find me?" he said, in a foreign tone of voice. That threw me completely.

"I asked a priest at the church," but he knew that already.

"You have a photograph of me," he replied. "You must have been given that by Fay. She must know I'm here. You came here on a tip off."

"She knows you are somewhere on the Costa Blanca coastline. I've done the rest myself."

"Are you a private investigator?"

"No, a property developer. I have no involvement with the police. I promise you that."

"He really is," said Kimberley, defending my honour.

"I don't want to know about your private life, Benjamin. That is your business. All I am here for is to ask you if you can help me. We seem to have opened a can of worms, and only YOU know what I need to know. You know what I am talking about."

"That land has been left that way for centuries," he said, finally joining the conversation. "It was left that way for a reason."

"Can you enlighten me?" I replied.

"Not really, just leave it the way it is."

"Bollox man! My company spent a lot of money with the intention of building a mini-complex of five multi-million pound houses. You can imagine, it is prime land for a business venture. The deal is done, we cannot backtrack now. But you can help us. What shall we do?"

"What are your plans for the Toll House?" he asked.

"Your wife says there are human bones in the cellar that you know about," I replied. "From what era? Do we phone the police or an archaeological society?"

"They are human bones, so regardless of age, you have to inform the police. Already your suffering has started, Mr Hampson."

"What makes those bones so important? Who is the skeleton in the pit? What about the tunnel system, Benjamin? You know more about that than anyone. Tell me what I want to know and I will tell you everything I know about the police."

"The tunnel is complex, beyond belief. You said in your letter that you have the three maps. Fay gave them to you, so she trusts you. The tunnel system is on three levels, built centuries ago, like an underground honeycomb that spreads right across the city."

"To Durham Cathedral?" I asked.

"Probably. Most likely, I'd say. The Cathedral has to be the nerve centre of the entire structure, the main tunnel. If it still exists! It is mapped but that doesn't say it is still there after 900 years, or whenever it was constructed. The other two were built later, one by the Coal Board, and the one that is six foot under the surface. That is a bizarre passageway linking crypts and tombs together. They don't spread far and they don't head in any particular direction. But they do link up with the coal mines more than once.

"Where is the entrance, Benjamin?"

"As far as the Cathedral is concerned, it is the exit rather than the entrance. Originally an escape route out of the Cathedral to Finchale Abbey to the north. Or was that a decoy? I believe no such tunnel existed, it was to throw people off the scent from Western Hill. I've measured the distance above land and Western Hill is 2.4 miles from the Cathedral. Add in the fact that the tunnel goes underneath the River Wear, and you are talking about an immense network that precedes anything like it by centuries."

"Fay said you have been down it." That put the cat amongst the pigeons. He thought before answering.

"Not really," he replied. "I found, what I think is, the Cathedral passageway, but I only got about half a mile then came back. You don't want to go down there."

"There is the old pirate map solution of an 'X marks the spot,' which would be perfect if we knew where 'X' actually is. You know where it is."

That wasn't a question, and he didn't reply. At this juncture I didn't know if I liked this guy or not. He was in this situation; in this pub; because he had been tracked down and his cover was blown. I needed information, and he did too. If he was anxious he didn't show it. But he had back-up and I didn't, and that must have relaxed him. If there was stress in this situation, it rolled off him like water down a drainpipe. But I was still unsure what 'Hinge and Bracket' were doing behind my back.

"What do you prefer … Benjamin or Sergio?" I asked. "You don't look like a Benjamin to me."

"My name is Sergio Segarra, and you didn't know that until yesterday, so how did you trap me down?"

It got really tense in that place, and I noticed Kimberley was on her phone texting her mother. I can only imagine the conversation they were having.

"Let's strike up a deal … you tell me where the exit hole is; what you found down that tunnel that scared the shit out you; and why I should fear Victor Schafer … and I will answer any question you ask. Is that a deal?"

He viewed the whole room with one sweep, his brown eyes settling on nothing, as though he was unconvinced there were only Kimberley and myself. Kimberley's texting started to un-nerved him, for sure. Then his eyes settled over my shoulder, on his two companions.

"Why don't you invite your friends for a drink?" I remarked. He looked at me with contempt, but I stared right back. It was not going as well as I expected, but I refused to be intimidated.

"Where is the exit hole, Sergio?"

He had many secrets locked away behind those eyes, but he was unsure about sharing them.

"You aren't a man of mystery anymore, Sergio. You help me and I will help you." I was bluffing because I didn't have much to give. Then he finally opened up.

"The map shows an arrow pointing north. Isn't that the give away?" he said, unlocking the puzzle.

"Not really. North is towards Dryburn Hospital," I answered.

"North is the Obelisk! That is why it was placed there, the North Meridian Mark."

The answer was right in front of me all along. Of course!

"It's bricked up," I replied.

"Yes, I bricked it up," Sergio said, "And that is how it should stay."

"What's down there Sergio? What frightens you?"

"What frightens me? The lot of it! The 'passageway to the dead' is your starting point. William Wharton was the High Sheriff of Durham in the early 1800's and he lived opposite Western Hill. Have you seen the little castle over the road? It's called The Battery because Wharton built it, and placed a massive gun from a ship on the doorstep. His fear was of the 'sub-humans' - his words not mine - that lived in that tunnel. The man built a castle in fear! The graveyard spreads right across the land you bought, and about forty crypts are connected by their own underpass. Try walking through there with a flash light and see if you can get to the end without heart failure."

"People lived in the tunnel?" I asked.

"That's what Wharton claims," came his response. "And trust me, they did!"

"What about Schafer?"

"He went by the name of Smelt. A Satanist with a crew of cut-throats and murderers, no-one had seen their like before. Those were desperate times, make no mistake, and those were the evil at the top of the food-chain. Nothing was beyond them. They held sacrifices; slaughtered animals and new born babies; virgins; all in an evening's fun. But they got him in the end."

"Who got him?"

"He was a Satanist. Who do you think got him?"

"Fay says, on an evening, she can hear the Last Rights being read when people were being hung," I replied.

"Yep, that's true. Who would issue the Last Rights? The church perhaps? Or the Freemasons? Reading the last rights to a Satanist, at his death, was like a coup d'atat."

Another piece of the jigsaw.

"Fay told me the story," I replied, "He was hung in a cage over North Road until he died."

"Not quite," came Sergio's response. "After three months, and near death, someone cut him down. He was one who lived in the 'passageway to the dead'. One of many."

We talked for another hour, and I assume Kimberley was close to falling asleep with the boredom of it all. But she battled through, didn't raise her head from her phone once, so I'm sure her mother was getting a running commentary, or alternatively, Facebook was very interesting that evening.

Sergio (and friends) left us, and as he walked away I was left with mixed feelings towards him. He had, supposedly, robbed his wife, but that was just one side of the story. I certainly wasn't going to ask him if he had. But he gave me every bit of information I needed, and made the whole trip to Spain worthwhile.

He probably only agreed to a meeting because of fear for his own welfare. But there was something inside me, some nerve ending somewhere, that made me feel a little bit sorry for the guy. He now knew the British police were closing in on him, but the fact he was Spanish – born and bred – they would have difficulty getting him on a plane back to Blighty. Perhaps that was a good thing for all concerned. Fay probably won't get her money back, but I think she was resigned to that a long time ago.

We left the pub and moved on to a music bar and I asked Kimberley if she was disturbed by the tales of horror and suffering. She played it down remarkably well, setting her face to 'casual indifference' as though she hadn't heard a word we had spoken. I could never 'read' that girl, and that was a big advantage she had over me, because she knew every thought that was going through my head. Was she a wizard of telepathy, or was I as transparent as a piece of crystal?

"What do you think of Sergio?" I asked.

"I liked him better as Sergio, rather than Benjamin," she laughed, and I couldn't figure that out, but I'm sure she had her reasons.

"I thought he was on a 'hair trigger' at first," said Kimberley. "You had him rattled, Dad, and it took him time to recover from it. He didn't want to open up, but you got it out of him. Would you say it was a success?"

"I got the information I wanted. That has to be a triumph."

"It's only a success if he was telling the truth."

And, of course, I gave her the last word. Because she was right.

CHAPTER EIGHT

"IT'S ONLY WHEN YOU GO TOO FAR … THAT YOU'LL FIND THE TRUTH"

I returned to work on the Monday only to find that Neil Furnell and his counter-parts on the Council had closed down all operations on Western Hill, pending their own inspection. It was a time-wasting ploy and we all knew it. Due to the bad feeling on all sides, I was given the task of being mediator in this battle of wills. I was asked to appease the situation, although it was more a case of "don't make it any worse." Bill McCracken's words – not mine.

Once again I was back at the Toll House.

The weather was 'inclement', which is a fashionable way of saying it was brutally wet. But the one pang of comfort I had in having rain drip down the inside of my collar was that the counsellor was just as unprepared for this sudden shower as I was.

"We're like two drowned rats," said Furnell, as we clambered through the long grass to get shelter in, what would have been, the living room of the decimated building.

"I actually brought my sunglasses out with me when I left the house this morning. It was glorious," he said, brushing the grass and weeds from his soaking trousers.

"I've no sympathy for you, Neil," I laughed, "You only live two streets away, you could get a coat."

"I will be heading there after this, I promise you," he smiled.

What I found difficult when conversing with Furnell was that my brain had been polluted. I genuinely like the guy, but business gets in the way. All of us in the office, are programmed to think - "Furnell – threat!" and it sticks. Alarm bells ring and red lights flash. We should all take care with word-association because it can screw up your subconscious.

"What's your plan for this then, John?" he said, looking at the walls of the Toll House with a smidgeon of affection. The rest of the room may have been cigarette-stained but two rectangular pieces of wallpaper stood out bright and bold where paintings or photographs once hung.

"I wonder what was placed there," he said, as though genuinely interested. "It must have hung there for years."

"A family photograph, perhaps?" I acknowledged, but we would never know, would we?

"I've grown quite fond of this place, Neil. Despite it striking the fear of God into everyone I mention it to. As they say in novels: 'If only these walls could talk'."

"I think Lawrence has a problem here. Are you just going to leave it like this?" he asked. "Or do you have a concession to flatten it?"

"You have the plans, Neil, you tell me, buddy. McCracken has the final word on this, not me. I'm just here to keep you happy."

"I guessed that," he laughed. "That's the dilemma. The Toll House isn't on the plans of completion. Did Lawrence do a deal with the church? I can't tell by the plans if he's going to move the bulldozes in, or if he's resigned to the fact 'it isn't ours, so bollox to it'."

"We could put a brick wall around it, I suppose," I replied. "But the trees hide it. Most of it, anyway. What does the Council suggest we do? I will be honest with you, it isn't our property, so in effect it isn't our concern. Ask the Roman Catholic church what THEY are going to do about it."

Then I thought about the bones in the cellar. They weren't our concern either, but it depended on how far the police wanted to spread the investigation. They could get the job closed down until the whole area was dug up for police analysis, or get the 'Time Team' in for an archaeological dig!

"Come on Neil, cut us some slack with this one. All we are doing is trying to utilise a piece of forgotten bogland and make it a nice place to live. Surely, not even Durham County Council can shit on that. Have a heart, buddy."

Neil wandered through the doorway (that had no door) and into, what I imagine, had been a bedroom. I followed.

"Do we understand the difference between priceless and worthless?" he said, placing the Toll House in a nutshell.

"Yep," I said, "If this was a 'whole' rather than a 'part,' what figure would the bidding start at to buy it? Half a million? You live around here Neil, what do 18th century houses go for? What's your take on the Toll House? You must know something about it."

"Nothing about the house itself. It is supposed to be haunted, but tell me an old building in Durham that isn't? The little castle over the road supposedly has the ghost of an old lady peering out the upstairs window every now and again. Grey face and long white hair, frightening the life out of anyone who passes by."

"I think I met her once in the Fighting Cocks one Friday evening when I was drunk," I joked.

"God, that place gets no better," he laughed. "Grab-a-granny night. That grey-faced lady will have been in there with her grandmother."

He was a decent guy. Good sense of humour, and fun to be with. He just happened to have it in for my boss.

Then, out of the blue, he gave me the go-ahead with our project: "I'm all for your plans, John. This area needs a face-lift to drag it out of the past. The council want the design to fit in with the surrounding area, but that isn't an issue here. You are building a complex all of its own, so your plans have been passed. We just wanted to know if the Toll House was your property."

Some good news for a change. We were back on track.

A couple of days later I was in the area, so I decided to pay Fay a visit. I had quite a story to tell, so I phoned her to ask if the kettle was on the boil.

"Give me five minutes," she replied. I was there in about three.

She opened the door and greeted me like a long lost friend, with a gentle squeeze and slight kiss on the cheek.

"I'm soaked to the skin Fay. I'm dripping on your floor."

Her home was luxurious, and I didn't really expect that. I had only been inside the house once before and that was through the back door into the conservatory. This was something else.

"What a beautiful home," I said, looking at the magnificent brightly coloured ornaments, in a room of white stone floor.

"You caught me off guard," she smiled. "I wasn't prepared for visitors, the place is a tip!"

"Far from it, it's charming. If you want to see a 'tip' you should pay me a visit."

"What's your home like?" she asked as though she was actually considering it.

"Nothing like this, I can assure you. I tend to think that 'home' is a state of mind. I can be anywhere and think I am home. Which probably suggests I don't have one. My 'house' is … businesslike. That's probably the best description."

"Bloody hell," she smiled, "That doesn't sound very enticing. Do you get many visitors?"

"Not really," and that did make me grin.

"What brings you here?" she asked.

"I've been to see Benjamin in Spain."

"Interesting, I thought you looked sun-tanned. What does my beloved husband have to say for himself? Any news on my money? Has he spent it all?"

"Do you know his proper name is Sergio Segarra?"

The kettle was boiled so she walked into the next room to make the coffee, leaving me wondering if she was in the slightest bit interested. About a minute passed, then she stood in the doorway to reply: "Are you sure we were talking to the right man? Smallish, 5ft 5 inches perhaps, stocky. I hope your trip hasn't been a waste of time."

"He is Spanish. I took one look at him and knew immediately. How long were you two together?"

"He is from Spanish parents, but brought up in England. He had an English passport. I saw his passport. There is no doubting that. We went abroad often."

"I suspect he has a Spanish one, too. I think he has been leading a double life."

"Did you see his Spanish passport?"

"No, but ..."

"He's obviously changed his name to avoid the police. He used his British passport to get out of the country because the police confirmed that he left as Benjamin Jones. Come on John, wise up.

What other bullshit did he tell you? I suppose he knew nothing about the missing quarter of a million. And I bet you told him the English police had tracked him down and were about to pounce. Did you?"

My silence said it all.

"Well there you go … you've done a great job wrecking everything the police have put in place. From the very moment that I lost all of my money I never thought I would see it again. But the police gave me a glimmer of hope."

I felt gutted for her.

"I don't know, Fay. I don't think he will have blown a quarter of a million living the lifestyle he is leading."

"He has a part-time job as a gardener. Doesn't that say he is skint?" she answered.

"Not necessarily," I replied. "Is that for money that he needs, or is it something he loves doing? It's not as though he is living a complicate existence in a complex life. He lives by himself, there is no other woman involved."

"I'm disappointed. Friendship is built on two things – respect and trust – and it has to be mutual. I trusted you, I told you where he was, but you didn't respect me. You gave the game away."

"Listen Fay, if I have blown it for you, then I am sorry. I realise now it was a betrayal, and I am deeply sorry."

"Was the journey worth it?" she asked.

"Shall I answer that?"

I sunk into the cushions of the lounge chair … and my heart sunk even lower. I was angry with myself, but more than that, I was embarrassed.

Suddenly the air was thick with the scent of coffee and she placed a tray with milk, sugar and two clay mugs on the table next to me.

"Well then, what did Sergio have to say for himself?" she asked in a sarcastic tone, picking up her mug then settling back on her couch. She looked every bit cynical, as if somewhat drawn into my response.

"He was very forthcoming and answered just about everything I asked. Do you want to know the details? Or shall I drink this and go?"

"Oh, I cannot wait to hear what he had to say. Don't skip the details."

I looked at her knowing I was on a hiding to nothing. The sarcasm just about filled the room. Was she really interested or was this just a mockery; a chance of revenge and a way to ridicule me?

"The gateway is the base of the Obelisk, that he filled in. He claims it is a tunnel system that honeycombs the entire city and 'probably' ends up at the Cathedral. He told me not to go down there."

"I'm not surprised," she replied. "He couldn't talk at all when they first got him out."

"Who were 'they'? The ambulance service team?"

"No, two men 'of the cloth' who went down to pull him out. Priests I think. They had ropes and flash lights. Nobody in their right mind would go down there if they saw the condition he was in when they got him out. He was covered in cuts, smeared in blood from head to foot."

"Was he taken to hospital?"

"Yes, the hospital is only 200 yards away. He was in there for six days. He had over 60 stitches in wounds to his legs, arms and head."

"I noticed a couple of scars on his arms. What caused them?"

"He wouldn't say. He told the doctors he fell down a hole, but they said they looked like animal bites. Are you seriously thinking of opening up the tunnel?"

"Am I letting my imagination run away with me?"

"Imagination, yes! You aren't stupid enough to think you can walk, and crawl on your belly, for two and a half miles in a coal seam that could collapse at any moment. All for what? To prove there is a tunnel to the Cathedral. Utter rubbish! You aren't brave enough! Being brave means being afraid, and I don't believe you would get twenty yards before turning back, because your fear hasn't kicked in yet."

"You don't know me," I said, defending my own corner.

"Let's see how brave you really are," she said, putting my courage to the test. "Come back here at midnight tonight and we will use the Ouija board and see if we can get Smelt to make an appearance. You never know, he might just want to meet you."

That was a statement no-one has ever said to me before.

How could I refuse?

"But first I think you should grasp what you will be dealing with," said Fay, clutching a hand-written manuscript she had taken from one of the drawers of a rustic solid oak wall unit.

"These are writings from Victor Schafer's book," she said, opening at page one. "The best bits, with Benjamin's comments after each chapter. Take it home, read it, and please return it around 11.30pm tonight. Drinks will be supplied."

I returned to the office to tell my colleagues know that the planning permission had been granted, and we were back in the building trade. I even got a handshake from Mr McCracken, who complimented me on my "sterling work and commitment", while giving me an imaginary back-handed slap across the chops by suggesting I "kissed-arse" getting Furnell to "see the light."

Do I lower myself to his level and give him a mouth-full back, or ride the waves? I wasn't in the mood for confrontation. Pass me a surfboard.

Back home I tucked into linguini with clam sauce, my own little speciality. My romantic meal for one. That was followed by an evening reading about the life and times of a Satanist. It was depressing reading:-

"I began to commit to paper some of the principal events of my life, merely by way of memorandums, to remind me of the difficult situations I had been in, to be suffered to perish in oblivion. As the reflections which I shall have occasion to make can be interesting to those who delight in following my ideas and sentiments. Where I was born has no relevance but I passed my days in a province on the banks of the Isar. Raised by my protector, but aged 11, I procured myself a master, and that, should I chance to displease him, I was in danger of meeting an early grave. However, young as I was, I considered it to be my duty to be ever assiduous in my efforts to please."

(Benjamin's comments:) Who this master was is open to conjecture, because Smelt gives him a variety of names. During the course of these strange writings, flitting from one time zone to another, I wonder if this gentleman (his master) had different personalities, or even if he was the same man.

"I should dream myself happy to live under the protection of my master, and would make it my duty, in earnestly endeavouring to deserve his kindness. Being at that time but a child, and not having arrived at that maturity of mind, my head was filled with the lively pictures my protector had given me."

(Benjamin's comments:) By those accounts he didn't have much of a childhood. The 'pictures' in his head could have been anything.

He was introduced to Satanism at an early age, with all its gore and carnage, and he was moulded and manipulated into what he later became. Take away the introductory first chapter, and the book is a do-it-yourself guide to demonic evil. Any sympathy the reader may have had for the author in the early pages quickly disappears, as chapter by chapter, page by page, he evolves into the animal he was destined to become.

His first taste of the 'extreme' was on a visit to Turkey with his 'master' when he was only 14.

"We received a visit from the Pacha of Hochim, a city about 20 miles away from us. This Turkish grandee, not more eminently distinguished by his rank of Pacha than by his service to Satan himself, invited my benefactor to visit his palace at Hochin. I was present at his invitation, and with great pleasure heard him politely request that I might accompany him, declaring that he would afford me entertainment. On our arrival we were received with all the honours due to the rank of king. As for me, I felt happy, and I was much caressed in the palace. How agreeably was I surprised when I beheld about twenty beautiful women, all graced with manners the most polite, and a behaviour the most tender and affectionate. I was fortunate enough to behold these exquisite specimens of beauty, and I bent in humble acknowledgement of their superiority. I shall not enter into a particular description of the special favours I received, but suffice to say only very special guests must have experienced such a particular honour."

(Benjamin's comments:) But that was just the first course. The main 'meal' was a young girl performing perverted sex acts with holy objects. Any image or token of Christianity. A gold cross, an image depicting Christ, anything blessed in the name of the Holy Ghost.

"I could not help being filled with astonishment at seeing such a practice. This girl must have undergone the most fatal reverses of fortune, and with all the faculties of her soul, she employed them with so much energy to promote the happiness of her audience. The image stuck with me of how she cavorted with a man of Asian authenticity. 'This is the man who shall be the Anti-Christ' she shouted, 'Recalled to the thrown, stripped of his crown of thorns and his consciousness of good'."

(Benjamin's comments:) Then, as if the depravity couldn't sink any lower, a newly born baby was brought to the alter, naked and crying. Smelt watched with "interest" as the young lady sacrificed the baby by cutting its throat.

"I was astonished at the appearance, the smallness of which I had no idea of. The strong curiosity in me gave way to the ecstasy I excited. Humiecka was the name of the executioner and she requested my company. I was the person she desired to see. She placed blood on my face and it possessed all the sentiments correspondent of the child's illustrious birth. I was reborn."

(Benjamin's comments:) Smelt talks about some form of disability he suffered, without going into detail of what it actually was. He struggled to walk, he makes that very plain, and he turned heads when people passed him in the street.

"I have experienced on my travels, that the public in general looked sharp upon my movements, asking me if I had suffered an accident. It was an accident that had thrown me into the bustling world. It would serve to show me the varied shades of human tolerance, and their ill example tormented me. I witnessed their intent towards my person, but they were too afraid to approach me. Who are they to judge me? Even the greatest Monarchs, who, great as they are, are not exempt from bowing before their tribunal. They will bow to me! I want to be an artist … of manipulation. Like strange paintings disguised by the artist in order to deceive the public eye … I have that power."

CHAPTER NINE

"NO TREE CAN TOUCH HEAVEN … UNLESS ITS ROOTS ARE IN HELL"

Anticipation is a nervous kind of energy, and visiting Fay's house (once again) did have me fluttering with curiosity. I wasn't exactly in the blocks and under starters orders, because I didn't believe this Ouija board stuff was for real. I had never done this sort of thing before, but I knew Fay could be extremely convincing, and I was sure to be in for an interesting evening.

What I knew about Ouija boards could be written on the back of a cigarette packet. TV programmes had revealed them as hoax spiritualist devices, full of tales of exaggerations and false claims. The story that sprung to mind was based in the 1920's. A lady claimed to be able to contact the dead spirit of the mother of illusionist Harry Houdini. Houdini proved it to be a sham and he began investigating the methods they used, becoming a self-appointed crusader against the charlatans. He called them "vultures who prey on the bereaved" and he organised an American tour proving to his audiences how they hoodwinked the vulnerable. Uses of the Ouija board were his primary target.

"I'm not here to prove or disprove anything," said Fay, after I told her the Houdini story. "You believe what you want to believe. If your mind is made up, I'm hardly going to change it."

We sat down in front of a wooden board that was placed on a coffee table, and the dimmer light was turned down to its minimum. The room had a 'cozy' feel to it, so I wasn't that concerned at first. So relaxed, another time and another place, I could easily have been sat comfortable watching TV. I had an easy-going 'let's see what this is all about' attitude.

"Bring it on," I thought.

"I read that Ouija boards cannot actually put you in contact with demons and the dead," I said to Fay, who showed a face of utter nonchalance.

"Well you have nothing to worry about then," she replied. "Chill out, man. Don't fight it."

"How do we start this contraption," I joked, "Do we have to wind it up? Or plug it in at the mains?"

Oh the fun we were having.

"The concept is pretty straightforward," she said. "As you can see, the board has the words 'yes' and 'no' in the top corners, and the alphabet in the centre, with 'goodbye' at the bottom. We place our hands lightly on this triangular pointer called a planchette, and the spirits – if they are active in here – will communicate with us. They will move the planchette around the board to spell out the answers to the questions we ask. Do you follow that?"

"Of course."

"But you don't believe in all this garbage, do you?" she said pointedly. "So nothing will happen. Just relax."

I needed convincing, but I had an open mind. I could feel my hand starting to shake as we both touched the planchette, and I looked at Fay trying to fathom if she was manipulating it. I don't think she was and she didn't say anything. After a minute or so it calmed down. Then soon after that the experience became mesmerising. Fay asked questions out loud, but didn't get any response. Then after 15 minutes or so, we drifted into a weird sense of serenity, difficult to describe. I felt I was floating and looking down at the board from the ceiling. Fay kept asking questions and, although I waited with bated breath for a reply at the beginning, that had left me. I wanted 'whoever' to answer. I wanted that presence to appear. I continued to feel myself drifting. Not just my mind, but my actual body seemed to be levitating. It wasn't of course, but I felt a floating sensation as though I was being carried around the room. I could sense involuntary physical movement in my arms and fingers. I cannot say it was an outside spirit, it was more a weird sensation as though my body was talking to me. I was being manipulated. I was moving, ever so slightly, without wanting to move. I started to twitch. Nothing too noticeable, but as though the nerve ending in my fingers and toes were marginally being triggered. If you have ever experienced the sudden feeling of jerking awake from sleep, that is the best description I can give you, although not as abrupt as that. My brain was giving me reflexive movements, but as though it was activated, or prompted, by another force.

Fay didn't seem involved in this, as though she was getting nothing back. But I was feeling something from somewhere. Time passed, I don't know how long but it cannot have been more than an hour, then she finally got a spark.

"Please contact us," she said, then I felt the planchette move. I could have been me moving it subconsciously, or it could have been her. Whatever. But the triangle moved.

"What's happening?" I said quietly.

"Something is here!" she replied, scanning the room but seeing nothing.

Fay was asking questions but my mind was unconsciously creating images of something that was not there. I saw a flash of light that was not from anything in the room, and I started to see the formation of a dark figure crouching in the corner. The shadow was a haze, fragmented, nothing that was a 'whole'.

My subconscious was pushing me to move the planchette. Fay went with it and didn't disrupt my train of thought. I know I was spelling out random letters but I had no idea if words were forming. It all seemed as though this romp into the 'dark side' was rapidly devolving into gibberish.

"Who are you?" she asked.

It made me aware I had no control of my movements. Paradoxically, the less control I thought I had, the more control my subconscious was actually exerting.

"Victor, is it you?" she probed.

Random letters flowed. Nothing making any sense.

"Or do you prefer 'Smelt'?" Fay said in an antagonising manner. Then suddenly it was no longer a game. The figure in the corner re-appeared – darker, bolder, more menacing. It still wasn't an actual form, more a shape made out of black smoke. But every now and again a part of it looked existent, as though it was mass and could be touched. The figure stretched out a hand, like a beggar on a street pleading for money. During which time the planchette kept pointing to three letters, over and over. I was communicating with something in my subconscious that I couldn't physically access.

Fay looked at the board, then looked back to the corner.

"Do you want us to go to the Toll House?" she asked. It didn't answer. I don't think it was capable of speech in that form, and I don't even understand what dimension it was in. How could something get into my mind and then suddenly become visible?

The low light flickered, my hand let go of the planchette, and calm returned once again. Whatever was sat in the corner had faded away and it's smokey image was gone.

"What the hell was that all about?" I asked, almost knocking Fay off her chair as I stood up.

"What just happened?" I said, "Fay … what was in that corner?"

"Nothing really. The individual sees what it wants to see. The mystery of the Ouija board is what lies within our own subconscious."

"You know what I'm talking about. You saw it, Fay! You saw the creature cowering in that corner. That was not in my subconscious. I did not want to see that and I didn't just conjure it up."

"So Mr Cynical," she replied, "Do you believe now?"

"What were the three letters that kept repeating? I couldn't make them out."

"T-O-L. He wants us to go to the Toll House."

"When?" I asked.

"Now!"

"You are kidding me!" I replied. "With the Ouija board?"

"I don't think we will need the board this time," she said, rather confidently. If she was as unnerved as I was, she had a resourceful way of hiding it.

"We are going outside?" I asked. "At 1.30 in the morning, to a place you say probably has the largest number of ghost sightings this side of the dungeons of the Tower of London?"

"Isn't it fun?" She said, picking up her coat and a flash-light before ushering me to the door.

―――――――――――――

If ever there was a right time for a full moon, I don't think that particular evening was it. Yes we had a sheen of light that glistened over most of what was before us, but did we really want to see what was there?

"The sooner this place is dug up, the better I will feel," I mumbled to myself. "It's like spending an evening in a graveyard."

"It is a graveyard, John," as if I needed reminding.

We moved into the copse towards the Toll House and blackness was upon us. The stillness of the trees seemed to suck the life out of everything around us. No rustling of leaves; no noise at all apart from the odd drone of a car in the distance. And I couldn't shake away that uncomfortable feeling that something was watching us. Fay hadn't turned on the flashlight, so what we saw wasn't much, but something was there. Then we heard the clunking of metal on stone, about 50 yards in front of us, as though a tin can was being kicked down North Road. It grew louder as though it was heading in our direction, then it stopped. The silence was almost painful, as we listened intently, like owls listening for mice. Then, I heard a voice. It rose and then fell, none of the words audible. At first it was a deep grumble, but it began to change tone and pitch, like an unpleasant lullaby from a bygone age. I froze, terrified to move a muscle.

From the blackness came a hissing noise, like nothing I have never heard before. It was almost upon us, I'd say three yards away, but I couldn't see a thing. Time stood still and I didn't move a muscle. Then I could smell the foul stench of its breath as it slowly moved to my left, still invisible. The smell was like rotting meat mixed with vomit. It pulled at my stomach muscles and I feared I was going to be sick. I was fighting with myself to stay perfectly still, but I knew I couldn't hold on much longer.

Then, after walking around me, it returned to hiss in my face once again. I could feel the vile smelling spit splash on my nose and cheeks, and some went into my mouth. I leant forward, cutting straight through the creature's space, then threw up on the ground. The beam from Fay's torch caught it's shape as it materialized before us in epic technicolour. It wasn't there long, two seconds tops, but it emerged from the dark like some form of deformed, disfigured being from the days of the Black Plague. It didn't run, and I wouldn't say it was uncomfortable at being seen, but something made it appear and something took it away, too. The creature was hideous.

"Is it still here?" I asked Fay.

"I don't know," she replied, before taunting it to reappear. "Show yourself Smelt, let's talk."

I notice my watch had stopped, frozen on the second the creature appeared. The air suddenly became cold and my body heat quickly deserted me, as I fought back another bout of sickness. I couldn't hold on any longer and I threw up again.

"Are you OK?" asked Fay.

"Yeah. What's happening? Is he gone?"

"I don't think he is ever gone. This is his home. We just have to goad him to show himself."

That made me most uncomfortable: "Are you sure goading him is what we should be doing?"

Suddenly the moon cast some light in the woodland and there was a semi-glow that showed the open mouthed face of the creature that was an inch from my face. A fully formed hideous, obscene face of the unholy was glaring into my soul. Wide horrific eyes bulged out from a face covered in sores and open wounds, a sight I could never even imagine unless I actually experienced it. After a moment of indecision, I took half a step backward, but he leant forward as if to grab me. I stepped back a couple of paces, avoiding any contact, and spoke slowly and calmly to him: "What do you want Victor?"

He turned his head skyward like a wolf about to howl, and I saw the scars of at least a dozen knife wounds across his neck that surely no man could have survived. My eyes were drawn to them in utter paralysis. No blood, just open lacerations so deep they must have severed major arteries. He tried to reply but I didn't think he was capable of talking. But he pulled out words from somewhere that were piecing and intense: "What … do … YOU … want?"

Fay looked on, some three or four yards from me: "Be careful John," she said in a quivering voice. Then gritted her teeth waiting for my reply.

"Are you a danger to us?" I asked, trying to keep my nerve.

"ARE … YOU … A … DANGER … TO … ME?" he screamed, in a tone that made me shake in my shoes.

"We are a danger to no-one, I promise you," I said, hoping a civil reply would get a civil response.

Then he moved towards my ear and serenely and quietly, as though talking in a library, he whispered: "Keep away from me, my associates, and this land."

That voice was not his. I promise you. I don't know where it came from, but unlike his previous words, he made no effort in saying them. Something came from within. He was a vagrant in soiled rags, with the body of a decrepit, weather-beaten, feeble man … but something deep inside was keeping him alive. Giving him immense power and strength far beyond his bodies capabilities.

He disappeared as quickly as he arrived, leaving a pungent smell behind to remind us of what really happened.

I fell back against the damp wall of the Toll House, the very spot where I had stood with the councillor the previous day. Shaking and petrified.

Fay moved closer so that I could feel her presence. She held my arm but stayed quiet, allowing me to stay lost in the moment a while longer. The tension was disappearing, I closed my eyes, and let my limbs fall loose. I had to waken my mind. But Fay did it for me.

"Come on, John, we've had enough for one night."

We returned to Fay's tranquil house, both of us having regained our composure. We went inside and I stood with my back against the door trying to make sense of what had just happened. Then without warning, a heavy rap on the door knocker nearly finished me off.

"God forbid!" I shouted.

I backed away. Fay looked at me, shrugging her shoulders, pointing to the kitchen clock. It showed 1.54am.

"Who would come calling at this hour?" she whispered.

"I'm not answering it," she mouthed, lip-sinking without saying the words.

I didn't know what to do. Someone was there, I could hear them trying to push open the door to see if it was locked.

Neither of us would commit ourselves. Then the letterbox opened, and the concerned voice of an old lady asked: "Are you alright Fay?"

"Oh it's OK, it's Lila from next door," said Fay, as she brushed past me to let her in.

"Hello Lila, what's up?"

"I just wondered if you were alright. I heard people climbing over your garden fence and I thought I'd better come and check on you."

The lady was 86 years old, yet she put her own welfare at risk to check on a neighbour who lived alone. Incredible. I had met this woman before, but I didn't know where or when. She may have had arthritic joints and a face with more lines than Paddington Station, but she seemed to have a sharp mind. Her speech was articulate and showed she was a lady of 'good breeding,' as my mother used to say.

Then I realised how I knew her. She was one of my schoolteachers when I was a child.

"Are you Mrs Moore," I asked, "You were one of my teachers in junior school."

Sadly she couldn't remember me, but a conversation commenced about the old and the new. Were the 'old days' really better? And why do we hear of so many bullies when "we didn't have them in our days." Mrs Moore's words – not mine. Perhaps the sands of time had clouded her memory, but I could name one or two.

The gentle lady made her way home, and we watched as she made it to her door. We were alone, finally, time for the autopsy.

"Well then Mr Hampson," said Fay with a touch of mischief in her voice. "Are you still planning to go down your tunnel?"

That experience changed my attitude to a lot of things, but first I wanted to know what the hell that creature was.

"That was horrific, Fay. How can you live next to that? He isn't dead. What does he want … or need? If he is dead then that sure isn't the Heaven they talk about in the bible."

I pointed in the direction of the Toll House and said: "You know more about that place than you make out. Never mind Benjamin, you know the score."

She didn't deny it.

"What is he, Fay? He isn't dead. What does he want?"

"Hang on, you summoned him! Does he want anything, or just to be left alone?"

"Can he harm anyone? Did he try to kill Benjamin?"

"Yes he can harm," she said, "But there is no logic to what he is … or what he has become. I don't understand how he can appear out of nothing, and you saw it, because he has that ability. We can smell him, so he has presence. He is a 'being'. You can often smell him before he appears."

"Yes," I remarked, "You can certainly smell him. I think the name 'Smelt' is rather apt. He stinks!"

I picked up the Ouija board and examined it.

"It's not anything special," said Fay. "It's just a mass-produced piece of wood that had no special characteristics about it. I don't know what you are looking for."

"You said you tried this before and he appeared," I commented.

"Yes, once before. He materialized very much the same as he did tonight. Not fully formed, cowering in the corner. It's only outside, by the Toll House, where he seems to come into his own."

"He must have been here as long as the Toll House," I said, calculating the years. "That makes him about 250 years old! That is just ridiculous! That means he moved to Durham 30 years before Victoria was crowned queen!"

I sat shaking my head, bemused by it all. Fay looked as if she had a lot to say but she thought better of it. Deep in thought but she wasn't going to reveal anything. I knew the Ouija board stunt would be an education, but I thought I had it covered. I was prepared to rip holes in the theory and prove it was a sham. She didn't coax me into anything … but something did. That woman is no fraud. But some 'being' took me by the hand and lead me to a ghastly place. I felt as though I was going through a type of indoctrination which I had to follow and obey. Something was feeding my curiosity with madness.

Finally Fay spoke: "He has been here a long time, John, tormenting and bullying the owners of the Toll House. Everybody who took it over has suffered. Something holds him there, and he wants everybody out. It's his."

"How does the Roman Catholic church come to own it?" I asked. It was something that had been bothering me for some time.

"They took over around 1810, just after they … or whoever it was ... cleaned out the Satanists."

"Did they have the right to just take it?"

"Own the Toll House? They are the church, John. In those days they ran rough-shod over anything that stood in their way. You know for a fact it is officially theirs, so someone signed the deeds over to them. It's tradition - the church has always ruled by fear. They still do today."

"So, when you say 'owners' that have lived there, I take it they were people who signed a rental agreement with the church?"

She explained there were many 'tenants' because nobody stayed there for long.

"I cannot go back beyond 1916," said Fay. "But I'm sure you will find references to the place in newspaper reports if you dig deep enough. There were many rumours and stories, but the trouble with folklore is that every new generation adds its own narrative and distorts the facts. But to have a story in the first place, proves there was substance."

"So, what happened in 1916? Why that specific date?"

"I have a collection of letters from the Great War. Romantic correspondence from the lady who lived there, to her husband-to-be, who was fighting in France. Benjamin found them hidden in a box tucked away in the wall of one of the bedrooms. Read them … read them all."

CHAPTER TEN

"ALL YOU DO IS SIT DOWN TO A TYPEWRITER - AND BLEED"

I took the letters home, and over the course of the following few evenings I read each and every one. They were like little individual notes put into bottles then thrown into the sea. The forgotten word, tossed to and fro by the waves for a century, then they came back to life once again.

We live in an era when letter writing is a diminished art. There is a charm to letters that texts and e-mails will never replicate. You can inhale a letter and draw the fragrance of the place they were mailed from. The feel of paper in your hand, bearing the weight of the words written from afar.

Letters from the Great War were a lifeline to soldiers, and their families relished news from the fighting on the front. Many letters were altered due to censorship by officials, who used a black pen or cut out any information they felt could help the enemy, should the letters fall into German hands.

Each writer told their stories with handwriting that showed their frame of mind at the time. Hastily scratched out words that may not have got past the censure, who would check every sentence. As for couples, it was a love suppressed because of prying eyes. Many had blotches where tears may have fallen.

The letters in my possession were bundled together in a soft muslin cloth, tied up with a red ribbon. There was I, interfering in a love affair that had died generations ago, written by a hand that was long dead.

"Your letter is written on cheap discoloured paper, but the words I read are priceless," said the lady to her soldier boyfriend. How about that for an opening line of the first one I opened?

Apparently the British Amy Postal Service delivered around 2 billion letters during the Great War. I held a batch that had arrived at the Toll House, plus the replies that went back over the Channel. All back together in chronological order.

In 1916 the Toll House was already 118 years old. Let's face it, 118 years is an age when many modern dwellings would have been built and demolished. It had already witnessed a lot. In theory it had seen many innovations in technology in those 118 years. But due to its location – on a bogland surrounded by trees – it would not have 'seen' anything other than perhaps the invention of the motor car. Possibility, in 1916, the only radical change to its structure since it had been built would have been running water. Council records showed it didn't get electricity until the late 1920's.

The thrill of sending and receiving letters in wartime must have been immense. Particularly to the soldiers who were fighting for their lives on a daily basis. It kept them connected to the home they had left behind, and every letter and parcel was vital to keep up morale.

It was a war when those at the helm didn't react to the death toll. Casualties were numbers on a piece of paper, never recognised as individuals. The warlords weren't able to cope with that kind of devastation, so they continued to throw bodies at the problem. Of course they had 'fear' of the enemy, but more 'fear' of the reaction back home.

Let me introduce you to Elena and Ted. Their secrets were theirs to keep forever … until I stuck my nose into such a beautiful, complicated, enigmatic romance.

Elena's letters (received from the front) had very few crease lines on the brown grainy paper, so the letters had hardly been folded and unfolded, but kept to last. Probably read less than half-a-dozen times, but memorized word for word, then hidden way in a tin box. Ted's letters were probably what kept him alive. Carried with him always and read often in difficult muddy conditions. Some words were tough to decipher, while some pages (I assumed) had to be cleaned with a damp cloth before he could make out the words at all.

Tales of love; hardship; war-torn France; happiness; oh yes … I nearly forgot … and a guy called Smelt.

25-year old Elena Nicolson was a nurse who worked in Durham hospital at the time of the letters. Born in the Toll House, she resided there after her father and disabled mother left to live with Elena's grandmother, five miles away in Chester-le-Street.

Her boyfriend of the same age, Ted Lawler, fought in the Northumberland Fusiliers battalion. Raised in the Durham pit village of Coxhoe, he signed up for duty before the first Christmas of the war, under the 'Pals Battalion.' It was a uniquely British phenomenon because the government didn't introduce conscription at the start of the war. Instead they organised local recruitment drives where friends, neighbours and colleagues could sign up and stick together in their own (as the title implies) 'pals' battalion.

Although Elena and Ted had corresponded throughout the war from 1914, the batch of letters that survived started in April 1915. There were 31 letters in total, Elena talking about her mundane life back home, and Ted explaining the tough life he was enduring on the battlefields of Verdun and Ypres before being captured by the Germans.

(April 1915) Dear Ted,

I hear from home that you boys are in the thick of it, is this correct? I have been comforting myself by thinking you would be in training for a month or so, but this morning's news has knocked me for six. I do hope you and the boys are alright. I feel so mean and heartless to be here in safety myself when so many of you are doing the opposite. Some soldiers from the Durham Light Infantry have been here for four days leave and they left yesterday for the front. Mother is well and Mary (the neighbour) is a perfect cherub and has kept her in amusement this day. Her laughter is infectious.

I do hope the Bosch learn soon that they have no chance against the Northumberland's and surrender soon.

Now I must stop, I expect you get heaps of letters, more than you have time to digest. Goodbye my darling.

Elena.

(May 1915) My dear Elena,
I am wondering if you got my last postcard. I suppose it went via Belgium, as most of our post seems to end up there. I wrote you a long letter of about 12 pages but the Censor returned it saying it was far too long and I was giving you too much information. That saddened me, but we understand they have a job to do.
I will repeat the news I put on the postcard as I never know what gets beyond the front line. I was wounded in my left leg. A bullet went in about three inches above the knee and came out the other side. But I am healing very well, even though I have not got the use of all of my muscles to my foot. But that will come with time so please do not worry. Around 30 of us were taken to a Catholic convent for medical treatment and I have been here three weeks now.
Can you please send me 100 cigarettes, along with items on a list I have sent you? I cannot tell you everything that has happened for fear this letter does not reach you, as space is limited. I will save it all for a fireside chat. I am limited in the amount of letters I may write, so you can tell my friends that I should very much appreciate a letter although I may not be able to reply. Rest assured that I am alive and kicking (with my one leg) and the other will heal very soon. I do hope things are good with you and your mother. I am expecting to be home in weeks, this war cannot last forever.
Give my love to all.
Ted.

(June 1915) My dearest Elena,
I suppose you have heard of my fate by now, from other sources, that I am a prisoner behind enemy lines. It is bad luck to be in this predicament, but at least I am alive. I almost dare not ask you, but did Patrick, Charles and Edward get back to the Battalion? I pray they are all alive. The German censors are very strict here, but I am away from Josefshaus (where I was captured), although I cannot reveal where. I am sharing a room with three Canadians. Please keep writing. Your letters are like the food of gods to me.

You said you were eating very nice chocolate biscuits and bemoaned the fact that you could not send them to me. That is not in the category of the impossible. You should try.

I would cherish a photograph of you if that is at all possible. Perhaps you could send me one on receipt of this letter. The book you sent to me was very good. Thank you, it was most enjoyable.

The quarters where I am living are a welcome change from fighting at the Front, so please do not worry about me. Your letters smell of that beautiful face powder you are accustomed to wearing when we go to dances. It is one of a thousand things that make the difference between freedom and imprisonment. The chief feature of this life is the absolute lack of anything to do, and the lack of any female element. The war will stop soon because the men will be so keen to get back to their wives or sweethearts.

The Canadian Officers can be annoying because they have an almighty opinion of their country, which is argumentative to a degree. They regard Canada as 'God's Country' but they overlook the fact that God also made a few more of the same. However, these incidents make no difference to our friendship.

A German student, who is training to be an officer, comes here quite often. He speaks English very well and it is most interesting to hear his views from a German standpoint. We are both convinced we are right, so with individuals in such a state of mind it is no wonder nations are fighting.

You must excuse my nonsense because there is very little to talk about here.

So many, many thanks. I miss you very much, and thank you for writing as regular as you do.

Yours lovingly,

Ted.

(November 1915) Dear Ted,

Thank you for the postcard. It was like phoning Germany and hearing you say "hello" or something. But you might at least have said what you thought of the photo I sent you. I expect you think it flatters me but dare not tell me. But you could have at least said something ....

It was this letter (No 6 in the collection) that Elena announced her fears at home:

"The dog has reappeared, but still it keeps its distance. As though it watches over me, but refuses to come when I call. It sits there, every day, looking and listening. The foul stench has returned, too, like rotting flesh. It makes my skin crawl and invades my nostrils."

Then in December 1915 she goes riding on Western Hill:

"Phyllis came over with Nero on Tuesday, and she tried to teach me how to jump. I just managed to scramble through the hedge, rather than jump over it, tearing my new habit. I rolled off Nero and onto my back onto frosty ground and I have never felt so disabled. Have you ever come off a 'gee' before? I lay and couldn't get my breath, then that man appeared again, wearing old, dirty clothes and stood over me. He would not reveal his face, which was covered in a filthy, soiled cloak. He had an interruption from something, and disappeared."

Ted obviously knew her predicament and commented on it regularly. He must have seen him, too, before he signed up for duty:

"The world seems no place for that man. He has so many stories to tell but he stays silent. I caught a glance of his face once and he has the listless eyes of the dead that I have seen so many times here on the battlefield."

Was it Smelt - in 1915? He would be 140 years old at the time of the Great War! Was Ted actually feeling sorry for the guy?

Being fed and watered by the Germans, away from shrapnel and gunfire, was not such a bad thing for Ted, as the war drifted towards the Battle of the Somme. He learnt of bad news from the Front from Elena's letters … often. His dear friends were dropping like flies. Elena wrote:-

"Mary is in black for Theodore, who was killed on a foreign field last month. He was in a serious condition and under chloroform when he died. But it was probably for the better because both his legs were taken off above the knee. Mary never really appreciated what she had. They weren't engaged but he intended to propose to her on his next leave. He left money in his will to buy her a ring. He was an awfully nice fellow."

Elena didn't seem to grasp how Ted was managing (under duress) behind enemy lines. She tried to elevate his sinking spirits, but often made it seem as though she was doing it for the praise he gave her, rather than from the goodness of her heart:-

"I saw the photo you sent me. It arrived this morning. You look so sad so I thought I would be specially nice to you to cheer you up. What were you thinking about? You mustn't forget to laugh. Why are you so solemn all of the time? I cannot remember when I wrote to you last, so I looked in my diary and there was no record. Sorry not to have written to you for a few weeks."

But life at home was starting to depress her, and she spoke of selling the Toll House:-

"What a silly letter this is but I have to get it off my chest. Dad still won't stay over here, and Mother won't come near the place. I stayed with them at Chester-le-Street last week. I was 'home' once again and it felt good. Too good. I fear for my life at times. I honestly do. The noises and the screams were back again last night. I can't take it much longer, Ted. My future is not in this house."

Ted's reply was short but enlightening:-

"I am sorry I am not able to answer all of your questions with a long letter because, due to new restrictions, we can only send one postcard a month. Sell the Toll House, Elena. It is an evil place, and I have said that to you countless times. As William Shakespeare once said - 'Hell is empty, the devils are here!' And I worry in case they are at your door."

Letters came and went, and the final one – No 31 out of a collection of 31 – was posted 8th December 1916. The Battle of the Somme was blazing like no war campaign before or since. On the first day alone, the British suffered 57,000 casualties, but Ted was miles away in the Rhineland. He was having it tough, but as soldiers did in those days, he made it sound as though he was on vacation at a Butlin's Holiday Camp to ease the worry back home. His last letter didn't get a reply:-

Dear Elena,
This is by no means the first attempt at writing this letter to you, but I hope this one actually gets to your letter box. Like you, I have thought a lot lately. About the war; you and me. You were funny in your last letter about the affection that has grown between us in the two years we have been apart. The fact is, I am labouring under

rather difficult circumstances in writing this letter. When we finally meet again, and I arrive at Blighty, can I meet you as my fiancee?

I would have much preferred asking you this question in person after having gauged your feelings on the matter, but 'faint heart never won fair lady'. So I am making the plunge and I can only trust that you do not think me too presumptuous as regards your affections. I am quite sure how I feel, and in very difficult times here in Germany, you have been such a brick to me during the whole time of my imprisonment.

Will you marry me?

The question remains with you.

Your loving servant,

Ted

The letter arrived at the Toll House but Elena didn't get to read it. She went missing two days before the postman dropped it through the letterbox. No-one ever saw her again.

The police inquest didn't throw any light on anything.

Did she run; did she hide? No trace of her was ever found. The only clue to her future (or lack of it) was the last entry in her diary:-

"I am in a place I don't belong. Going on with my life and trying to be someone I'm not sure I want to be. I cannot recognize the person I am anymore. But when it's two in the morning and I can't sleep, I start missing the old me again. I miss myself. I miss the place I call home. I miss the people and the feelings I had back then. I hate it, and I hate myself for this. There are a lot of 'things' that aren't how they should be. As far as I am concerned, I'm glad they are finally over."

The case was left open. No death certificate and no body. I checked with the local newspaper about the disappearance and there was a report in the Northern Echo the Christmas she went missing:-

"Saturday December 23rd 1916 Elena Nicolson left her home to visit her aunt in Chester-le-Street. The report of Miss Nicolson's disappearance stated that she was seen boarding a bus at 10.15am wearing a green lacy shirtwaist and a long narrow skirt. Her father was to meet her off the bus but she didn't arrive. She suffered from paralysis and could hardly move her left arm, a distinction that

police hope will help elicit sightings. Her father has offered a £100 reward for information leading to her discovery."

There was no footprint or headstone to pursue Elena, but the war records revealed a lot about Ted. I went through the Army archives, and although I originally thought he got off lightly during his three year stint in German hands, that was far from the case. His letters hid the truth. Soldiers in that particular POW camp endured "de-nutrition and methodical exploitation." They slept in hangars or tents, and dug holes to keep warm. Many suffered pulmonary illness including Emphysema.

Ted was awarded the Military Cross for outstanding bravery at Ypes, although records suggest he didn't attend the presentation because of illness. Like so many soldiers who had endured the Great War - "the war to end all wars" - he was never the same again. He returned to his home village of Coxhoe but died a month later aged 29, in December 1918.

Although Elena was never seen again, after Ted's death, letters started arriving at the Toll House purportedly written by her hand for her boyfriend. Yet Ted never actually lived at that address while he was alive. They were stories of their relationship recounting their happiest days. Three or four arriving each year, hand delivered, yet nobody ever saw who pushed them through the letterbox.

The final one was dated December 8th 1921, five years to the day that he proposed to her.

It read:-

"What I really want from you this Xmas Ted, is actually quite different from other years. Well, this is desperately what I want. I would like three wishes that will last forever.

1. For you to be my Prince.

2. To buy a castle.

3. For you to ask me to marry you.

Please do,

Elena xx"

CHAPTER ELEVEN

"IF OPPORTUNITY DOESN'T KNOCK – BUILD A DOOR"

Durham County Council had granted James (our boss) his wish and our building programme was finally underway. The designs for the manor houses had already been completed, with the company deciding on five dwellings that were going to be state-of-the-art. Our biggest, most expensive project to date.

Financial advisor Alan Ravenhall admitted he was rather jealous: "I've always wanted one of those, you know," he said, pointing at the artist's impersonation of how they would eventually look. "A house that rich people buy when they get paranoid about getting rid of their money before they pop their clogs. Too much dosh in the bank so they build themselves a fortress with tall electric gates, and more security gadgets than a military compound. Yeah it's a prison, but it's a beautiful prison."

Within the week the site was being cleared by a swarm of men in hard hats wearing 'hi viz' canary yellow waterproof jackets. There were bulldozers, cement mixers and a large excavator tearing the place apart. Bushes were uprooted and rocks thrown to one side as the monstrous steel jaws and hydraulic arms of the machines ate up the earth. A merciless onslaught that destroyed three or four hundred years of growth, effortlessly. By the end of the third week the area looked like a clearing in the Amazon rainforest, giving ourselves the platform to transform a wilderness.

For the first time in centuries, the 90ft Obelisk revealed itself to the world in all its splendour.

"The idea of Obelisks originally came from the Egyptians," said Ravenhall. "They placed a pair at the entrance to their temples. Something to do with their sun god."

"Have you been researching Egyptian history, Alan?" I laughed.

"Not so much 'researched' as Googled it."

Ours was built for a different purpose. But if I believed what I was told, it was the gateway to a remarkable secret.

"Hey, you're back again!" said Mrs Woodhouse as she opened the front door with a spurt of enthusiasm. "I am so happy to see you again."

"How is the old gentleman?" I said, greeting the lady with a peck on the cheek.

"Not too well, John," she said, seemingly slipping into an anxious ambience. "The doctor came to see him yesterday."

"Perhaps I should have left it," I replied.

"He wants to see you, so I cannot see what harm it will do."

I didn't realise he was laid up in bed or I certainly wouldn't have made the journey. I walked into the bedroom and I saw a steely man struck down with old age. He was a pale figure of the guy I had seen only a month previous. At 82 years of age you would expect a withered look, but he was deteriorating too much, too soon.

His eyes lit up at the sight of me, and that was a blessing.

"Hello my good friend," he said, holding out his hand to greet me.

"What's this all about William? Have you slept in?" I joked.

"Rose has stopped me smoking in bed. Ridiculous. She says I'm senile and I might burn down the house. Rubbish. If I burn down the house it will be on purpose! I've still got my mind, but not much else is functioning. Some parts of my body are falling off!" he said, laughing so much I thought his false teeth were going to shoot out of his mouth.

William had phoned me asking if I could visit him because I had left his book behind at my last visit, and he claimed he had more information about the Toll House for me. He was like a worn out book, himself. One I could turn to for inspiration. He genuinely wanted to help, as though being actively involved in a project was keeping him functioning.

I gave him an update on anything and everything involving Smelt, and he was fascinated (perhaps even excited) by the fact I had met him face to face. His health was obviously blurring at the edges, but his mind was very much alive.

"Who got to Smelt at the end, William? Who put him in the cage?"

"I don't honestly know. Either the Masons or the church. He had enemies on both sides."

"Would the church go to such extremes? Did they have 'heavies' in those days?" I asked.

"You must be joking," he replied. "There were more bloody gangsters and murderers in the church than in the Mafia! The church rule by fear, and they have done since the start of religion. What is religion? Moses was supposed to have written the first five books of the bible in 1300BC, yet there is no proof that Moses ever existed.

The New Testament was written no earlier that 100 years after the death of Jesus, so none or the writers were alive at the time he was performing so-called miracles. The bible wasn't published here in England until 1526, and that included 'add-ons' by another section of religious people who didn't know what they were talking about."

"So you are not a believer, then?" I laughed.

"No, and I never was, not until now. Your meeting with Smelt puts a whole knew slant on it."

"How do you mean?" I asked.

"Because Satin, or the Devil, are biblical creations. The concept of Satanism is an invention of Christianity. There was no Devil until the bible invented him. As the bible was adapted and expanded through the creation of folklore – people telling their own far fetched tales – the Devil became more of a demon. The whole point of the exercise was to terrify people, so that they could be 'saved' by God."

"What are you getting at?"

"If Smelt is part of Satanism, and that was his sole intention when he was alive, he is doing a good job of promoting it now he is dead. The point I am making is simple – if we have a Devil – we must have a God!"

"You are saying that Smelt is the Devil?"

"What do you think he is?" he said, throwing the question back at me.

"I cannot explain him, William. I cannot explain what I saw."

"If you have bulldozers on that land, you are going to dig him up," he said, reminding me of the fears I had right from the start. "You are going to release him … and possibly a lot more like him … because they have been living amongst the dead in that tunnel system for centuries. 'Each crypt is linked' - the words of William Wharton in the 1850's. They terrified him, so he built a castle. Those houses you are building on Western Hill – are they castles? They will need to be."

"What do you suggest I do?"

"The Toll House seems to be the key. He conducted sacrifices there, and he fought his battle with the church from that location. Every person who made that place a home was made to suffer. You only have to look at the census records to see who they were."

"Who took it over after the lady in the Great War?"

"Lady Jane Coddington. She is featured in my book 'Durham's Darkest Mysteries,' a book you left behind on your visit here."

"Yes, I was so wrapped up in our conversation I left it."

"It could teach you a lot. I suggest you read it. It's on the bookshelf over there. It will give you a run-down on Lady Jane's time there?"

I picked up the book and took my glasses from the inside pocket of my jacket.

"William," I said apologetically, "You don't mind if flick through this right now, do you?"

"Not at all dear fellow. ROSE … PUT THE KETTLE ON!" he bellowed down the corridor. And soon the kettle was on the boil.

Lady Jane Coddington - 'Durham's Darkest Mysteries' by William J Woodhouse.

Lady Jane Coddington was next to reside in the Toll House, some five or six months after it was, assumed, Elena would not be returning. The Lady had properties in abundance, her father made his money from shipping, but she required a 'folly' close to the heart of the city for the hot summer of 1920 to entertain friends. She was very much a lady about town, who mixed with the gentry, boasting that film actors Charles Chaplin and Douglas Fairbanks were close friends who she visited regularly in the States. Those two gentlemen were Hollywood royalty at that time, and as she liked to 'name-drop', those were the names that would get a jaw-dropping reaction.

A film critic who knew her from her frequent visits to London theatres in Covent Garden, Soho and Dury Lane once described her as "the archetypal English rose" with "porcelain skin, ashen and bloodless." She was, herself, a major celebrity – in her own mind! She paid the reporter to promote her status in the capital, although nobody of high standing really knew her.

There was no proof that she ever met Chaplin or Fairbanks, but no doubt she convinced herself, in her own little world, that she had. Just as Jozef Bruwlaski borrowed the title of Count, Jane unassumingly bought the title of Lady.

"Leave me to my eccentricities," she once said. "Because I wallow in them."

The summer of 1920 went well for Jane. People who knew her painted a good picture of fun and laughter and her head seemed to be 'in the right place.' It was May 1921 when things took a turn for the worst. Although she was married, her husband was rarely at home. A man of limited resources (he was actually an animal trainer at a fairground when she met him), he struck lucky with a chance meeting with Jane at a carnival in 1918. They were married within the year. While Jane entertained in her folly that summer of 1921, Ronald made regular trips to the French Riviera, making the most of his new found wealth.

It didn't take long for her to realize her life was ebbing away and her marriage was becoming a sham. She was 31, childless, and her wealth was proving more of a hindrance than a luxury. According to friends, she suffered with horrible bouts of depression and she started to spend more time at the Toll House, at one point saying it was the only place she could 'find herself.' Lady Jane, who had a medical history of being mentally fragile, was teetering on the brink.

Disaster struck one May evening when Jane's best friend, Eleanor, collapsed at the door of the Toll House and died of unexplained injuries. Her neck was broken as though she had been strung up from a gallows, and there were rope burns on her wrists and neck. Yet Lady Jane swore on oath that Eleanor simply collapsed as she walked out of the door to go home. Nothing more – nothing less – a simple fall.

The autopsy described it as a hanging, and a crime investigation was immediately launched. Jane's mental health descended into slow and excruciating torture. She insisted the house had become sentient and 'angry', which didn't help her medical case, and one doctor suggested she was insane and appropriate action should be taken.

One evening everything came to a head. She had a breakdown and relatives were called to the Toll House because she deteriorated so rapidly, there was fear she wouldn't see out the night. While under sedation she suffered disturbing subjective symptoms, spasms and convulsions that were later described as 'possession by evil spirits,' but denounced by the family doctor as being a religious hoax.

A priest was called that evening, much to the annoyance of the doctor. There was a lot of strange activity in the house, and several family members left in haste. The doctor claimed Lady Jane was "not of sound mind" and he was concerned that the priest was "influencing her behaviour." He said Lady Jane was: "Confused and disorientated under medication and open to the power of suggestion. She was an ill, delusional patient that should not have been subject to forcible physical restraint that cause intense, angry confrontations. The priest was trying to perform an exorcism yet she descended into madness, slow and excruciating."

Much to the distress of himself, and the anxiety of others, Jane's father said that evening: "Most people assume they can at least recognize themselves in their offspring. But what if you don't? I don't recognize myself in my daughter. I don't recognize my daughter!"

The priest said: "Pivoting on the idea that we are often blinded by the features we cannot see, some psychic power was at work."

Something put the woman through unimaginable sexual abuse, while the priest and doctor stood back helpless.

The priest said: "What could anyone do when a room drips with ominous meaning and horrific intent? I don't believe Lady Jane was possessed by demonic spirits, but I believe she was raped by one. Was she emotionally and mentally disturbed? I believe so, but that didn't influence what happened. An invisible demonic entity invoked supernatural powers on her. Scratch marks suddenly appeared on her face and naked body, and troubled onlookers were flung towards walls and windows. It was impossible to conduct an exorcism because, at one point, I found myself pinned to a door by my throat. Lady Jane was manipulated like a rag doll, forced up against a wall 2ft off the floor, her arms out stretched like Christ on a cross. Family members ran while the doctor collapsed, struck in the face from an invisible attacker. There was more than one entity in that room. Two or three concealed figures that never showed themselves."

We don't really know what happened that evening because we only have the information from character witness reports, and that's not much. Only the priest and the doctor actually wrote down accounts, the doctor reporting: "Rape can be categorized in different ways, mainly by the reference to the situation in which it occurs. First you need a victim, which we have. Secondly you need a rapist, which we don't have. I believe the victim was incapacitated but I don't know how or by who.

But, the hideous activity only stopped after half-an-hour of carnage on a young woman's defenceless body. I was struck unconscious by something (or someone) that didn't want to be identified. I cannot give a description."

Lady Jane recovered from her ordeal in time. She made good again, and friends said she "recaptured her sparkle." Some claimed her mental state improved, while others refute it, so we can only wonder. But Lady Jane returned home to live with her mother and father and vowed never to return to the Toll House again. She meant every word.

Whatever happened that evening was meant to be laid to rest and never spoken of again. But there was a footnote that meant the opposite.

Jane's husband was having an affair, and if anyone is going to 'sponge' from their wife, I assume the 'sponger' may as well dip his foot in the Mediterranean and be done with it. Ronald (the husband) was getting by quite nicely living it up in their holiday home in the south of France, reportedly seeing a French courtesan called Adele. Then he received a letter from his dear wife saying the marriage was over:-

"I have just realised that the most dominant part of a horror story is the suspense before the horror starts. Not so much before, or after, but smack bang in the middle. You and I have not had sexual relations for many months, Ronald, but does it matter? I thought we both wanted children, but things change. People change. Am I faithful? Yes I am, one hundred percent. Are you? Can a foetus be an effective horror story? Oh it can, for sure. Especially when it is growing into something paradoxically different to what everybody else produces. Nine whole months of anticipation, with the horror growing inside. I have tried to figure out what put it there, and what it will turn into. I'm not the virgin Mary, but that is the closest comparison I can come up with. I'm pregnant, Ronald. Don't worry, you needn't seek out an explanation for Adele, I already know about your French Molly. You and me ... we don't have a bridge to build. We have a bridge to burn."

I turned to William, who was sat up patiently in his bed looking out of the window, and I spoilt his concentration: "The chapter on Lady Jane ..."

"Yes, interesting isn't it?"

"What happened? Did she have the child?"

"Oh, that's another story," he said, smiling to himself.

"You can't just leave it there William, there has to be a conclusion."

"It's further on in my book, another chapter. Jane left the Toll House and a married couple called Kieron and Clara O'Brien arrived from Kilkenny. You should read that, too. Very compelling reading. Take it home with you."

I let the book fall closed. It made an exhausted sound like a puff of air. It had a battered cover and dog-eared pages, obviously well read.

"Do you read this often?" I asked.

"It's been loaned out a few times. People don't always treat books with the respect they deserve."

Then I changed the subject.

"Do you think I should explore the tunnel, William? I'm temped."

"For what reason?" he replied.

"I don't know. I get a 'calling' to check it out. No rational explanation."

"What did the guy in Spain say about it?"

"He said it's a death trap and he would never go down it again."

"There's your answer."

"Yeah but it's easy to say that," I said, foolishly trying to convince myself the risk was worth it. "Come on William, give me an excuse to go down there. You are the Cathedral expert. You know the place. Give me a justification to risk my life."

"Oh I could do that very easily," he said, looking me straight in the eye as though he was checking to see how determined I really was.

"Go on … I'm all ears," I replied.

"The person you want to talk to is the Spanish guy. He knows what's down there, as a threat, and he probably knows what's at the end of the tunnel, too. It's all to do with Henry VIII and Ann Bolynne."

"Henry VIII?" I asked. That was a whammy I wasn't expecting.

"Henry wanted to marry Ann and the pope wouldn't allow him a divorce from Catherine of Aragon. Henry split from the Catholic church and ordered the 'Dissolution of the Monasteries,' which involved taking away their income and stripping them of their assets."

"Yeah, that's when they arrived and reputedly smashed up St Cuthbert's tomb," I said, remembering my history lessons from school.

"Yes, that's what they did. But Durham, being so far north and one of the last to be raided, the Monks were tipped off in advance that Thomas Cromwell's men were on their way. Gold and treasures were hidden, but Henry meant business. If any treasures were concealed and then recovered, heads would roll … literally! It was rumoured that there was a tunnel stretching to Finchale Abbey. It held the most treasure, but due to rock falls and coal mining catastrophes, the gold was lost forever as the passageways crumbled."

"So where does that put 'our' tunnel?" I asked. "Isn't it probable that ours suffered the same?"

"Yes it does. But, and there is a big 'but' … your tunnel is a hell of a lot nearer to the Cathedral. To get from Finchale Abbey to your Obelisk the tunnel goes under Brasside, Framwellgate Moor and Aykley Heads. That has to be two miles at least. I don't believe they would build a secret tunnel that far. The treasure was placed somewhere between the Obelisk and the Cathedral. Considering the Cathedral entrance was totally blocked off, you have the gateway to a fortune."

"What's the down side" I asked.

He laughed at the thought.

"There are many 'ifs-and-buts' along the way, and the treasure was most likely recovered centuries ago, but there was no record of it being found. That gives you a chance. A slim chance, granted, but the opportunity is knocking."

If opportunity doesn't knock … build a door.

CHAPTER TWELVE

"BLESS THIS HOME – AND ALL WHO ENTER"

I remember Kimberley's words so well when we were heading home from the holiday in Spain. I said: "I got the information I wanted. That has to be a triumph."

She replied: "It's only a success if he (Benjamin) was telling the truth."

That daughter of mine is always honest and sincere, even when it is detrimental to the cause. She means what she says, and it scares people at times. Emotions on full throttle - forget the fine tuning.

Benjamin didn't have to meet us that evening. Yes, curiosity played a major part, but I wanted to give the guy credit. Because I thought he gave us honesty at his expense. We gained a lot, and I include Kimberley in that because she played her part in extracting the maximum we could from an emotionally charged situation. What did Benjamin walk away with? The knowledge the police were on his tail, and very little else. Yet he told us the truth.

I ran through this with my daughter during a phone call, but she wasn't as forthcoming with the compliments: "Honesty? He stole a quarter of a million pounds from his wife! Get a reality check, Dad."

Point taken, but if I was going to go tunnelling in a grisly hell-hole fighting demons and dragons, I needed to know what to expect. And he was the only guy who knew the score. I had a record of the phone number Benjamin used to contact me in Spain. I only had to press redial. He didn't answer my first call so I left a message on voice mail explaining why I wanted to talk to him, saying I would phone back on the hour. I was at home, and that hour dragged tediously, as once again I listened to the monotonous beeping tone, nervously waiting for a Spanish voice. Finally I got a reply.

"Benjamin, I'm sorry to disturb your evening buddy, but I would welcome a quick chat if you could manage it."

"OK, what can I do for you?"

"I hope you are keeping well, my friend. Carrying on from our conversation in Altea, can I talk to you about the tunnel system on Western Hill."

"You aren't seriously considering going down there?" he remarked. "I thought I'd put you off that idea."

"What inspired you to go down, Benjamin? What was your motivation? Curiosity or financial gain?"

"What would be financial about going down a tunnel?" he quizzed. But he knew what I meant.

"Gold or treasure, perhaps. Did that not tip the scales?"

He didn't reply for quite a few seconds, before finally saying: "What do you know about the gold?"

"I'm just grasping at straws. What about gold from the Henry VIII's Reformation in December 1539? A historian I know 'suggests' there could be hidden treasures in one of the tunnels worth millions. Do you know anything about it?"

He gave out a slight chuckle before enquiring about my research: "I've heard of it. What historian?"

"William J Woodhouse. The gentleman claims it could have been recovered at a later date. So I thought I'd phone you and pick your brains. Do you know more than me?"

"I know William," he replied. "Well … I don't know him, but I know of him. I would imagine that treasure was recovered a few years after it was hidden. It had a death sentence! If Henry's assassins found hidden loot the monks would have gone to the gallows. So they wouldn't have been too eager to retrieve it. But there were traces that some treasure was left. In 1910 the Coal Board stumbled upon five gold coins dated around the time of the Magna Carter. They claimed their digging impacted an old escape tunnel, but it collapsed and made the area unstable. It was too dangerous to continue excavating and they abandoned that seam. How true that is, we don't know. They could have found the gold and cleaned up for all we know."

"Being honest, Benjamin, is it worth going down there?"

"Nobody knows what treasure it was. There wasn't an itinerary list because it was secret. It's a comic book story that all boys grow up with. All kids want adventure.

"If you were a betting man, what are the odds of finding it?" I asked.

"Odds of it being there I'd say 3/1. Odds of finding it … about 1,000/1. On the positive side, remember St Cuthbert's body was hidden from Cromwell's men, so they obviously had a hiding place. Probably many hiding places."

"And the negative side?"

"It's two miles from Western Hill to the Cathedral; crawling on your belly; kicking away rats the size of cats; then deciding which tunnels to take. I suspect it will be more nearer the Cathedral than the Obelisk. Will you get to it? No chance! Don't get pound signs in your eyes, John, because nothing is worth the risk. I mean it. There are things down there you don't want to meet. Forget it."

The plan was to phone the guy, get assurances, then the rubber could hit the road. The brakes were back on.

_____

If only I'd taken William's book home when the kind gentleman offered it to me on my first visit, I could have saved myself a lot of leg work. I poured myself into that book, it was everything I needed to know. The chapter on the Toll House had a vice-like grip on me. The twisted reality of those people that had suffered there, could never be underestimated. They were all characters that could have come from an Edgar Allan Poe horror book, yet I could relate to them all and feel their pain. It was terrifying stuff. The sort of book I wanted to put in the freezer and then move in with someone (anyone!) because I didn't want to spend the night alone.

The world is a dangerous place to live, not because of the buildings, but because of evil people. But was the Toll House evil? I couldn't make up my mind. People that lived there should never have opened the door to a subsidiary evil, because greater ones inevitably crept in with it. Does that make the house evil?

Kieron and Clara O'Brien - 'Durham's Darkest Mysteries' by William J Woodhouse.

In November of 1923 an Irish couple called Kieron and Clara O'Brien took down the 'For Rent' signs and moved their meagre possessions in through the front door of the Toll House.

Many years later they featured in a book that made them notorious figures in horror circles nationwide. The author claimed that they arrived in England from Kilkenny. But I think he just pulled that town out of a hat, because they were Irish-American, and arrived in England from New York.

The trip took six days on the RMS Mauretania, in choppy Atlantic seas, as the couple looked to start a new life in a new country. They picked Durham, of all places, because Clara's mother lived in Durham, North Carolina, and they thought it would be a lucky omen. Kieron and Clara could have come from Hell for all I know ... because that was where they were heading back to.

When words fail us, or we see more than words can ever explain ... that's when fear leaps far beyond anything speech can accomplish. I say that about this couple because they were not really of this world. They were Bonny and Clyde without the firearms, but with a hell of a lot more firepower. Evil was an aphrodisiac to them, the more extreme, the better.

The author of that notorious book also wrongly claimed Kieron had spent time in Alcatraz Federal Penitentiary in 1920. Alcatraz wasn't opened until 1934. The prison he was referring to was Eastham Prison in Texas. The toughest prison in America at that time, and probably the toughest in American history. It was where Kieron suffered physical and mental abuse in a penal institution that was filthy, dangerous, overcrowded and neglected. A place where the prisoners maintained their own (kind of) order. It had a gang-controlled hierarchy where the low-status, weak and vulnerable inmates were made to suffer. Kieron just happened to be the weakest of the weak.

After serving two years for a gun felony, he was released having suffered the humiliation of rape and brutality that we can only imagine. His final two months were in solitary confinement for his own protection. He lived from day to day knowing that tomorrow was never guaranteed. Although he saw out his time, he left knowing survival shows little sentiment when you have a fractured mind.

We know nothing of Clara's early life. She fabricated so many stories it was impossible to work out what was fact and what was fiction. But we do know that they met due to a Lonely Hearts advert placed in the New York Times by Kieron that read: "Toe-rag seeks witch who hates everyone and everything."

The advert drew curiosity from one or two 'hopefuls', but genuine interest from Clara. They were made for each other. Psychologists must struggle to explain how a macabre love can overpower decency and humanity, for a partner to risk all for a crooked purpose. But Clara did. All for an emaciated, malnourished skeleton who weighed in around 8st. Kieron looked like a refugee from a prison camp.

Somehow they had money, and lots of it. No-one knew where it came from, but a 'blind man on a galloping horse' could see it wasn't legitimate. So when they arrived in Durham, the Toll House was well within their budget for renting purposes. Regrettably, they never hit it off with the neighbours.

Kieron had a low IQ, bi-polar syndrome, and a high drive for sexual deviancy. Not a good combination, particularly when his wife was just as perverted and twisted as he was. They first tried choking each other while making love, and other ways of asphyxiation. When the thrill from that faded they introduced a third party. It wan't long before they prayed on young vulnerable women, often the homeless and the desperate. Clara was the key to it all, portraying a loving caring face to entice the weak and defenceless. It cannot be termed 'abduction' because the 'victims' were offered a warm room for the night, and a high percentage of them took it. Some stayed more than one night and some actually moved in. Rooms were selected for different practices and the Toll House became a sadistic, warren-like sex shop. Their home became a macabre menagerie full of people at all hours of the day and night, engrossed in bizarre and perverted sexual activities. Clara worked as a prostitute from their own bedroom, not only for the money, but simply for the gratification.

Police were regular callers to investigate allegations of child abuse and prostitution but, for whatever reason, no charges were made. Kieron and Clara proved a powerful duo at denying and deflecting, although it was suggested 'favours' were often given to satisfy the curiosity of the Old Bill.

But then things changed, and even the mists of time wreathed around this deviant couple couldn't cloak the brutality of their crimes.

When others claim to finding God, Kieron found the opposite. He had a vision one evening and it took him to another level. He started practicing grotesque ritualistic devil worship and some of his lodgers became followers. He claimed he heard voices that told him he had to arrange Satanic sacrifices, and he got so wrapped up in the moment, he prepared for it. Clara, too, "heard the voices and had a vision," and from that moment it was guaranteed that their relationship was not going to end well.

The first atrocity connected to the Toll House was the story of 19-year old Charlene Appleyard who spent three months with the O'Brien's when they took her off the streets where she was working as a 'lady of the night.' She left the house, for whatever reason, and returned to her hostel in the city. Then two days later she was arrested on suspicion of burning her three-year old son in an alleged satanic ritual. She was found sat on a chair in St Mary's Church next to the altar of Christ, holding her son who was totally burned black.

The newspaper reported (April 4th 1924): *"Neighbours called the police, who arrived and found a metal tub with blood evidence in her home, as well as wood and a lighter. Witnesses claimed she was repeatedly saying phrases in Latin when she was found. They don't think she acted alone because they said there had seen several men and women leaving the house, and had heard the tot's shouts. Miss Appleyard went missing but was later found in St Mary's church clutching the child. Police believe that the woman may have some psychological problems and authorities have been called. The investigation is ongoing."*

Meanwhile, back at the Toll House, blood was the meal of the day. Clara told a 'follower' she had learned how to drink blood from a human without piercing an artery. But after dabbling in that art of extracting blood, things turned deadly when the couple claimed they had "orders to kill" from Satin.

The victim was 38-year old prostitute Mary Hatfield, known locally as 'Hatty'. She was not a resident of the now-brothel, but she worked there most days. Clara later said that they had selected her as their sacrificial victim because she was "the most lewd of the girls and will do anything, so she will keep Satin happy."

It was a brutal slaying. While Kieron had sex with her, Clara attacked her repeatedly with a claw-hammer. Cracking open her skull, then stabbing her several times with a kitchen knife. Apparently, or so she told the police, she drank Hatty's blood while her husband continued having sex.

The police report claimed there were 66 stab wounds. Her butchered body was found several miles away by a dog walker on the heathered grassland known as Waldridge Fell. Local man, Barry Bonarez, was arrested but later released. A walker had seen him on the Fell splattered with blood, carrying a gun, but he had been killing vermin.

As the days rolled by, and the constant threat of being caught, Clara became more and more unstable. Kieron, on the other hand, fell further into lust and debauchery. At that point he genuinely believed he was acting as a "tool for Satin." In his mind there was nothing wrong with killing. It was all for the sake of sacrifice and "the dark book", and the voices grew louder and louder in his head.

"If you run someone over with a car, you don't prosecute the car," he told his wife (and Clara later repeated those words in court).

Clara was soon diagnosed with mental health issues and was evaluated after she began attacking passing pedestrians in the street. Her hallucinations became more frequent as she told doctors she was in direct contact with the Devil. She asked doctors and nurses to visit the Toll House and see for themselves. Nobody did. She was sectioned.

Kieron's love affair with Satin developed to such an extent that he started to believe he WAS Satin. He 'befriended' an elderly down-and-out in the city and invited him back to the Toll House. But in time he tortured and humiliated the defenceless old man, helped by a young prostitute called Amy Davies, who had enough mental problems of her own. The litany of cruelty included several anti-religious symbols branded on to his back with a hot poker, broken ribs, and his feet put in scalding water. He suffered regular beating, but during the course of one hiding, Kieron was mysteriously thrown across the room and pinned up against the wall about 10ft off the floor. Amy described it as: "As though he was doing it to himself … no-one was there! After several seconds he crashed to the ground. There was blood coming from his eye sockets and mouth. He was dead!"

His injuries were too many to list. Just about every major bone in his body was broken, and he had internal injuries as though he had been hit by a steam train.

Clara later admitted to killing Hatty, but pleaded 'not guilty' to murder, saying she was instructed to do it by Satin and "it had to be done."

Look at enough killer couples and you start to notice similarities – most killers flee broken homes where violence and sexual abuse are norm. The biggest and most finite commonality between them is that they almost always turn on each other when they are caught. But not in this case. Kieron wasn't alive to blame anyone, but Clara would not have a word said against him.

CHAPTER THIRTEEN

"STOP FEELING THE STORM – BE THE HURRICANE!"

The fox terrier bolted out of the undergrowth and legged it towards Fay's house.

"It always heads off in that direction then I lose sight of it," I told one of the labourers on site. "Did you see where it went when it got to the fence?"

"See what?" he replied.

"The dog!"

"What dog?"

"You are kidding me. The dog that shot out of the long grass."

He gave me a raise of the eyebrows and 'that look' that makes you doubt your sanity. We've all had it, when its time to shut up rather than dig a bigger hole. Perhaps he didn't have "the gift" … or perhaps I was losing my marbles.

The landscaping was coming along well. Five acres is a decent bit of land and the guys did a great job in a short space of time. It was amazing how quickly they could move when the foreman was on site. The idea was to dig the foundations for all five houses at the same time, then erect the buildings after that. James decided it wasn't practical to construct one house at a time. He wanted all of the clients to move in when the entire job was completed. It made sense. Who would want to move into a multi-million property when the location looks like Baghdad on bonfire night?

I wanted to be on-hand throughout the first stage to see what they dug up when the machinery got to work. The land was as old as Father Time and, despite safety checks and land surveys, I had a strange feeling that anything could appear. The first foundation went as planned. Although no maps showed any sign of buildings on Western Hill apart from the Toll House, old bricks from a bygone age were brought to the surface. I rummaged through everything they dug up, and the brickwork was a Victorian underground tunnel that was a drainage system for the old Catholic church. It was probably a dig that members of 'Time Team' would have found riches from a by-gone age. Old pins, arrow heads and pottery, while I was looking for the obvious, a treasure chest. Sadly, I didn't find anything older than a pitman's leather boot that was probably no more than 1910. Thankfully there wasn't a foot still in it! That would have been another 'tools down' and work discontinued for the day.

The second foundation didn't go so well. The survey showed the land was all rock and shingle when it wasn't. The excavator dug four foot down and then nose-dived into a cavern, which caused mayhem. All the while, my imaginary friend (the fox terrier) looked on from a distance.

The first task was to get the excavator out of the hole, then we had to examine the cavity to see how far it stretched. I stood on the bank and looked into the crevice, then I could feel the ground underneath my boots give way. I gasped, my arms flailed as I tried to grab onto something to keep me up, but a trap-door seemed to open and gravity took me downwards. After a few moments I splashed into frigid cold water right up to my chest, knocking the wind out of my lungs. I splashed around for a while, trying to drag my feet out of the mud but only making matters worse. It was more of a drama that it needed to have been. I wasn't going to drowned.

"Are you OK Mr Hampson?" came the cry from above.

"Yeah, see if you can find a rope," I coughed and spluttered.

I could feel wood underneath the mud, as though I was stood on a wooden plinth. But as I tried to feel how solid it was, by stamping on its surface, the wood cracked and splintered into pieces. I dropped down another 18 inches or so, and now there really was a drama. I dropped below the water level. I wasn't particularly concerned about a little bit water over my head, but alarm bells would ring if I went down any further. It was only when a piece of old clothing floated past my face that I realise I was stood in a coffin. Then bones and body parts swirled around my arms and chest, like a clip from some horror movie. At least, stood in a coffin, I wasn't liable to drop any further. I could get my head above water easy enough, but the thought of taking a mouthful of water filled with decaying flesh was stomach churning.

I could hear music playing from a nearby radio up above, and the most bizarre thoughts flashed through my head as I bobbed up and down gasping for breath. I closed my eyes but all I could picture was Smelt's face, then I could smell his stinking breath. That never-to-be-forgotten acid stench of vomit.

My heart was hammering inside.

"Keep your mouth closed!" I kept reminding myself, but the smell was churning my stomach. My head was pounding, every cell of my body screaming for oxygen.

I could feel something brushing against my face and I opened my eyes.

"Grab hold! Grab hold!" bellowed a voice from above, as he dangled a rope noose into the water. "Put it over your head and under your arms!"

I did as instructed, and he (and his fellow workers) dragged me to the surface.

Still the music played, getting louder and louder as I was pulled to the top. It was a rap artist who sounded like a child chanting a repetitive nursery rhyme. But, for some unknown reason, I felt like singing along.

My next thought was one of embarrassment. I was soaked and covered in stinking mud, and I was sure half the work force were fighting back tears of laughter. I looked at their faces and I could sense their thoughts: "The boss has fallen down a hole! I wish I'd videoed it for Facebook or Youtube. We might even have got £250 for the clip on TV."

I thanked them for the help, but deep down I was mortified. I stood up and scraped the mud off my trousers.

"Wait till the boys in the office hear about this," I moaned to myself.

The O'Brien's made the Toll House notorious in the 1920's. Although 'notorious' is probably not the right word. Let's try 'shameful.' Their illicit acts of sexual promiscuity and genocide turned the place into a Freak Show. The blame should stop with them, but in the eyes of the public, the church was responsible in some degree, because they rented it out. What went on in that house was hardly a secret. Some of the neighbours even suggest the church was involved in its sexual degradation, although that was never proven. It was fervently denied ... as you would expect. It was then that the Freemasons stepped in. Two-peas-in-the-same pod, the Masons and the church had a curious relationship. Trying to take the pressure off the Catholic Church, the Masons offered to buy back the building, but no deal was ever struck. The church knocked back all offers, but many thought it was only a propaganda exercise anyway.

It was a full five years before anyone made it a 'home' again. The image of the building was shamed and tarnished to the point that residents in nearby homes organised a petition to get it pulled down. That was flatly refused by the church and the council. But with all eyes focused on what was going to happen, the next tenants had to be squeaky clean.

Henry Gelston - 'Durham's Darkest Mysteries' by William J Woodhouse.

This time the church took care of its own, and a young priest called Henry Gelston arrived at the door of the now infamous, House of Horrors.

He was a military chaplain during the First World War, and although Catholicism was very much a minority religion in the British Isles at that time, the Catholic faith rose during the conflict.

The chaplains were very much at the 'sharp end' of the battlefield. Although the official ruling was that they were not to go to the frontline, and unlike the Anglican chaplains who stuck by the rule, the Catholic chaplains simply ignored the regulations to give the last rights to dying soldiers. The rule was relaxed in 1916 and they could all 'do what they had to do' in the midst of battle.

At the start of the war it was felt chaplains would be a nuisance and it would be bad for morale if one of them happened to get shot. They were excluded from combat and not officially part of the army because they weren't conscripted. But Gelston was also a stretcher bearer, never more than 100 yards from the front line. Described at the time as "a life saver, rather than a life taker," the stretcher bearers couldn't carry guns, and they were an inspiration to many soldiers. Gelston was so enthusiastic about the khaki uniform he rarely wore his clerical collar while on military service, preferring to be indistinguishable from his fellow officers. Considering he couldn't carry a gun, and couldn't be distinguished on the battlefield as a man of God, that was courage of the highest order.

Although not officially a soldier, he was presented with the Military Cross for bravery at the Somme when he lost an eye from grenade shrapnel helping a dying soldier.

That soldier was Bartholomen Gelston, a Sergeant in the Yorkshire Regiment known as the Green Howards. The name gives away the tale … it was Henry's older brother.

The story goes that Henry found him in a pitiful state, blown up by a mine, impaled on barbed wire about 50 yards from German lines. An arm and leg were not quite amputated, but hanging onto his body by scorched skin and God's will. Bullets were flying front and back of them as Henry pulled him to a bomb-hole. Carnage was raging all around them. The slaughtered were hushed; the dying made it known they weren't quite ready for that same graveyard.

Henry said: *"There were buttercups and forget-me-nots, and the sun shone just like back home when we played football with wooly jumpers for goalposts. Bart was happy to see me, and I say that with tears in my eyes. He smiled, then looked up at the sky looking for God.*

"He didn't want me to give him the Last Rights, he just wanted to talk to our mother. Then he convinced me she was there. He spoke of their love in such a meaningful way it was as though she was listening and talking back. Obviously I couldn't hear her, but as sure as God made little apples, HE could! I've seen a lot of strange things on the battlefield, and this was just one of them. I cannot explain the reason for angels; dead men walking; and my mother laying our Bart to rest, but they happened.

"He wanted to end it there and then, and I could understand why, because I'd have wanted the same. 'Finish it!' Bart said, and he meant it. The bugle didn't sound; the pipe organ didn't play; but I placed a handkerchief over his eyes and sang a song: **Abide with me, fast falls the eventide; The darkness deepens Lord, with me abide; When other helpers fail and comforts flee: Help of the helpless, oh, abide with me.**

"Then I pulled the trigger."

The general rule during WW1 was that, if you were on a battlefield, you were buried where you dropped. Sometimes shelling actually stopped to allow both sides to dispose of their dead.

Henry took Bart's dog-tag, pay book and personal items … but took the unprecedented step of cutting out his heart and placing it in a mess-tin … to take home to be buried on British soil. During a spell on leave back home, Henry organised for the heart to be buried in the family burial plot at a special service conducted by himself.

Many soldiers failed to re-adapt to normal life after the war, and Henry suffered with mental trauma. He struggled to sleep in a bed because he had spent four years sleeping on the soil of a damp, rat-infested trench. Sleep became sporadic as he was tormented by visions and nightmares of his brother's last moments.

He returned to his home town of Leeds after the war and then moved to Durham in 1931, taking over duties at St Cuthbert's Church in the city.

Described as having "the height of a giant, but none of the bulk," we can assume he would be handy at getting a tin of beans off the top shelf in a shop. One of his congregation portrayed him as "soft on the inside, although he looked tough and composed on the outside. He carried a number of scars on his face, and always wore a black eye patch."

Another claimed she was constantly drawn to those scars: "I tried not to stare but I kept finding my eyes diverted to his face. Such a handsome man disfigured in his prime. His face must have been a daily living reminder of the horrors of war."

Despite his heart-rending appearance, Henry became the pillar of the community. Humble and respectful, he was devout to his faith. One of his flock said: "He never judged harshly and always showed you the right way back to God. He could shine a light when there was despair."

Sadly, he suffered despair himself, and that became apparent after three months in his new parish. If his scars were a daily reminder of anguish, his mind tortured him on an evening. He revealed to his congregation that war was never far from his mind, and he suffered sleepless nights, dreaming about one particular soldier.

He died under suspicious circumstances in 1932, having been at the Toll House for only ten months.

———————————————

That particular chapter offered more questions than answers, and I phoned Mrs Woodhouse to ask if William was healthy enough to take visitors. The last thing I wanted to do was interrupt his sleep pattern. I was intrigued with the story of the soldier, specifically as there was no conclusion. William left the reader hanging. How did he die?

Rose said William was having "one of his better days" so I told her to expect a visitor. Thirty minutes later I was at the door, wrapping the brass lion knocker, and I waited. The door opened and quickly Rose gave me an update on her husband's condition.

"He's OK, John. He's still bedridden, but a lot perkier than yesterday. He won't take his medication, that's half the problem."

I walked into the bedroom and he was out of bed, rummaging amongst a mound of books on a table.

"I thought you were supposed to take it easy," I said, rushing to steady him.

"I've had enough of it," he said, holding one particular book, then manoeuvring his way towards his armchair. He grasped me with his left hand and I decided to take him wherever he wanted to go. He was determined he wasn't going back to bed.

Settled in his chair with his knees covered by a red and black woollen cover. He struggled to get his breath. Obviously he wasn't as well as he had convinced himself.

"I hope you are taking your medicine," I semi-joked, trying to make light of it. But whatever the doctors were giving him, he needed some immediately.

Rose was flustered, and I felt for her. She was trying her best to keep the old guy content and happy, but it seemed to be a thankless task. It was only when she had gone that I mentioned it: "You need to take your medication, William."

"Has Rose told you that?" he said abruptly.

"Rose doesn't need to tell me, I can see by your face. You are not a well man, and she wants you to get better."

On the wall was a row of diplomas neatly hung in line, and I noticed him letting his eyes roam over them. I could only imagine what he was thinking. Life was passing him by, and he knew it. For a few seconds I regretted intruding on his moment of reflection, feeling he should be alone. I stood back trying to read his mind. Whatever was flashing through his brain didn't seem welcome. Was it time for me to go?

We needed a conversation to bring him back. I told him one of my eccentricities: "I take my painful memories and place them in an imaginary box and visualise it being cremated. It works wonders for the conscience."

He thought deeply but didn't answer.

"You seem lost in thought," I said, leaning forward to hold his hand.

"Does cremating your memories create a mess?" His mind was still alert.

"I give it the same reverence as a funeral for a friend, but without the tears and trauma. Does it heal me? To a degree. Death is the same as life, William … all a con."

"I will find out myself soon," he murmured, looking rather sad and defeated.

"You wrote about Henry Gelston in your book," I asked, hoping to drag William back into the present.

He wasn't that responsive at first, so I threw him a curved ball: "Is it his voice people can hear on Western Hill reading out the Sacrament?"

He turned and gave me the strangest look, like a ventriloquist's dummy with eye-popping intensity.

"Perhaps."

"What happened to him William? You spare us the details in your book. The ending is far too abrupt."

"I wrote a follow-up book, but nobody believed it and it didn't get published. Here is the manuscript. I hunted it out for you. It's called 'The Unwritten Tale' because I knew the publishers wouldn't touch it."

He handed me the papers. My very own instalment, for my eyes only.

Henry Gelston - 'The Unwritten Tale' by William J Woodhouse.

Henry was not the only priest to make his home in the Toll House in 1931. There were at least four others. The Roman Catholic church went for Victor Schafer head-on. His satanic presence had the appearance, rightly or wrongly, of being irremovable, and he was dug-in for the fight. But the church and the Masons knew he was the catalyst behind all the Toll House murders and it was time to 'take him out.'

They put together a sanctified Task-Force involving ministers from Britain, France, Spain, Italy and, most intriguing - the Vatican. The conquest against Smelt was so important it was sanctioned by Pope Puis XI, himself.

Incidents happened immediately. Smelt was 'encouraged' to make an appearance at the Toll House but the exorcism went gruesomely wrong. He was not alone. Eye witnesses claimed the Vatican priest had been "sucked out" of one of the windows when Smelt fought off the exorcism. In a matter of one minute after the frenzied attack the priest was found hanging outside, by his feet, from the archway linking the two buildings. His hands were bound together and his mouth gagged, but there were black sockets where his eyes had been poked out in a brutal attack. He was 10ft off the ground with a wound from his cut throat to his lower abdomen. The blood flowed freely from his cut neck like rain dripping down a window pane, and formed a massive pool on the ground. The cut was so severe it was millimetres away from being a full decapitation. The entire crime scene stunk like an abattoir. And more tragedy (and blood) was just minutes away.

The French priest, who was conducting the exorcism, cried out for a confrontation. He tried taunting and humiliating the creatures, luring them into the open, but he was no match for whatever charged at him. It wasn't as brutal as the previous death, initially, becoming a war of minds. Smelt snarled and gloated – the priest mechanically quoted extracts from the good book. Smelt was unmoved as the priest continued his chanting. Then the holy man could feel his heart bouncing off his ribcage. Fast at first, then progressively slowing down as the hammer of time ticked and tocked. Slower and slower. He tried to suck in air, but none came. His eyes bulged. He realized that he was about to die, It wasn't his heart that would kill him. His chest collapsed, he raised his head to scream, but then an almighty explosion, sending blood, flesh and shards of bone shooting in every direction.

There was no spooky skeleton in a black rope holding a scythe. The Grim Reaper wasn't going to catch that man's soul.

Smelt and his compatriots disappeared into the night.

The mission failed. If they were going to achieve anything they would have to be stronger than the 'life-form' standing in front of them. Religion, in the form of exorcism, was not the answer. Smelt had a surge of energy that was more pure than anything the priests could conjure up. It gave a fire, a passion that went from spark to bonfire within milliseconds. The men in their religious robes were powerless.

Several days later Henry wrote: *"One great tragedy of our existence is that often, the Devil, the liar, the Satan, the divider, believes more in our identity in Jesus Christ than we do. We have fallen for the lie that to be heavenly minded is to make us earthy good. But the truth is, it is only when our vision is expanded beyond this life that we are given his Holy Spirit. Tonight is the night, beloved. Time to realize exactly who I am."*

Make of that what you will. That particular evening Henry chose black cassock with white Collarino collar, rather than armour plate and chain mail that probably would have served him better. I suppose the church preferred the classic bible hero in black, rather than the gun-wielding psycho with a tank. Armed with nothing more than a bible, a wooden cross and a prayer, he went into battle.

Smelt was summoned outside the Toll House and words were exchanged. The demon never spoke more than one syllable at a time. He grunted and groaned, a faceless ogre hiding under his soiled, grubby hood. While the priest was unreadable, no fear, no emotion. Was there a minimal sense of mutual respect between the two of them? I doubt it. There was only going to be one winner.

The priest raised his cross, pointed it to the sky, then he tried to summon the powers from the heavens. The rain started to fall, floating down in gentle waves as the wind started to rise. Together they painted a new picture on the priest's scarred and chiselled face like sacred drops of tears mourning the moment.

Smelt stood motionless, like a statue repelling anything a statue was worthy of. The wrong side of righteousness; without morality or rectitude. The rain spattered off his crimson hood, the droplets scattering rather than soaking. Heavier and heavier it fell, until it was torrential. Thunder cracked like two juggernauts colliding head-on, and the two stood face to face, both trying to avoid the gaze of the other.

Lightning struck Smelt, and he crumbled to the soaking grass, clutching his chest, and finally, showing his repugnant face to the priest. A sudden gush of pain jolted through Smelt's body, paralysing him for a moment, then as he tried to stand, his arms lost tension and his legs buckled. Another crash of lightening bolted through his body and the bag of bones and grotty clothes fell to the ground.

All the while the priest held high his wooden cross, praying to his maker. Smelt had no response. There was no honour, no code, all that mattered was the victory. All exits were covered and I don't think surrender came into the equation. All that was needed was the final blow. The hammer of the Gods.

Gelston pulled Smelt's knife from it's case on his belt, threw down the cross, and clasped the dagger with both hands. Smelt eased himself up onto his knees and leant forward, displaying his back, giving the priest a bigger target. Whether it was meant, we will never know. Gelston pushed the hood back over the head of his victim to hide his face, like a firing squad execution, then raised the knife high. The rain fell like God's own Sacrament, each drop a letter in the verse. But the priest duplicated it for good measure.

"Oh Holy ghosts above, I call upon thee as a servant of Jesus Christ, to sanctify ..."

But before the knife came down between the shoulder blades, a bolt of lightening thrust into Smelt's body knocking his life's blood out of him. He rose up, took his final breath, and crumbled to the ground.

Gelston continued with the Last Rites, uttered the final word, then threw the knife into the bushes.

The priest declined the 'coup de grace' to end the suffering, preferring to leave it to those better equipped.

Now we have to ask ourselves, was Smelt truly evil from his birth, or was he transformed? He wanted to see how long his victims could live while he was slowly disembowelling them. He wanted to see the light go out in the man's eyes while he examined his innards. The face of evil!

Gelston turned towards the Toll House and trundled his way back to the door, leaving all the death and destruction behind him. He had sat at the table and played poker with the Devil. Picked up his hand and even though he had a 'full house' the Devil said: "You can't win, boy!"

What now for the Toll House? Was it really evil? Or are we all evil ... and goodness is a choice?

The priest turned the handle, pushed open on the door to the Toll House, then a presence came from behind and whispered in his ear: "You can't win, boy!" and the knife was thrust into his back.

CHAPTER FOURTEEN

"LET YOUR DEMONS OUT TO PLAY"

"So, Smelt killed him?" I asked William.

No reply, but it didn't really matter. We both knew what happened.

"I see why you didn't print the end of that chapter," I said, "It's not quite in the same 'voice' as the rest of your book."

"No-one would believe it! " William added.

"What's your take on it, William? Assuming Smelt is still wandering on Western Hill, as indeed he is, what can stop him?"

"There are two things we have to take into consideration. Number one: If an individual was going to achieve anything they would have to be stronger than the 'life-form' standing in front of them. Smelt is not a life-form. He is officially dead, but no-one seems to have told him. I know that sounds ridiculous, but he is in a kind of limbo. His soul – if he has one - hasn't moved on. That is the key."

"And who has the key?" I asked.

"I don't know what the key is as yet. But we will get there. Trust me. Then we have question Number two: You asked me if it was Gelston's voice you can hear on Western Hill reading out the Sacrament. Personally, I think it is. But it could be some sort of video re-run, where a specific moment in the past is shown again. That could explain ghost sightings. There is a cellar in York where countless people have seen a Roman battalion, in full uniform, march right in front of them. Out of one brick wall, straight through the other at the end of the room. Like a re-run of an army on the march two thousand years ago. Perhaps some kind of energy force unintentionally presses the 'play' button."

———————————————

I'm not an unkind sort of person. I don't kick puppies and I try not to lash out with unkind words. I do have feelings, like us all, and the story of the priest touched me deeply. William brought him to life, then took him away with a pen and a knife. The guy was gone.

"There is more to the Toll House than just Smelt's presence," I said, feeling the place had an 'evil' all of its own. "Why was the place built, William, and what 'pull' does it have over the Roman Catholic church. Why don't they pulled it down and sell the land? My boss must have given them a hefty offer, just to level the place and tidy it up!"

"The Freemasons were more than umbrellas and bowler hats in 1798. These days we have 'fake news' and the majority of us presume the government and the media should never be trusted. I do have a habit of taking an instant dislike to politicians … because it saves time! The very fact they want to rule the world should be enough reason to banish them from trying to get started. Money buys power. There are secret societies we know of, but that is the cover! It's the ones that we don't know about that are the true 'secret' societies. The Masons were the real movers and shakers of the era, because they had different levels of mystery and concealment. Then there was God's banker, the Pope, leading perhaps the most corrupt cloak and dagger institution in the history of this planet. Christianity gave us a set of values, in exchange for your wallet. Every war is fought over religion and nationalism – because both hold the purse strings of power."

"That doesn't explain the Toll House, though," I suggested, knowing he was going to get round to it … eventually.

"The Toll House was built as a meeting place for the nameless puppet masters of real power. The Polish Count is one we know of, and Smelt was another. Don't underestimate either of them. The Count is buried in the doorway of Durham Cathedral, no less. Not bad for a guy who played the part of the colourful, penniless dwarf musician who was always on the cadge. In truth, he had the financial backing of British, Polish, French and Austrian royalty! Smelt had a band of gypsies that probably had almost the same power over the Mongol Empire as Kublai Khan did in 1260! Where did he get those people from? Smelt's secret society in Germany, and then London, is the real deal … because they genuinely were secret!"

"That is what I don't understand," I replied. "Different religions under the same roof."

"That got me too. Who owns the Toll House, and who wants it, is up for debate. The Masons had it; the church took it; and Smelt made it his home. If possession is 90% ownership – the Pope can wave his rosary beads until he is blue in the face – Smelt has moved in, and he ain't going anywhere soon!"

I was fascinated to know who was next to go into battle with the Toll House, and William returned to his tale. Next to pay the rent was a former naval officer called Joseph Hedley, who was a bit of a local celebrity having sailed the seven seas - and found himself shipwrecked in the lot of them. Let's just say "he could tell a good tale." Born in India, son of a British Army Major General, he was a well travelled man. A widower, his wife sadly died of malaria in Central America when she was infected by a mosquito bite during a sea voyage through the Panama canal. Or so he claimed. They went on a sea voyage and she never came back.

Joseph Hedley/Edward Peele - 'Durham's Darkest Mysteries' by William J Woodhouse.

Joe Hedley was a charmer, for sure. Described as having a "twinkle in his eye and a voice so warm it could almost spontaneously combust". I usually like that – but the more I read about Joe the more I suspected he had more than a droll air of power about him – he was just plain creepy.

He ended his sea-faring days and moved in at the Toll House in May 1933 with his partner of three months, Eliza Dixon. Her portrayal in a book published in 1934 was not a pretty sketch: "Her voice was a baleful cackle suppressed from behind chipped teeth that looked like broken piano keys."

In the first week of their residence Eliza stumbled upon a gold locket in the garden when she was planting shrubs. At first she thought it was broken glass as it glinted in the summer sun, but then she unearthed the gold chain as she scratched in the soil. It was an exquisite piece of jewellery, dated from around 1880. The front featured a bold Coat of Arms design which was surrounded by leaves and chrysanthemum flowers. During the Victoria era, the chrysanthemum flower signified 'love.'

It wasn't until the jeweller, who was valuing the piece, prized open the tiny lock with a knife that the contents could be revealed. Behind the tiny petite glass window were strands of blood-stained blonde hair. There were no signs of who it belonged to, no signature or engraving.

Eliza, surprisingly, wasn't too spooked by the hair, or the blood, and claimed the locket as her own.

"Finders – keeper – losers – weepers," she told Joe.

She wore it constantly, opening it regularly like a child with a new toy.

Within days of moving into their new home, they replaced a lot of the dated furniture with Art Deco. Out went anything religious, and there was a lot of that, to be substituted with modern Gatsby drawers, Cavendish oak tables, and a French Royere Cerused bed. The house was finally moved into the 20th Century, whether it (or the owners) liked it or not.

Sadly, the mood of the new 'home' didn't stay 'homely' for long. The doors would open and close, and furniture (modern or not) had a habit of refusing to stay where it was put. The grandfather clock, which had been in the house for as long as anyone could remember, would vibrate until it stopped. Then, randomly start ticking again. The floors would creak at night and Eliza, who had now reached the point of packing her bags and leaving, insisted it was the noise of spirits roaming the rooms.

Certain evenings, a breath of stagnant air would whip through the bedroom, what Joe described as "stinking like a festering dead corpse."

The local gossips told Eliza the history of the location and that just about tipped the scales. One old lady told her: "That building grew out of the ground – it wasn't built."

That was it - Eliza wanted out!

"It's haunted, Joe, I can feel it."

Joe would have none of it (at first), but agreed a compromise, saying he would hire a medium to find out why peculiar things were happening.

"There is nothing that cannot be explained," he said, making his stand. "There are no ghosts here. That's just the tales the neighbours tell to keep the rabble away from the place."

That very evening, Eliza lay in bed, determined to see a ghost to prove her point. Every time Joe dozed, he would get a dig in the ribs.

Then around 1am, they both drifted off into a deep slumber. Eliza's head started swimming, hallucinating as though she was climbing a mountain, suffering because the air was too thin to breathe. She was in the Death Zone, without oxygen, gasping and coughing. She saw a thin mist moving before her eyes, but she was unsure if it was real or a dream. She tried to scream out, but no words would come. A light appeared, it flickered but it was distant, too far away to focus on. Then a sickly smell hit her nostrils, vile and offensive. Not unlike the stench earlier in the day. But no matter how hard she tried, her eyes were clamped shut. Panic hit her like a hammer striking an anvil.

A voice whispered in her ear: "You had better know the rules, Lady. You have one hundred moons. Stay beyond that … and you come with me!"

Then, as though someone had snapped their fingers, Eliza opened her eyes, straightened up in bed and looked around. Darkness, nothing more. She could breathe perfectly normally and the smell had gone. She began to cry, although she wasn't sure why. And Joe slept through it all.

As good as his word, Joe contacted a Psychic Medium to ease his partner's worries. Simply called 'Jasmin', the Psychic came highly recommended (as they usually are) by friends and relatives. That "gifted clairvoyant" walked up the path to the Toll House wearing a black robe made of a soft satiny fabric that reached the ground. Apparently "a puff of wind swept through her long white hair, making her look majestic, as she walked up to the door as lightly as an acrobat."

She gave her credentials verbally: "I realized my spiritual ability from the age of 7 and that was nurtured by a gypsy my grandmother knew. I also work with tarot cards, crystals, tea-leaves and the power of the Earth."

All legal and above board, Jasmin wandered the house from room to room, doing what Psychics do. The main bedroom had "an aura about it" she said, and there was a presence of "a young girl" in the room down below, which was the cellar. She acted very matter-of-fact about most things; did a tarot reading; gave Eliza a "lucky stone" and was happy to take her money and leave. But Eliza asked the lady if she could return at night, when "the real activity takes place."

Jasmin agreed to go back that very evening, if her palm was "crossed with silver", as you would expect from a business woman.

Later that night it soon became apparent that the girl underneath the floorboards was very much real. Jasmin continued to get a "pull" directing her into the cellar. The trapdoor was raised and she trudged down the steps, rather confident and assured, determined to get a connection with the young lady. However, when she got a reply, that courage evaporated. If the truth was known, Jasmin didn't usually get replies.

The medium described the bond with the young girl as unnerving, verging on intimidating. The child was desperate for her story to be told, and she said she yearned for the return of her necklace, which had been taken from her. The way it was described, it seemed very much like the one Eliza had found. When it was produced, the medium got a flurry of activity.

"She says it was given to her by her father when she was ten," said Jasmin.

Then the full story unfolded, through Psychic association and newspaper reports:

The girl was called Isabella Iles, who went missing on 17th of February 1881. Her parents (Rab and Florence), although never married, separated when the child was just a few months old. The mother was a live-in house-keeper for Mr Iles, but their affair proved an inconvenience to the man of nobility, and he moved her out rather quickly. Florence took Isabella to live with her, but Rab would see the child every weekend. Rab was a businessman and had money ... plenty of it, while her mother was one step away from the notorious Work House. That 'one step' was the meagre finances Rab gave them to keep the 'authorities' away from their door. It was a difficult world of two contrasts for Isabella, from posh to pauper from the time the sun rose to the time the sun set. Loved by both, we imagine, but Rab had perplexing ways of showing it. It was after a holiday with her father in the Lake District, that the kid was abducted, when she was returning to her mother in Durham.

A 12-year old witness reported seeing Isabella walking through the city centre being dragged by a well dressed gentleman, who constantly kept telling her to "shut up!". Police launched a search of the city, but young Isabella just became a statistic, as many kids (some as young as four) were reported missing in those dark and desolate times. For some of them, the Work House was the best place. At least it kept them alive.

Isabella's father offered a reward for her safe return, but all leads proved futile. He dealt with the loss and uncertainty as best he could, but her mother died less than two months later. The official verdict on her death certificate was Tuberculosis, the biggest killer of the day, but from the time of the child's abduction until her death, Florence spent every hour of every day looking for her daughter. Little known to her, but Isabella was less than two miles away, hidden in a room called "The Chamber" in the Toll House.

The tiny room, that was the cellar, was the child's entire world for eight years! Her abductor (Edward Peele), would allow her periods of time upstairs in the house, but she always had to return to the "Chamber" to sleep. That was where she stayed when he went to work as an undertaker.

He told her that if ever she escaped there were madmen from a local mental institution who would catch her and eat her alive. Her life became one of extreme submission to her captor. She was regularly beaten, sometimes so badly she could hardly walk, her hair was shaved, and she was chained to the wall as she slept. But, surprisingly, the relationship was never sexual, which was one gift sent from Heaven. The only comfort she had was a small fox terrier dog she was allowed to keep.

Peele tried to crush all hope from the girl, telling her that her family had refused to pay a ransom of ten pounds to take her back home, saying they were "happy to get rid of her."

Her life, she believed, was not worth ten pounds. As well as the physical and mental abuse, there was the torment of loneliness. Her little dog was her whole life. After six years, when she was 16, she even yearned for the company of her captor, so she could hear someone talk to her. Anything to preserve the illusion of normality. Her one grace was that Peele taught her to read, and he gave her books and newspapers, so the teenager could educate herself.

One evening when Isabella was allowed upstairs, she tried to get out of a window and Peele caught her in the act. He took her to a sink and pushed her head underwater until she lost consciousness. When she woke he had a double-barrelled shotgun pointed at her head, and he told her: "I will blow your brains out if you try it again."

On March 1st 1889, Edward Peele died suddenly. He failed to turn up for a funeral he was conducting, and one of his fellow workers went to the Toll House to seek him. The stranger heard cries from below the floorboards, and the rest is history.

18-year old Isabella weighed less than seven stone when she was found by police. She was formally identified by her gold necklace, that displayed a coat of arms and contained her hair. After her release, she buried it next to the Toll House as a grim reminder of her days there. But sadly, her little dog ran off when the police first arrived, and was never found.

Throughout the ordeal she never gave up. The police were astonished by her intelligence, considering her isolation, but predominantly by her compassion towards her captor. Isabella cried when they told her Peele had died, and she referred to him as a "poor soul" who "did his best" for her.

She was taken to her father for an emotional reunion, then surprised everyone by insisting she wanted to go to Durham for Peele's funeral. No ransom money was ever asked, but when Isabella told her father the story that she didn't feel she was "worth ten pounds", he accompanied her to the funeral. As the coffin was lowered into the grave, Rab threw a ten pound note on top of it, and shouted: "There's your money you Son of a Bitch!"

CHAPTER FIFTEEN

"AS WORTHLESS AS A DEGREE FROM FRAUD UNIVERSITY"

"You didn't think Jasmin the psychic was the real deal, did you William?" I laughed.

"I don't trust the lot of them, John. Tarot cards; tea-leaves; crystal ball. It's all bloody rubbish."

"She found the young girl, though."

"She did indeed. Although I didn't publish it, she found Smelt, too!" He said, pointing a finger at me as though another theory was about to be brought to the table. So from the pages of William's 'Untold Story' the tale continued.

Joseph Hedley - 'The Untold Story' by William J Woodhouse.

After her 'success' at connecting spiritually with the little girl, Jasmin became an unlikely local celebrity. She made headlines in the local newspapers, and a column or two in the nationals, too. She made a lot of money from the articles, plus 'every man and his dog' suddenly wanted a Tarot reading.

That woman was psychic dynamite, and I'm sure it would of stayed that way, but for a young reporter with the Northern Echo called Robert Catchside.

The 18-year old rookie reporter had ambition. He was very keen to progress in journalistic circles, hoping one day to catch the eye of an editor from Fleet Street. When he was sent to Durham to cover the Toll House story, it was a step in the right direction. It was big news. Certainly a step up from women's coffee evenings and charity events to raise money for a new roof for the church. Young Robert had (almost) hit the big time.

Eagle-eyed and bushy-tailed, Robert was on high alert, and it was during an interview with Jasmin, that he noticed she mentioned quotes from Isabella's's father that the medium couldn't possibly have known. Too much information coming from a spirit of the dead. He returned to his office desk and pondered for a while, before deciding to research the story from grass-roots level. He looked for an article in the Northern Echo of that period (March 1889) to see if that could shed a light on his curiosity. Anyone could have access to back copies of the Northern Echo at their Darlington branch, so long as they signed the visitor's book and gave the reason for their research. When he signed the book he noticed the name Maria Barber. Maria Barber was actually the lady he had interviewed. Her pen-name was Jasmin. Clearly she had read the 1889 article just days before she visited the Toll House. She knew about Isabella and Edward Peele in advance, but she must have been incredibly fortunate that Eliza just happened to have found the necklace.

Robert met her again and approached the subject discreetly, suggesting perhaps she had embellished the tale. He didn't want to claim the entire incident was a hoax. He hoped she would come clean about the whole incident. However, although Jasmin admitted she did know about the young girl from newspaper articles, she pressed the point that they did make contact with the girl.

"I'm confident I could do it again," she said, trying to uphold her reputation. "I'm happy to go back to the Toll House and talk to her, with you watching my every movement. I am not a con artist Mr Catchside, and I will prove it."

The scene was set. Robert positioned a Box Brownie camera at the hatch to the cellar, and one inside the room itself, both triggered by a wire and a thumb switch. He knew a photo of a ghost would net him a fortune, but Jasmine made it clear that nobody had seen the ghost of Isabella during the last encounter.

"She didn't appear in any form, she only spoke, so I think getting a photograph of her is very ambitious," she said, giving herself a 'get out clause' should nothing be recorded.

All was quiet in the Toll House, only Jasmin and Robert were present. But despite repeated calls for Isabella to appear, and much to the frustration of the Psychic, the teenager remained silent.

Robert suggested they try other rooms.

"She spent 99% of he time down the cellar," said Jasmin, "But once, when she was allowed upstairs, she tried to escape out of a bedroom window. Peele caught her and nearly killed her. Perhaps there is an energy in there."

They went to the major bedroom and Robert set up his cameras once again. Darkness had set in, so Robert wanted light on the subject. The bedside lamp was switched on, but it gave more of an atmospheric glow than any brightness.

"Is that it? The best light we can get?" Robert asked.

"That's the only light," replied Jasmine. "We can try candles, if we can find some."

There was a candelabra on an oak dresser at the back of the room and, after digging around in the drawers, Jasmine found a box of 'Bryant & May's safety matches.' Robert lit the three candles, not that it made much difference. Then suddenly there was a sensation; a spooky grim atmosphere; and the temperature dropped to chillingly cold.

Almost immediately Jasmine picked up on it, claiming there was a very strong spirit presence in the room. That was no hoax. Robert recorded later that the look of terror on her face said it all.

"She is here. Something touched me … like rain … as though it would go right through my skin. She is trying to contact me."

Cameras clicked, and Robert stepped back to the wall to give the lady some space.

"That's strange," she said with a tremble in her voice.

"What is?" asked Robert.

"She has never touch me before. Hang on, she's touching me again. Running her finger up my arm. Oh my God. I've never experienced this before. She is sucking in breath. I can hear her."

The camera continued to click.

"Ask her something," whispered Robert, as he stepped nearer to the door, feeling the courage drain from his body. He wasn't quite sure they were being made welcome.

"Isabella, is that you?" asked the Psychic. "Please talk to me."

Her eyes fell to the floor, looking at her brown leather shoes.

"I can't move my feet Robert, honestly, I cannot move."

The bedside light began to flicker, as though the electric power was being drained. It stuttered for a few seconds, then cut out altogether. Robert was now stood in the doorway, and Jasmine caught sight of him edging away.

"Don't you leave me Robert! Don't you even think about it!"

He gave her no words of encouragement, he simply stood there, with his hand on the door handle, trembling from head to foot.

"I can smell something," she cried. "A stinking smell. Can you smell it Robert?"

He didn't reply.

"Isabella, please talk to me," she pleaded. "Oh my God. Something is lifting up my dress. I can feel its hands on my leg. I can feel it! Don't! Please don't touch me."

Then she got her reply, one syllable at a time, with a deep mechanical drone: "Darling, I've missed you. We are going to have the best time."

A strangled cry filled the air, that Robert later described in his statement as: "A cry you could only imagine when her lungs were empty and she had nothing more to give. Her dress was raised, her under-garments ripped from her, and what happened next … well, I cannot describe it. There was no shape or form; no-one I could see; just Jasmine writhing against the wall. Fighting for her life, being pinned back, her head constantly banging against the wall. Her life's blood was sucked out of her as she rose, slowly, higher up the wall, some 4ft from the bedroom floor. Her arms were out-stretched, as though forced, re-creating Christ on the cross. She gasped one long last breath, then something – something I couldn't see – slashed her throat and blood gushed everywhere. I couldn't see the person who did it, and I couldn't see the knife. But I know one thing, she was dead before her throat was cut. And in a strange way, I thank God for that. She was certainly dead before her body crashed to the floor."

Robert continued his tale: "I escaped from the room because there was nothing I could do. My feet slipped as I scurried down the stairs, trying to get hold of the banister, but I must have fallen down a dozen steps at least. My knees bent and I plunged head-first, crashing my forehead into the concrete floor. Blood was running into my eyes but my heart kept telling me to keep moving, 'do not stop!' It was all or nothing. I had to get to my feet or reap the consequences. I swear I saw a silhouette on the wall, although the shape was nothing I could describe. My ankle was twisted, but, despite my injury, I moved quicker than I have ever moved in my life. Finally I could smell his breath as though his face was inches away from mine. A smell of vomit and death. A combination right out of abattoir. I was desperate to get out of that hell hole. I stretched my hand towards the door handle, grasping in the darkness. 'Please God, let me live!' I cried, and I genuinely mean – I cried! The door opened and I charged out into the woods outside, in no particular direction. It didn't matter. I tried to throw myself forward, dragging my crippled leg behind me, shouting and bawling in a trembling panic until I reached the street light of the road."

Robert made his way into the city before collapsing 200 yards from the police station, where he was found by a stranger, who notified the constabulary.

"I felt safe – for a brief moment," he recorded, "But I didn't really escape anything. Whatever was pursuing me, gave me my freedom. At the base of the stairs it could have ripped me limb from limb. But, for whatever reason, I was allowed to scramble away like a minnow thrown back into the river by a fisherman."

The police went to the scene of the crime, and took samples, swabs, photographs, and a carcass away. They probably thought a stretcher was more dignified than a body-bag, although all dignity had been ripped from that girl's body long before the Plod arrived.

Robert was in a quandary, and a big one at that. He was witness to a murder, but, as is so often the case, when you want the police to be 'human,' all you get is the dark blue uniform and shiny black shoes. There were two people in a house and one got murdered. How do you get out of that one? No witnesses, just a cock-and-bull story of ghosts and demons and a corpse half-way up a wall. That was his alibi, and he found it difficult to make it stick.

Sergeant Roger Haswell was a strong believer in public service and he did his job to the best of his ability. He saw the worst of people on a daily basis and I'm sure it tested his faith in the goodness of the criminals that were brought before him. To him, the victims were always on the right side of the law and they deserved justice. The Sergeant was proud to be a police officer. In an ideal world he would fight for integrity, honesty and decency, and be the one to bring evil to its knees. He saw Jasmine's blooded and mutilated body – and he saw the guy who was in the room with her at the time.

Robert was not going to walk away from this. His whole case rested on photographic evidence, the film in his two cameras, but both were over developed and showed nothing more than black prints. The young journalist was put on trial for murder.

He spent close to a year in prison while his lawyers fought his case. In which time he wrote his memoirs for his newspaper. Not much of a story from an 18-year old who had never travelled; married; divorced; or had children. Hardly a classic tale from behind prison bars like Adolf's 'Mein Kampf' or Mandela's 'Conversations With Myself.' But the end of his story was spectacular … he was hanged from the gallows at Durham prison on March 13th 1934.

The campaign for justice, led by family, friends and the local newspaper, fell on deaf ears. Perhaps if the homicide had taken place in modern times the forensic department, with recent developments in science, would have saved him from the noose. But in 1934, with no authentic alibi or 'legitimate' reason why someone else could possibly have done the deed, Robert was deemed guilty by association.

He had a tough time in Durham prison. Not so much suffering at the hands of fellow prisoners or from prison guards, but from voices. Like most of the older jails, Durham reputedly had many ghosts of previously condemned criminals. Sadly, Robert let them inside his head. Several times he was found on a morning, crouched in a corner crying in abject fear.

The last words spoken by criminals before execution stand like the scribbles on suicide notes. Words from those poor souls, remembered by their family and friends for eternity.

I'm sure the hangman had many convicted criminals proclaim their innocence for the thousandth time, while others told their mothers they loved them. Poor Robert did both. And he meant every single word:-

"Mam, Dad and sis, look me in the eyes. I have tears, and I am afraid. I love you so much. I did not do that dreadful act, and God will have mercy on me, because he knows I didn't do it! Good people are always so sure they're right. But to the jury that convicted me … you are so wrong!"

William handed me a blue plastic folder: "Take this, I've prepared it for you."

I opened it and found a detailed chronicle of past events at the Toll House since Jasmine's horrifying death. I didn't read it there and then but I imagined it would scare the socks off me when I did.

"What do I do, William?" I asked, closing the folder and placing it on his bed.

"As regards to what?" he replied.

"The land we are digging up," I said, flicking through the photo gallery in my phone. "This is the hole at the Obelisk. We both know what is down there. Do I go looking for it?"

"There are more than mine shafts," he replied. "It's a grave yard, too. I cannot suggest anything. You do what you do. As the saying goes – in the age of information - ignorance is a choice. Remember that. You can continue building your houses oblivious to the consequences, and I would probably recommend that. Look at poor

Robert. His tales of ghosts didn't do him much good, did they? Nobody believes it John – only you and me. I've shown you the hidden history of the Toll House but it's hidden for a reason, because nobody with a single brain corpuscle in their head would believe a word of it! The next chapter is about to be written. Don't be part of it."

"I thought you were behind me on this? Encouraging me to dig for gold. Come on William, you are my protagonist. A leader of men. Don't fail me now."

"Yes, I was behind you," he said, switching his stare from the steely-eyed 'man of the hour' I imagined him to be, to an old gentleman lying in his sick bed.

"I know what your future holds," he said, "and I don't need tea-leaves or tarot cards. You refuse to take the easy answer, John, I'm just offering an alternative. A 'get out of jail free' card. It's a cemetery, but it ain't God's acre. It's a necropolis full of evil, and hidden bodies don't always stay hidden."

I didn't peruse it. I gave him the last word. It was the very least I could do.

CHAPTER SIXTEEN

"A NICKEL AIN'T WORTH A DIME ANYMORE"

A happy ending is always reserved for the last page of a book. But I'm going to ignore protocol and slip a happy ending in right now. Whether or not you regard it as being 'happy' is your perogitive. Because this particular story made someone extremely happy – and it had an ending. So let's just ride with it.

I received a text from Fay the following day after my visit to see William, asking if I could pop over her garden fence for a little chat … and a coffee of course. I was on site, keeping tabs on our work force, while seeing what the planners had come up with to solve our pot-hole dilemma. Several well-educated University graduates formed a 'think tank' to come up with an intellectual, cultivated sophisticated answer … which was … "bung the hole up with cement"!

Was there really an alternative?

One problem solved, I walked the 50 yards (or so), leaped the fence, on course to solve another.

Fay opened the door, with a face full of fireworks and enthusiasm, like a kid on Christmas morning.

"Thank you, John. You have turned my life around, and I don't know how to thank you."

Not the welcome I expected. But I was pleased (whatever I had done) to be part of it.

"No need to thank me, Fay. Not all," I joked. "What have I done?"

"Look," she said, handing me a photocopy of a cheque.

I took the glasses out of my pocket and saw that Benjamin had written a cheque for £198,000.

"You convinced him to pay it back," she said. "It's short of what he stole, but it's still a lot of money. I never dreamt he would return any of it."

"I'd try and cash it first, if I were you. You could be in for a mighty fall."

"It cleared this morning," she replied, "That's only a copy to keep reminding me it actually happened. You got me my money back."

"Well, not exactly, Fay. It's nice to take credit when it's due, but not in this case. I think the threat of deportation could have had an influence. Or, maybe he has realised the error of his ways and turned over a new leaf. It happens, even to the strangest people."

"I never ever thought I'd see that money again," she said. "This is one of the happiest days of my life."

There were things I could have said, principally the fact her husband took it in the first place, but I didn't want to spoil the euphoria of that moment. I let her wallow in the satisfying happiness that only money can stimulate.

"I'm middle-aged John. Heading beyond that now. I'm not stoney broke, I'm financially comfortable I guess, but getting that cheque has made me a better person. Because I despised that man for what he did to me. I hated him from the bottom of my heart. Even though it is only getting back what he took, I feel vindicated."

"He is middle-aged, too, you know. Perhaps its a time in his life he wants to right his wrongs."

But then it made me think about myself. Had I reached the dreaded 'crisis' stage yet. Do you trundle onward to further maturity, becoming the acceptable face of old age? Or tread the other path? Some say it is trying to relive the teen years, when really that person hasn't changed at all. It's those treading the first path that have changed ... into old age.

Then I thought of William in his sick bed, having to face his own mortality, all the while fancying another turn on the swings? That guy had a brain full of life – sadly his body wasn't up to pace.

"Are you willing to forgive and forget what Benjamin has done?" I asked.

"There was a letter with the cheque," she said, holding it in her hand. "He seems sincere."

For a moment I thought she was going to hand it to me. But after giving it a few seconds thought, she neatly folded it up and placed it back in the envelope, to be read another day. There was obviously something in there she didn't want me to see.

"The police will still prosecute him, you know?" I said, letting her know that the matter was far from over. "He broke the law and the police have gone to a lot of trouble to track him. They have used a lot of resources and they won't let him off the hook."

Fey let it brush by her as though I hadn't spoken. She was always selective in what she wanted to hear.

The next couple of weeks were 'interesting' on a personal level. Kimberley found love (again) and her mother was not particularly enthusiastic about her choice of partner, suggesting we (her and I) meet for a chat. But I didn't feel that 'we' were in the right place emotionally to sit together at a table.

"What if we argue, like always?" I asked.

Although I was always concerned about my daughter's welfare, I thought Kimberley and I were close enough to deal with whatever problem either of us had, together. Did I really need advice from a third party ... even if it was her mother? But, to keep the peace, I agreed, and she came to my house one evening.

"I think this place could do with a bit 'de-cluttering', don't you think?" she said as she entered the room. Obviously not too impressed with my house-work.

"Well actually, I've just cleaned up!" I replied. "It's lived in; it's clean; and I kind of like it that way."

It's always nice to start on a good footing, and it was, shall we say - 'absorbing' - to be told my house was just shy of being a hovel.

She put her hands on her hips and she cocked her head to one side, her usual stance for a lecture, so I immediately put myself on the defensive.

"Are you happy with your life, John?" she asked, her eyes shifting from one piece of 'clutter' to another. Inwardly that woman hated untidiness. Outwardly she hated it even more!

"I am very happy in my own little world, Susan. It doesn't take much to put a smile on my face."

"Where did you get the clock from? I don't remember it."

"Susan, why are you here? Ignore the clock and what is in the room. Just tell me, why are you here? It's not about Kimberley, so obviously its about us."

"What do you think of me?" she asked, placing her arms outstretched. "Tell me what you see."

I am not the best at giving compliments. She had made the effort, so perhaps she deserved more than I was giving her. I needed to think. I couldn't afford to get it wrong.

"What do I think? I think you are a beautiful lady. Kimberley takes after you, and that is the best compliment I can give you. You take my breath away, you always have."

Was that good enough? Was it over the top? That woman frightened me.

"So why are we apart?" she snapped back.

"Because you kicked me out of the house! You live with another man, Susan. Bloody hell, girl."

"He's gone," she said, giving me a look as though it was my fault. "He left a few weeks ago. I couldn't stand him any more."

"So this conversation is not about Kimberley's boyfriend at all, it's about you being lonely?"

"I just want to know how you feel about me?" she said, giving me those deep blue eyes. Typical Susan, if you want something, just flash the eyes.

I was growing more and more uncomfortable and struggling.

"Where do we go with this?" I thought to myself. She stood there like Ingrid Bergman in Casablanca, her black dress hanging eloquently from her shoulders, yet hugging every curve below the waist. You can never be under-dressed with a little black dress. I've always thought that. I met her gaze with a smile, then shook my head. "What do you want from me, Susan? Are we kidding ourselves here?"

The conversation flittered from past to present. How we met; how we parted; and most things in between. Our first kiss; our last kiss. The beauty of the birth of our daughter, and Susan reminded me how much that daughter misses her father. That is always the twang on the heart-strings of any parent, and it got me.

"Kim said your trip to Spain was the best time she has ever spent on holiday with you. That was nice."

"Yeah, it was special," I recounted. "A lot of it was work, rather than a holiday, but she was amazing. Moments I will treasure."

"Come back, John," she said, and I think she genuinely meant it. I didn't reply.

Time passed, we sipped wine, we laughed and we cried. All the while she had me transfixed. It was like the grip of tiger. Once she got her claws into my skin she was never going to let go. Susan had my head spiralling in a hazy cloud of rainbow colours like a puff of marijuana. She sat opposite me and folded one leg over the other, dangling her black stiletto shoe off her quaint little toes. Knowing she was in complete control of herself ... and me.

"You look at me," she said, "And nothing has changed, John. You are still my 'other half', and always have been. My soul mate. In life I believe you have to try every path, and knock on every door, and you've done that. I'm just waiting for your return."

But, was I ready to return?

The black stilettos swung it ... for that particular night ... I was.

One of the documents included in William's file was a return to the story of Lady Jane Coddington. She was pregnant when we left the tale, but William was reluctant to tell me the outcome when I visited him. But all was revealed in papers in his blue plastic folder.

Lady Jane Coddington - 'The Untold Story' by William J Woodhouse.

Lady Jane Coddington was very much a lady about town who mixed with the gentry. But the events at the Toll House in 1922 put paid to a lot of things in her life ... including Ronald, the unfaithful husband, who was passionate about spreading his passion on the French Riviera. They never actually divorced, probably because he was entitled to half of her wealth if they did, but he was given a generous pay-off on condition he never 'darkened the door' again. And as far as we know, he never did. He may have gone back to fairground rides and training exotic animals. We will never know.

Jane moved to the country with her sister, Catherine, to a stately home called Mill's Manor, about ten miles away from Durham. Exquisite grass land covering around ten acres. The interior of the manor featured Jacobean furnishings and French paintings. But money cannot buy everything.

Jane was in an unhealthy mental state before the pregnancy, and her letter to her husband showed how terrified she was once the foetus started to grow. She was in an even more unhealthy mental state after the event, spending long months in hospital.

During the pregnancy she came very close to having an abortion, but a dream changed her mind. Although back street abortions were illegal in the 1920's, money could make doctors 'sympathetic' to a women's plight. Legal operations were performed. However, her date with destiny was cancelled last minute when she claimed to have had a dream that she called a 'visitation.' The apparition urged her to see out the pregnancy, which she did, but evil thoughts were never far away. Would the experience be the beautiful gateway for new life coming into the world, as the 'visitor' said in her dream? Or the ninth circle of Hell, which was how she felt herself? Whatever the outcome ... Jane was going to face it.

Giving birth is completely unique for every woman, but Jane's delivery was about as exclusive as it could possibly be. Her mind was not in a good place.

She described it as: *"I had to have an out-of-body experience because I felt I was dying. It felt like someone was pushing forcefully from the inside against my spine and twisting it at the same time. I escaped my own body because the pain was so intense. I actually yelled at the nurse to stop using her nails to pull me apart, but she said she wasn't even touching me! But something was. So I had to leave my body."*

The baby arrived with a misshapen head, peeling yellow-tinged skin, swollen eyes and bright red birthmarks. Those are common at childbirth – so the little girl was declared 'normal'. She was named Paula.

We don't know much about Paula's baby years, other than she didn't see much of her mother because Jane spent a lot of the first 18 months in hospital. After that, Jane described Paula as being "very clingy", as though that was a problem. However, considering there was no father figure, the child was sure to cling to whoever gave her affection. But Jane continued to have doubts about what the child would become.

Her sister, Catherine, claimed Jane was a "cold mother" who would only show attachment in the company of others: *"She often ignored the child's needs, and that bordered on child abuse. There was always someone on hand to pick up the pieces, but Paula wanted her mother. Neglect can negatively effect a child's emotion, behaviour and development, but surprisingly Paula progressed beyond her years. She could read small words at the age of three, when my child started reading at six. I suppose all children have imaginary friends, but Paula would stand in a specific corner of the living room and hold a conversation with 'her friend' for many minutes. That particularly disturbed her mother more than anything else. Once, when Jane scolded her for talking, I saw the look of evil in that child's eyes when she stood her ground and replied: 'He hates you mother!' That child really meant it. I have never felt the need to argue with my children, but that was a mother who was put in her place."*

On her fourth birthday, Paula was allowed a family party at the Mill's Manor. Guests arrived with gifts and money but Paula seemed unusually despondent, sedate even.

Catherine: *"It was a day I will never forget. Jane took centre stage, as usual, because she loved a big crowd. Poor Paula could not get a look in. All dressed up for the occasion, but the child was pushed in the background and made to feel a little bit useless, neglected even. The more Jane drank, the more she grumbled and complained about motherhood. I don't know what Paula was thinking at that time, and nobody should underestimate how bright she was, but I think she knew she was an 'inconvenience.'*

"I was uncomfortable with the atmosphere so I told all of the children, about a dozen of them, to go and play in the garden. They seemed happy enough, entertaining each other, laughing and shouting ... all but Paula. She stood looking into the wood transfixed. Loneliness is a crowded place – but that kid did not seem alone. I can't explain the ambiance of that moment. The garden was noisy with chattering, screaming children, but Paula was transfixed, whispering to herself.

"I returned to the house, but 15 minutes later one of the parents noticed Paula was missing. The gate was locked so she must have climbed over the fence, but none of the children could remember seeing her in the garden at all. They were otherwise occupied with swings, games and toys. The search was on."

The landscape was not a particularly massive area to search, but there were streams and a river that could have enticed a youngster. The police were called and the entire sector was examined by sniffer dogs and a search team. All that was found was the child's pink hair bonnet, snagged on a branch of a tree. She could have wandered down a lonely road, but how far could a wandering four-year old get without becoming conspicuous? Obviously far enough to get lost.

The search brought nothing, although it was curious to note that at no time did Lady Jane join the search team in their efforts, while most of the revellers did. There was a mixture of emotions from the mother, bordering on the uncontrollable, to the bizarre. But she never shed a tear, which was noted by the police. The days passed without a single confirmed sighting. The detective on the case, Detective Constable Brian Russell, suggested the possibility that Paula was kidnapped for ransom money, specifically as there had been a high profile case in the news at that time. One child abduction in London had seen an MP asked to pay kidnappers £10,000 for the safe return of his son. Sadly the job was bungled by the Metropolitan Police and the MP never saw his son again.

Days turned into weeks, and no ransom note was delivered, no phone calls made. That ruled out a kidnapping. Then Detective Constable Russell turned his attention on Lady Jane. He suggested she could have set up the "perfect alibi" by organising the party, with scores of witnesses present, then organised the child's disappearance. But the policeman couldn't make the accusation stick. No court case was ever brought, and no-one was ever charged.

July 16th 1932 – Move forward ten years. Lady Jane is now 37, still in a marriage of convenience, but in a relationship with a Durham banker called 'Richie' Richardson-Winter. He was so good – they named him twice.

No children, but all was well in Jane's world of globe-trotting and sun-worshipping. She no longer talked about her 'close friends' Charles Chaplin and Douglas Fairbanks. Maybe because they had slipped out of vogue … or maybe she didn't know them in the first place.

One particular Saturday was nothing special – raining cats and dogs with thunder imminent – and Jane and Richie managed to get to the County Hotel in Durham before lightning struck. They took a window seat and ordered a meal.

"Did you know that King Charles 1st hid in this hotel before his arrest for treason?" said Richie, making idol chatter. "I've just read it on that picture frame on the wall."

"Did you know I don't even know what treason is?" laughed Jane, fiddling with her knife and fork in readiness for her meal.

"Hello," said a little child who mischievously placed her hands onto the table.

Jane turned around to see a young girl dressed in white.

"It's my birthday today," said the little girl. "I'm four."

"Paula! WHAT THE HELL?" shrieked Jane.

"What's up?" asked Richie, looking at a lady he thought had just seen a ghost.

"Paula … Paula … come here!" said a woman dressed for the weather, trying to bring her child to order. "Stop bothering people, we're going now."

"Errr … excuse me," said Jane, rising to her feet. "Is this your child?"

"Yes, I'm sorry if she has disturbed you. She can be a right little madam at times."

"She is remarkably like a child I used to know," replied Jane, leaning forward to take the girl's hand. The child stood motionless, as Jane knelt down and looked her in the eye.

"Your name is Paula?" she asked. The child nodded, still standing statuesque.

"Do you know me?" quizzed Jane.

"Excuse me," said the child's mother, wondering where this was going. "We have an appointment. We have to make tracks."

"She looks remarkably like a child I lost a long time ago."

"Oh, I'm so sorry," said the lady. "A loss is a terrible thing."

"It was more than a loss, dear lady, it was something that was never explained."

Jane continued with her questioning: "Do you know me, Paula? You do don't you?"

Once again the child didn't answer.

Ritchie tried to ease the tension that was starting to become a little bit concerning: "I'm sure Jane is getting your child mixed up with someone else." He said to the child's mother. He laughed, but it just made it worse.

"Don't patronise me!" said Jane very slowly and resolute. "This is my child!"

The lady grabbed the little girl by the hand, easing her towards the door.

"Come on Paula," she said. "This lady doesn't know what she is talking about. Let's go."

"Please!" said Jane, "Can I ask your daughter one question?"

There was a strangled silence, that grew more intense by the second. The woman wasn't quite sure what was going on but she wanted to get the last word before she left: "This is NOT your daughter! Do you understand?"

She opened the door and the rain gushed in, knocking her back a step.

"Paula, what happened to your pink bonnet? The one you lost on your birthday?"

"She never had a pink bonnet," was the ladies reply. "Leave her alone!"

"Paula, do you remember the bonnet? Please tell me. The pink bonnet."

"I lost it," said the child. "I lost it in the trees."

The lady bundled her child out of the hotel and onto the street, then upwards across Elvet Bidge, paddling their way home. Jane stood by the bay window, watching and wondering, until the mother and daughter disappear into the crowds of umbrellas and overcoats.

CHAPTER SEVENTEEN

"STARE LONG ENOUGH INTO THE ABYSS AND ..."

My ex-wife was back in my life, 'sponsored' by Kimberley of course. There seemed to be a quest from someone to have us reunited whether I liked it or not. I was happy to plod along, even though it wasn't the romantic novel my daughter was hoping for. The two basic elements that comprise a Mills & Boon novel are a central love story, and an emotionally satisfying ending. The publishers would have to wait.

Kimberley and I sat in our favourite cafe in Durham, the air thick with the aroma of strong coffee and oven baked bread. It was our father-daughter dinner break together, something we did regularly if we were both in the city.

"How's the new boyfriend?" I asked

"He's gone," she replied. "Not my type."

"Your mother was concerned about you."

"I shouldn't have introduced them," she said. "I knew she wouldn't like him."

"What happened to Kevin? He was nice," I asked, digging up the one male associate of hers that I actually liked.

"We are just mates. Nothing other than that. We are going to different universities next term. He's hoping to go to King's College in London, so we have made a list of things to do and places to visit on day trips before we go our separate ways. Edinburgh, York, Blackpool."

"He's a nice kid," I said, sensing there was an undercurrent there. "Just friends?"

"Yeah. No more, no less. You two always got on," she said. "He thinks the world of you, Dad. I like him a lot, but we don't want to spoil the friendship."

"Spoil the friendship? I think you are smart enough to know that first love never lasts. There's a big world out there."

She seemed undecided whether to continue the conversation about Kevin, or switch it. She stumped for the latter.

"How do you feel about Mam's ex-boyfriend, Steve?"

"I never really liked him, but then again, I wouldn't would I? Someone moves in with your wife. It's never a comfortable situation."

"Can I tell you something?" she said, and I knew she was going to tell me anyway.

"Howay then, but I don't think I'm going to like what you are going to say. Be tactful. Think before you speak."

She can rush in where angels fear to tread, that girl.

"I came across a shoebox hidden in the wardrobe under Mam's clothes. Whenever she was depressed she would write you a letter about how she felt, sealed it, and then hid it in the box. It was her way of getting over depression."

I didn't know how to react to that.

"I didn't realise she was depressed. How often was that?" I asked.

"Quite a few times. I opened some of them – and resealed them of course – but I was going to post a couple of them to you."

"What benefit would that have had?" I asked.

"I don't know why, but I thought about doing it," she said, shrugging her shoulders. "I almost did."

"I never stopped loving her, Kimberly, but I did things that ripped us apart. That's difficult to forget. There are two things to look at. One - I'm not the guy I was before, because I don't get drunk. Two - I'm not the guy I was before, because I've moved on. What's going to hurt your mother worst - the day she kicked me out; or the day I came back?"

The weeks rolled by and the houses on Western Hill started to take shape. But finances started to bite hard. Money was released at key points of the project, so we had to complete two of them, pronto, to raise the capital to fund the whole scheme. The pressure was telling on the boss, and he couldn't complete the job quick enough.

The Obelisk was now in a clearing, detached from the rest of the construction site, looking (probably) as bold as it had since the day it was erected. It still wasn't visible from North Road, but dead trees had been cleared, in and around it's base, and finally we could see what the Victorians had seen all those years ago. The bricked-up entrance was more conspicuous than ever, and it dangled like a carrot every time I caught sight of it. My mind was made up – I was going to tempt fate and go down there. Obviously I needed to prepare. Preferably with someone who knew what the undertaking involved. Someone trust-worthy, with experience in tunneling and caving

So many thoughts; so many emotions. Expectation, precaution and foresight were just three, but they brought an amazing feeling of courage inside me. First of all I had to build my confidence and go into it believing the 'object' was going to be achieved. I had to be fearless, but not to the point I was untouchable. Then I had to convince myself I was in the right - ethically and morally. Where does the law stand on Property Developers going plundering a Cathedral's long lost treasure? What would I do if I found it? I hadn't even thought about that. However, even if I was in the wrong, there is always contention on the degrees of wrongness.

I remember William giving fair warning of the dangers: "We are not meant to wander underground amongst things we don't understand. There was a monster down there. Always remember - stare long enough into an abyss, and the abyss will stare right back at you."

———————————————————————

Poor William was admitted into hospital on one of a handful of visits that confirmed to me his health was in decline. He knew it himself.

"I'm worse than ever!" he moaned, "I won't see Christmas. Don't put my name on the Christmas cards, Rose." I wasn't sure if that was a grumble or satire. He had a wicked way with sarcasm.

It was now September, and his wife was determined he would see Christmas.

He was always keen to talk about the Toll House, and it was on rare moments like that when his spirits rose. It was remarkable. I asked him about Lady Jane Coddington and the incident in the Royal Hotel, and he said it was something that had gripped him for decades.

"I think we have to grasp what Lady Jane was all about," he said, pointing his finger in a pose I had come to love. Breaking into school-teacher mode gave him his platform: "That was a woman who claimed she was best mates with Charles Chaplin! It could have been true, and who am I to doubt her, but she was very talented at bending the truth, then believing her own stories. Although I took ever story she told tongue-in-cheek, some incidents were genuine and established as fact by authentic witnesses. There WAS a ghostly encounter in the Toll House and she DID have a child, of that there was no doubt. But, on the other hand, perhaps there was an affair with an unknown gentleman and the whole pregnancy story was fabricated as an excuse for her husband. God only knows what he thought about it. We don't know. Those were strange times, and she was a strange woman. 'Richie' Richardson-Winter claimed that the Royal Hotel episode did happen. He was very persuasive at the time, and I'm not sure what he had to gain by telling a lie. But Paula would have been 14 at that time, and the child was only four. We are asked to believe that the kid was like Peter Pan, stuck in a time warp, refusing to grow old. She went missing on her birthday and her mother saw her again, exactly the same day – ten years on - as when they parted."

"That is a difficult story to believe, William," I said, knowing he would fill me in with further details.

"I tried to trace the kid on the 1931 census, when she would have been one year old," William replied. "But records for the 1931 census were destroyed in the Second World War. None remain."

Despite his frailty, the old man loved to tell a tale. He couldn't muster a tight embrace or a firm hand shake, but he found joy in reflecting his thoughts.

"How far are you with my book?" he asked. "Have you read it yet?"

"Yes, I have, William," I replied. "You paint an incredible picture. The research is meticulous and brings the Toll House to life. A mysterious and magical structure, with its glamorous guests and hidden secrets. And the end? Well that is still to be written."

"Who was next up for residency when we last spoke?" he asked, trying to remember the date.

"We got to World War Two and a guy called Alfred Sawyer."

"Oh yes," he smiled, "Alfred Sawyer and Viv Inglis. What an odd couple those two were!"

From the memoirs of my dear friend, the story continued - *Alfred Sawyer and Dave Inglis - 'The Untold Story' by William J Woodhouse.*

The war years 1939/45 were difficult times for Durham city, but the Toll House spent most of the conflict uninhibited, apart from Freemason functions and activities, when they hired it. Then, during the closing months of the war, it received its first new tenants for almost a decade. An ex-convict called Gilbert Cooper arrived (along with his friend) a month after his release from Strangeways Prison, following nine years in custody for abuse against women. An ex-priest, he originally resided in Cumbria, and he had a trail of offences going back decades. Some men aren't looking for the simple trappings in this existence of ours. No, some men just want to watch the world burn in Hell.

Whatever happened between the journey from Cumbria to Durham must have been life-changing, because Gilbert Cooper arrived with the new name of Alfred Sawyer. A name to hide the past and confuse the present? More likely to conceal what he had become, under the knowledge of the basilica. Whether a man is a criminal or a man of the cloth is purely a matter of perspective. He was in Durham, aided by the Church. They knew his past, but gave him a clean canvas to paint another picture of madness.

His side-kick (although not necessary his partner in crime) was Dave Inglis, a character right out of a William Shakespeare play.

"Must you with hot irons burn out both mine eyes?" said Arth to Hub in Shakespeare's *King John*.

Dave Inglis was that man. He had made his fortune gun-running in the Spanish Civil War for the Anarchists against General Franco's army, until he was captured loading up his boat in Morocco. Franco's boys were a strange bunch. They spared his life, but Inglis would never see the light of day again. They blinded him.

He returned to England where he joined the Priesthood, under the guidance of Cooper. Even though the world (and the police) caught up with Cooper, and their lives were thrust apart, Inglis visited the convict in prison on a regular basis (assisted by Inglis's brother).

They remained pals, and the blind man, who was no longer part of the church, was quite possibly the only friend Cooper had during his nine-year term behind bars.

'Anonymity' was their watch-word in the early period of their stay in the Toll House, and Sawyer managed it, let's say 'under duress,' rather than effortlessly. What better place to hide than in a house in the middle of a copse? But a name change doesn't change a personality. Alfred Sawyer was no better an individual than Gilbert Cooper. He was suffering a slow death, feeling his mind break just a little more each day. Medication brought little relief to the deprived mind of a psycho, and only morphine quelled it for any length of time. His prison record was deplorable. Women-beaters were not segregated in the 1940's, and to murderers and cut-throats, there was no lower form of life than anyone who beat up women. So, he was beaten to within an inch of his life many times, spending weeks in the prison hospital, never once forming a friendship with any inmates. The abuse he inflicted on women was a matter of opportunity, it represented a need to dominate and control. But Sawyer (as I will call him from now on) was never of sound mind. He didn't realize he was doing was wrong. He genuinely believed that he was showing affection. That was why he continued to offend time and time again. He understood that society deemed it wrong what he did, but he couldn't understand why. The police report concluded: "He is highly unlikely to be rehabilitated," but no-one listened.

He served his time, and they let him out! Sawyer was free to roam wherever … whenever.

Was he as naive as the prison system had us believe? I honestly don't know.

Inside that house were two strong people who knew what they wanted …. but neither knew what they needed. Poor Ingles was balanced somewhere between Heaven and the deep blue sea, dealing with his violent, disturbing and bizarre room-mate on a daily basis. Ingles was still of the real world, for a while, but he knew he was dealing with a guy with a serious mental issue. It was when it all became 'normal' to Ingles that the pair went beyond hope.

The blind man had physical problems, and the fact that he couldn't leave the house alone was intimidating, particularly because Sawyer wouldn't take him very far. It was at that point Ingles claimed to be able to talk to the soul of the house, and (I imagine) get a reply. The ability to sense spirits is called 'clairsentient' and Ingles claimed he developed it himself when he was in the Priesthood. He would describe the feeling as being like: "A heavy cloak suddenly falling over the room, because the increased energy has entered the space." And he had a way of communication: "In order to connect with the spirit you have to raise your energy and the spirit has to lower theirs, to put us both on the frequency chain."

Ingles was talking to Smelt, but he didn't know what the hell he was dealing with! He said he spoke to spirits - often. Some were happy, some were sad. But, according to the man who couldn't see, one of those spirits was extra special because he made contact by touch. The sad fact of the matter is, both Sawyer and Ingles were as mad as shit-house rats. And the day two charity workers came calling, one of those rats opened his jaws.

There was always a path to the Toll House, right back from the days of horse-drawn carriages. But in 1945 it was badly overgrown and didn't encourage any visitor to venture beyond the cobbled road. Although no wooden notice stopped anyone dead in their tracks, there was an aura about the place suggesting that no-one was welcome. However, two ladies, oblivious to auras and warnings, found there way onto Western Hill.

Anna Cartwright and Simone Costil were collecting clothes for a children's war-time charity when they happened to go down the wrong overgrown track. Friends 'forever', but that was before they learnt that 'forever' can be so heartbreakingly short.

Their car was less than 150 yards from the Toll House, within ear-shot, but when the cries rang out, Hell was reeking its revenge.

The Toll House appeared out of the branches like a white-washed cathedral. Anna peered through the window, and Sawyer manifested himself out of the darkness of the living room like a gargoyle from Gothic architecture.

"Come inside ladies," he said, opening the door with scrawny filthy fingers like Fagan from *Oliver Twist* rounding up his gang of thieves. His filthy dark hair, as oily as a Ford 8 dip-stick, strung over his blood-shot beady eyes. His mud brown shirt was probably the one he slept in the night before.

Simone spoke afterwards about the tragedy saying that Anna was always his target, and Sawyer acted alone. Ingles was nowhere to be seen. Sawyer enticed both of them down the cellar, where he told them he kept children's clothes. Then he tricked Simone, bolted the trap-door, before dragging Anna into the master bedroom.

Nobody could possibly imagine the kind of thoughts that slipped through his warped delusional mind. Whatever it was, didn't register a spark. Not a heartbeat. He stood there brain-dead holding the knife that had penetrated her heart. No sexual encounter, but he did what he did best, beat up a woman.

On an ordinary Friday afternoon on sunny Western Hill, Anna Cartwright was slumped on a chair. Her face sunken and bruised; her mind cold and haunted.

On an ordinary Friday afternoon on sunny Western Hill - 30 seconds later - Alfred Sawyer was forced against a bedroom wall, and his entire body levitated up to the ceiling. His eyes started to pop out of their sockets as his face was slowly crushed, from either side, by a force so fierce he choked and probably swallowed his tongue. Smelt's party trick - the hammer striking the anvil. Sawyer's brain was squeezed out of his head through his eye-sockets.

Police broke down the door to find the poor lady where Sawyer had left her. But the psycho's mutilated body was still suspended from the ceiling, hanging by some invisible force. Two police officers stood watching as the crushed figure, dripping with blood and urine, shook and swayed. They were powerless to do anything. Suddenly, in one heart-stopping finale, the bag of bones clattered to the floor, bouncing before it settled in silence. But only for ten seconds … before the body levitated, then shot forward, head-first, crashing through the bedroom window.

At the inquest in court many weeks later, PC Derek Hilditch reported: "How can we appeal to the court to accept our account of events in good faith when we don't believe it ourselves?"

PC Malcolm Chapman added: "Scientists claim we only use 15% of the true potential of the mind. This court is going to have to open up the other 85% of their minds if they have any hope of believing what we are going to tell them."

Nobody knows what happened to Ingles. He was never seen again. Perhaps Sawyer killed him and left him in a shallow grave in the woods. If he did, it was never found. However, the blind man claimed he made friends with Smelt. Now there's an interesting meeting of minds that opens up a whole world of possibilities.

CHAPTER EIGHTEEN

"ALWAYS KISS YOUR CHILD GOODNIGHT"

The more I read William's tales about Victor Schafer, the more I felt relieved. Relieved in that I was still alive! Smelt threatened and intimidated me during our short spell together, but I walked away with my throat still in the place it was meant to be, and my eye sockets full of eyes.

"So, William, perhaps Mr Smelt has a good side to him? And I mean that as a question rather than a statement."

The thing about William was that the words he replied with were always worth the question in the first place. I don't know what gripped me the most, his intelligence or his imagination.

"Don't let sentiment come into it," he replied in a sharp tone. "Underestimate him at your peril!"

"What do we do about him, William?" I asked.

"We have to re-evaluate everything about the fellow," he replied. "He is in a form we know nothing about. Alive or dead, it doesn't matter. He is what he is and he is here! What I do know is that he is tied to the Toll House and he doesn't wander far beyond that. The Toll House is his life's blood. He gets to the Obelisk, which is the gateway to the tunnels, but that's about it. I assume he is the Gate Keeper, and I don't believe he has the power or the strength to go much further. He shows up in Fay's house, but only when summoned, and you told me yourself that he was very weak and only appears as a shadow. So, I assume, 50 yards is his limit. Get beyond that in the tunnel and the threat goes away. I'm not suggesting that all will be sweetness and honey down there, but you needn't fear Smelt."

"He gets a power supply from the Toll House that keeps him alive."

"It seems that way, John, and that brings more questions to the table. Why does the Roman Catholic Church refuse to bulldoze the Toll House? It has no practical use and what do they gain by rejecting offers for that small piece of land? I don't believe the theory that if you destroy the Toll House you destroy his lifeline. It's what is in there that regenerates him. Perhaps something tucked away in a hidden room? Are those old bones in the cellar his? I don't know. I'm just throwing suggestions at the question."

"There seems a 'bond' between the Church and Devil-worship," I said. "They are the opposite ends of the spectrum."

I started a fire inside the old man.

"No, no, no. You don't understand, they are two peas in the same pod. You cannot believe in one without the other. Heaven or Hell? Is there any difference? The bible created them both. Three thousand years ago neither existed, so what has happened since? The Church started to point fingers. Witches were either burned or drown. What are witches? Women that were not under the control of the Church. It only took one shout of 'witch' and the crowd would become fearful enough to attack. That is one hell of a powerful 'spell', one word that can turn a crowd of religious soulful people into a sea of zombies baying for murder. The crowd kill ... in the name of God. Who is God? The conductor of an orchestra? Are we the orchestra? The ones bound with duty? The Church like to believe that."

"Why does the Church benefit from keeping Smelt alive?" I asked. "Where is the logic?"

"I can only surmise they benefit because they have a Gate Keeper," he pointed out. "The religious artefacts that were put in the tunnel system are probably lost forever. Nobody can get to them from the Cathedral side, I'm convinced of that, or they would have retrieved them centuries ago. Something happened, a collapsed mine or tunnel, or maybe all the escape routes from the Cathedral were closed off. If you have an escape tunnel out of a building, that tunnel can let your enemies in. Maybe the treasure was looted. That happened to the burial chambers in the Valley of the Kings in Egypt. As for Smelt, if the Church cannot get to it, isn't it handy having a doorman that stops everyone else?"

Whether it was intended, or not, I was starting to see the whole tunnel 'adventure' in a more positive light. Fifty yards isn't that far in a race, but it's a long way to travel having the son of Satin trying to rip out your wind-pipe. All I had to do was get a move on.

For as long as people have been walking, communicating, and struggling to survive … they have been constructing homes. A cave in a rock face, a mud hut, it didn't take much, but some modification always took place.

These days all the graft and hardship of house-building is done for us. Construction sites are dangerous places, which is why everyone who enters such an environment is requested to wear a hard hat. The words 'hard' and 'hat' are self-explanatory.

Thankfully, JL Property & Developments had an exemplary record with safety over the years, despite the nature of the beast. Assembling large buildings is hazardous, due to heavy machinery, dangerous tools and large vehicles. Labour statistics show that almost 20% of deaths in the workplace happen on building sites. Falls, not surprisingly, are the commonest cause of death.

I mention this because, despite our vigilance, preparation and foresight, we suffered a week of perplexing accidents that grew more curious by the day.

One of our hired staff, not part of the usual crew, drove a digger beyond the Toll House fence and into the building itself, demolishing one of the stables. As Alan Ravenhall, commented: "It could have been a lot worse. How can you ruin a building that's a ruin itself?"

A bodged up job of 'righting the wrong' was the best we could do. A bit of cement here, and a brick there, the boys rebuilt the stable.

"Does it stand out?" asked Bill McCracken.

"It looks as much a ruin as the rest of it," I replied, trying to make light of it. "It is our boys doing the building!"

It bought a laugh, at least.

"Well tell them not to over-do it," he replied. "We don't want it looking better than the rest of it."

Another problem solved. But then things went strangely wrong. Incidents happened without explanation. The next day scaffolding on one of the houses collapsed and two roofers fell to the ground, luckily escaping serious injury. All bolts and joints had been checked that very morning, yet the entire structure subsided. That was just the first of a series of episodes of dangerous practice that blighted the site. We had one case of electrocution when a worker touched an exposed power line; two workers were hit with falling power tools (when they insisted there was no-one up the scaffolding above them);

one suffered an arm injury when he was crushed between a wagon and some immovable object; and one worker somehow shot himself with a nail-gun! Half the workforce ended up in hospital. No deaths, thankfully, but a couple of compensation claims landed on my desk pointing the finger of blame at myself.

There is no way a site manager can prevent every accident, but the men were dropping like flies, and questions were being asked. McCracken took me off the job, which I found embarrassing, and we had a blazing row over it. Another argument I was never going to win. So I was moved to a single house construction in Sedgefield five miles away. I was out of the firing line, but I was bitter that the blame was pushed onto me.

James Lawrence took me to one side: "It's just temporary, John. I'm not saying you cannot do your job, mate, its just that McCracken feels we need more experience at the top level. Nothing personal. It's like bloody cowboys and Indians on that building site at the moment."

I was in no position to argue.

A lot changed over the coming weeks. It was now December. Susan and I became an item (of sorts). Not living together but seeing a lot more of each other. Something I will go into more detail later. But poor William was on the slippery slide, refusing to go into hospital when summoned, and making life very difficult for Rose. I would visit him twice a week, but sometimes I had to leave because he was so fragile. Some days he would be brimming with life, laughing and joking, then other days a sea of depression would flood over him like there was no tomorrow. The doctor explained his mood could depend on his medication, but alternatively his medication often depended on his willingness to take it. He was in the process of dying and each day was a battle of will. His attention span was still strong, most of the time, and rarely did he lose his thread when telling a story. But when he did struggle, it was painful to watch. One day he said he felt like he was a guest in someone else's dreadful body.

The last couple to officially take up residence in the Toll House and be on the electoral role were a married couple called Martha and Reg Pascoe, and I spoke to William about them. But first … from the

memoirs of my dear friend, the story he put in writing – *Martha &*
Reg Pascoe - 'The Untold Story' by William J Woodhouse.
From 1950 to 1955 there was a growing clamour by local residents to
have the Toll House pulled to the ground. Petitions were signed and a
local counsellor, called Jennifer Bennion, made it her battle cry to
have the building, and its stigma, removed from Western Hill.
However, no matter what argument she put to the Church, they
refused to budge. At one point, as a propaganda stunt prior to local
council elections, she handcuffed herself to the metal gate leading to
the front door of the building. She posed for photographers and gave
her story to local reporters, saying she was fighting for "the decency
of the good people of Durham city." It was all for publicity, of course,
and the handcuffs were off immediately after the final click of the
photographer's shutter. Later that year she fell foul of the law and
was charged with tax evasion. She kept her job (for a while), but all
credibility went out of the window, and her campaign dwindled away,
along with her career.
In 1956 Martha and Reg Pascoe arrived from Liverpool to start a
new life in Durham, having allegedly made their money from
property. It was all a cover. They were actually gypsies on the run for
theft, having set up a business stealing tractors and farm machinery
and shipping them to Ireland. They had a record of moving on from
town to town rather quickly, so it was no surprise when Reg fled
from Durham shortly after he arrived. His wife tried to deflect police
interest by changing her name to Martha Godfrey, and decided to
stay. At that stage there was more to it than keeping one step ahead
of the law, their marriage was on the rocks, too.
Martha acquired a lodger called Dumitru Georgescu, a Romanian
gypsy she had known from Liverpool. Apparently he was a bit of a
legend amongst the travelling fraternity because of his association
with sawn-off shotguns, and the people who used them. A nice guy
to know in an argument, but did Durham need a gun-slinger?
Martha and Reg were officially 'over' as a married couple, but the
break wasn't as clean as the pair of them would have liked. Martha
was pregnant and want-away Reg was the father. He agreed to pay
for his child's upkeep and made arrangements that he would visit the
mother and baby periodically.

Young Sean was born a healthy bouncing 8ld 3oz baby, and the mother forwarded photographs to Reg. He had given up the 'tractor business' and was now living in Cork. He was a very proud Dad, and often wrote to say so.

Reg arrived for a sort visit a couple of months later, spending the day with Martha and his son. Christmas was coming up soon and Reg wanted to make sure his child wanted for nothing, handing over money for presents and clothes. The ground rules were set, Martha insisting she was not having a relationship with Dumitru (and that was genuinely the case, he was only a lodger), and the child would be brought up knowing who his father was. As far as broken marriages were concerned, little Sean would have the best of all worlds.

Although visits to Durham were always fleeting, Reg did make the effort four times a year, although he was never allowed to go to the Toll House. That wasn't so much of a concern to him, because he didn't want to meet Dumitru. Martha, on the other hand, always refused to go to Cork, no matter how much Reg sugar-coated it with the offer of money and accommodation. That did tear at his heart strings because he wanted more than just photographs to show his own parents, often saying that the child needed to meet it's Grandparents. It was never an ideal father and son relationship, but it was amiable for quite some time, and took a while to get complicated. It was quite a few years before the serious problems surfaced.

On one visit the child (who was now four) questioned his Dad as to why he always called him Sean, when his real name was Peter. Martha stepped in quickly, laughing off the matter: "You are Sean, you know that."

The child threw a tantrum: "You are not my Mam and you are not my Dad. I don't want to be here. I hate you!"

No matter how hard she tried to comfort the kid, he would never settle in front of his father. Making visits awkward and stressful for everyone. So Martha suggested Reg stopped the visits: "He doesn't know you and perhaps it is for the best that you don't come back. He will always be your son, and you can continue to help raise him financially."

It wasn't until Reg got back home to Ireland that doubts crept into his mind. He started to wonder what sort of life Sean had with Dumitru. Everything was changing, and Reg wanted his son … for good!

He wrote a letter to Martha saying he was going to contact the authorities and put in a request for custody of Sean because he didn't think his child was being brought up in the right environment. She went on the defensive and made a call to Ireland: "Don't contact me again Reg. Not by letter or in person. You do not have a child. You never did. Listen to me … you do NOT have a child."

Reg immediately phoned Durham police. He wanted to know where his son was. He was concerned there may have been foul play, saying: "I think her Romanian boyfriend could have killed him."

Reg drove to Dublin then caught the ferry to Holyhead, before returning to Durham by train to help with investigations. Martha was taken in for questioning and throughout the 48 hour ordeal she insisted she had never gave birth to a child. Police Sergeant Paul Astley took Reg in a small room to explain her plea, and the consequences.

"According to her," he said, "You don't have a son, Mr Pascoe. Martha claims the entire story was made up to get money from you."

"But I saw the child, I saw him grow up from being a baby," Reg insisted.

"That was not her child, Mr Pascoe. That was her friend's baby. She would baby-sit the child on the days you came to Durham."

"So her friend was in on this, too? Is that what you are saying?"

The sergeant paused for a moment: "I'm not in a position to comment on that because the 'friend' claims she knows nothing about this. Whether she is being economical with the truth, I cannot say at this moment. But the child in you photographs are certainly her son, Peter."

"I've lived my life for almost five years believing I have a son, and it was all just a story?"

Reg sat and stared at the floor. In the eyes of the law he was made to look a fool. What was worse to accept – not being a father in the first place – or going through all of the emotions of being one, only to have them all ripped away?

"I don't know what to say Mr Pascoe," said the officer.

"I don't believe it. It's all fabrication, and I need some answers. Have you checked for a body in the grounds of the Toll House?"

"There is no body, sir," he replied. "There never was, I'm afraid."

"Can I ask you, will you please check that ground? Please. I have come a long way and that would help put things in perspective. Something tells me my son is buried there."

"If it makes you happy, sir. I will check today. I will go round with one of the dog handlers."

Reg was a shell of a man looking for a reason to believe in. He lit a cigarette, threw the spent match on the floor, then blew the smoke towards the ceiling.

"My wife did that to me," he said, but the officer didn't respond. "She crushed me. What happens to her and the Romanian now? Will they be charged?"

"She embezzled money through false pretences," said the sergeant. "That's the charge. But the Romanian had no part in it. They are not a couple, Mr Pascoe. He is only a lodger. I can promise you that."

"There seems to be a lot of people walking away scot-free, from what I can see," replied Reg, obviously wanting some retribution. Who could blame him?

"No man nor woman can be judged a criminal until they are found guilty," said the sergeant. "Is it better to risk saving a guilty person, than to condemn an innocent one?"

Reg didn't feel the need to reply. He left the police station, threw his cigarette butt into the gutter, then headed for his Durham hotel.

Room number 3 in the City Hotel in New Elvet Street. Handy, spacious and comfy. Reg kicked off his shoes, lay on the bed, then drifted off to sleep.

Four hours later there was a rap on the door. A young lady made herself heard: "Excuse me sir, there is a phone call for you down stairs. It is very urgent. It is the police."

Reg stumbled down the tight stairway, feeling his footing rather than looking where he was going. The lady handed him the chalk black receiver and he heard the voice of Sergeant Astley: "Can you come to the Toll House Mr Pascoe? Immediately. We have a body for you to identify. A young child, about four years old."

———————————————

"Oh, dear me. A sad face not what I want to see when I open the door," said Fay, looking me up and down. "What's up with you? I want the happy version. The one with the instant smile and the cheeky eyes."

"I'm off the building site, Fay. Bombed off the job," I answered, and my face wasn't going to get any happier.

"They've sacked you?" she asked, pulling a quizzical face.

"Almost," I said, taking off my coat and placing it on the hook on the wall.

"There cannot be an 'almost', they've either sacked you or they haven't."

"I've been transferred, which is a bit like 'gardening leave.' Any excuse to get me off the job."

"What are you going to do?" she asked.

"I'm going down the tunnel. I've decided to take the plunge."

She looked at me as though I was spinning a yarn. Slowly she sipped her drink, placed the cup back on the saucer, then gave me a look of distrust.

"You are going down the tunnel because you aren't sure if you have been fired, or not! Am I hearing right?"

"No, the tunnel has nothing to do with the job. It's something I need to do. Well, what do you think?" I asked.

"Shock doesn't quite cover it. Why? What's changed your mind?"

"I spoke with the old guy, William, and he claims Smelt is tied to the Toll House. We don't know how, but it seems he only travels about fifty yards away from it. As far as this house."

"Are you sure enough to stake your life on it? How are you going to bypass the first fifty yards? Go down in a tank?"

"I don't know. That's why I'm here. Do you think Benjamin would help? He has experienced those first few yards."

"Then they took him to hospital!" she exploded. "The only advice he will give you is – don't do it. He's already told you that."

"But I feel passionate about it. I need his help."

"You haven't got his number," she replied.

"I do. He phoned me in Spain. It's logged on my phone."

"If you feel that way, go ahead."

I phoned him there and then.

After the preliminaries I asked for his help: "I am serious about it, Sergio. I want to try it. Can you help me?"

He knew the background so I got straight to the chase and asked him what I needed to know about the dangers. He was polite and affable, as I expected, but he wouldn't go into detail about what was down there. That was disappointing, to say the least. The call lasted less than five minutes and he said he needed time to think. Think about what?

"Well then," said Fay, after I had turned off my phone. "What did the man say?"

"'Don't be a fool,'" I replied. "That's basically the jist of it. He wouldn't recommend it, put it that way."

"I told you," said Fay with a certain look of mischief. "You are on your own. You aren't so keen now, are you?"

Back home Kimberley came to visit, and I made an evening meal for two ... out of a box.

"Dad, what is generally regarded as food to some people - may not be food to others. What is it?"

"Hey, it's going to be great. Add vegetables and its transformed. Just drink more wine and it will taste great! Miracles can be performed. Look what some people can do with five fishes and two loafs."

We spoke about the tunnel business; lost treasure; Sergio; and Indiana Jones and the Temple of Doom, although not necessarily in that order. I did point out that Indiana Jones had more idea of lost treasure than me. Kimberley agreed.

"I need Sergio's advice, Kimberley."

"Would you want him here? To do it with you?" she asked.

"In an ideal world ... yes!"

"Would he come here? Would you pay for him to come here?"

"I'd pay for his flight and accommodation, of course I would. But it's all hypothetical anyway. He isn't interest. I couldn't even keep him on the phone for longer than the time it took him to say 'no'."

"Give me your phone, Dad," she said. I handed it to her. "I'm going to ask him."

I left her to it.

"Hello. Mr Sergio, I am John Hampson's daughter. We met in Spain on our holidays. I'm fine thank you … thank you for asking. I hope you are well. Can I ask if you, sir, would you help my Dad go looking for treasure?"

CHAPTER NINETEEN

"AT THE END OF EVERY LIGHT IS A TUNNEL OF DARKNESS"

Although Susan and I were back "as an item", as they say in rom-coms, we hadn't moved in together. Progress in motion, because reunions can be emotional things, so far better advance with baby-steps. My idea, not hers. Particularly when the pre-internet concept of keeping a physical diary kept getting a mention. My God, diaries can tell a good tale. In my day, girls had them and boys didn't. So, Susan had one and I didn't. Of course they are one-sided, that's the whole point of them, and the pen has the last word.

Well-thumbed passages got an airing, the quotations of choice, and I don't know how we were such an easy going couple, because I didn't seem to get a look in. She played on the 'opposites attract theme' - she was good and I was bad - when I always thought that we are two-peas-in-the-same-pod. See how wrong I was? I always felt there were enough good times in that book to out-weigh the bad. It seems I got that wrong too.

Did the separation do us both good? That's difficult to answer. Susan seemed to think I spent the entire time in a coma, because I didn't go out often. That wasn't necessarily the case, because I belief had at least one eye open most of the time. So much for the coma, I had a drink problem to sort, and that ended well.

I wasn't all bad, I don't think. I grew out of my 30's with a hard heart, and I'd put that down to her. She has never experienced a lonely life. There has always been someone there for her, Kimberley or her boyfriend, and that covers over a lot of cracks mentally. However, that said, my daughter did spill the beans about her mother's depression. She said Susan wrote letters to me in her dark moments, and tucked them away in secret. If there was a love-triangle going on, it would have been nice to have know about it.

Were we discovering true love at last, and a new perspective on our relationship? Too early to say. Binning the diary, and getting rid of my dark past, would be a good start. I don't want to be someone who always has to be accountable for a past that I've worked so hard to put it right. A new day – a new dream. We move on with our lives.

Having said that, we still say those three little words, and when she says them with meaning, I still get a speck of dust in my eye.

He said he wouldn't make it to Christmas, and as always, he was right.

William J Woodhouse passed away, quietly, on December 3rd in his own house, on his own terms. Although we are often reminded that funerals are a celebration ... that one was different. I didn't feel like celebrating, and none of the congregation did either. Outside of my own families bereavement, it was the most moving occasion I can remember attending. He was a guy I will never forget.

The funeral service gave us all our own memories, dictated by the man himself. If he was going to have a farewell … he was going to be the conductor; the orchestra; and the soloist. Leonard Bernstein would have been proud.

Rose bowed to every request, but sentimentality was hardly William's thing. His speech, read out by Rose herself, was short, polite and respectful. But all his true thoughts and feelings were delivered in person, to those that mattered most, before he died. The 'laying to rest' was for show. The black clothes, the grim faces, and the red eyes were for the moment. The grieving would be done later.

Our last get-together was strange. I watched his whole world dissolve around him. It melted away as the pain tore through his body, and he couldn't fight it any longer. The medication took over and he slipped into a hazy trance as though his brain was being removed while he was awake. It probably was, and it was a memory I could have done without. I kept convincing myself he wasn't gone, just out of reach for a while.

He was my inspiration, and I took his passing very badly. I called back to his grave the following day. No maddening crowds and everything had been ticked off his funeral 'to do' list. Just me and him. I told him one day I would grieve for him, but first I needed his spirit with me on the most crucial part of "our" journey. I couldn't do it without him. We planned it together and I needed guidance to see it through. I picked up the note from the flowers I had placed there the day before, and when my words wouldn't come, the tears did.

A week later the postal delivery service brought several cardboard boxes to my doorstep, the items William wanted me to have. The presents varied in size and value, from books to medals; maps and diagrams; to a keyboard with the attached note "You know what it's worth – make sure you get the right price."

The riches he had amassed were for his pleasure, and his wife often told me he took a moralistic view on wealth: "He hated greed and over indulgence, and what he bought for himself had a purpose."

He was untouched by wealth's corrosive, addictive effects.

I was honoured to be offered his gold watch, which was probably worth more than my car, but did I deserve it? I felt it should have gone to a family member, but Rose insisted I take it. However, the gem in the legacy (as far as I was concerned) was his teaching – my learning. Detailed works about the Toll House and my proposed trip underground. Writings both past and present. Theories, proposals and ideology on Smelt and his band of brothers.

"If Victor Schaefer hadn't have existed, I'd have invented him," said William in one passage of writing, which suggests admiration when surely none was deserved. But he claimed we (himself and I) lost the plot because we studied Smelt as a human being, rather than the devil he always was.

"His goals, ambitions and desires were always power-driven, but not necessarily for his own gain. Yes he flaunts his virtuosity, but he will do whatever it takes to win the war. Of course he is a success because he rides rough-shod over space and time. Is he immortal? Does he have a timeline? Whoever created him crafted a masterpiece. But is he still trying to win a war he has already won? Because that will be his downfall."

Kimberley and I stood by the 'Arrivals' board as the passengers trundled past us, most of them homeward bound met by enthusiastic relatives and friends. Kids with beaming faces reunited with granny, the odd straggler heading home from business. That was Newcastle airport at mid-day, with heavily armed security forces all looking and listening. One security guard was dangling an automatic rifle by his finger, probably believing he was giving the commuters a sense of protection, but he had me on my toes hoping he knew where the safety catch was. He looked more like the Milky Bar Kid than an officer of the law. It was high alert, either a terror threat or some dignitary arriving from abroad.

Just then Kimberley caught sight of our own V.I.P., and she raised her hand to attract his attention.

"He has arrived Dad," she said in a flutter of excitement. "I told you he would be as good as his word."

I didn't doubt her for one moment, or him. I had paid for the flight so I assumed he had nothing to lose, well … apart from the small matter of getting arrested on arrival for being on the airport wanted list. I just prayed the security around us was not for him. But surely Newcastle wouldn't roll out the heavy guns for a guy who had stolen from his wife, and paid it back?

Sergio was back on English soil. Under a different name, with a different coloured passport, but let's not nit-pick.

Fay didn't seem so enthusiastic about our visitor from a sunny climate, but I didn't expect her to be. Hopefully their paths wouldn't cross during his visit, or perhaps they had arranged a meeting of their own.

The plan … oh yes we had a plan … was for him to stay at the Radison hotel in Durham for three nights, during which time we would prepare to change five hundred year old history. Perhaps.

"Hello my friend," he said, dropping his luggage to the floor, looking relieved that we were there to greet him. But it paled into comparison as to how I felt that he had made the effort. He shook my hand vigorously, greeted Kimberley with the usual traditional Spanish greeting, then we ushered him out into the rain towards my car.

We settled on calling him Sergio, his wish, Benjamin was now officially deceased.

———————————————

The building site was on-going, but with building work delayed for a weekend in preparation for more heavy machinery, we had a window to work with. Friday night right through to Monday morning. There was always a security guard on duty but Len was a good friend of mine, and he was on the rota for that weekend. If push-came-to-shove, I'm sure he would lend a hand with our equipment, if it was required. Obviously we wanted to keep it very much 'hush-hush' so we would have to come up with a decent excuse for what we were doing.

Kimberley was the link "up top", manning the walkie-talkie, so we had a fair chance of a phone connection for some of the route. Although 500 yards was probably the limit. We had no chance of getting a signal connection with our cell phones underground.

Fay wanted to be involved, and that made everything a whole lot easier and far more practical for many reasons. She knew the background, and didn't need a crash-course in either history nor demons, to understand what we were up to. Plus her house was on-site, or as close as we could hope.

The reunion with her husband was interesting. They preferred to meet on neutral territory, in a restaurant in the city, and all went well by all accounts. No punches were thrown, and knives and forks were used for food only.

Susan was kept in the dark about all of this, which we felt was for the better. I told her Kimberley and I were going away for a weekend break in Edinburgh, which she took without question. At least that was her on safe ground and away from the stress of it all. Kimberley, although not the sort of girl I wouldn't trust to keep a birthday present a secret, was focused and rational. She was a major player in the whole scheme of things, and clued up about everything. She was to stay at Fay's house throughout the course of events and the plan was to relay all information back to them. I don't suppose there was much they could do in an accident, apart from phone the emergency services, and that would be a last resort.

I viewed Sergio as the brains of the outfit, and I believed he was going to be the difference between success and failure. I insisted he was the captain of the ship, the commander of the fleet, and whatever he said must be the final word. The plan was laid, we collected our tools, and set off into the unknown.

I had known about the entrance to the tunnel for many months and I had prepared for the day we went underground. Weeks before I moved two concrete slabs out of the base of the Obelisk with a JCB and I replaced them with a wooden board and placed house bricks on top, hiding the entrance to the tunnel. The doorway to the Obelisk was different to the hole underground. They were two different entrances to two entirely different places. Although the tower had been an actual dwelling for some poor soul, he hadn't found the way into the tunnel. However, he had left behind all manner of junk. Hypodermic needles were my main concern, and there were many of them. Broken beer bottles, old cans and shards of glass. But I removed all of the rubbish a week before our decent.

We removed the bricks and it only took us two minutes to open up the passageway. A new world awaited.

"This is for real," I mumbled to Sergio, but I had the feeling I was a lot more enthusiastic about that entrance than he was.

"This is the difficult part," he replied. "We have to be vigilant. Keep watching and listening. If anything moves, we tell each other. OK?"

"OK."

We ventured underground and all of Williams thoughts and fears came back to me. Particularly one quote: "If you feel you don't fit into this world you were born into, create your own. Because Smelt did!" And we were stepping into that world.

That was Friday 6pm, early evening. Len Whitley was the security guard, who was well aware we were "doing jobs" out of hours, but he had the good sense not to interfere with the boss's business. So he didn't know the precise nature of the job. He sat in his cabin as happy as a pig in muck. He had his feet up, coffee in hand, TV switched on, oblivious to everything going on around him. In other words - a typical security guard.

We had prepared long and hard. We both had the full set-up of equipment, including a hard helmet with a headlamp; appropriate underwear (you cannot underestimate good underwear); kneepads; elbow pads; gloves; boots; waist-belt carrying spare batteries and tools; walky-talky; six-inch knife; and a whistle. The walky-talky was our link to Kimberley and Fay, but only for a short time. We understood that. Then we were on our own.

We lowered ourselves further into the darkness, dropping down the last few yards to hit the ground. We steadied ourselves then meandered along a narrow path for about twenty yards then noticed two side passages branching off to the left and right.

"Don't concern yourself with those," said Sergio. "They are two crypts linked together by a path. Two of the many we will come across. I hope you aren't squeamish. The smell can make you feel very nauseous."

I cast a look down the passage-way on the left and it seemed murky and foreboding, about as endless as the very one we were heading down, only a lot tighter to squeeze down. A black expanse of nothingness apart from a dead decaying rat that I noticed half submerged in watery mud.

Already I was doubting my sanity. "Remind me. Why are we doing this?" I asked, as I tagged along, following the torch light in front of me.

"Curiosity?" Sergio commented, although he knew as well as I did, it was more pure greed.

"Yeah, I can go along with curiosity. And we know what curiosity killed."

Another opening to our left-hand side, seemingly an open invitation to deviate off our track.

"What's down there?" I asked, like a parrot reciting the same phrase over and over.

"Same again, a crypt," he replied. "Do you want to see it?"

"Not particularly."

"Come on, let's take a look," he said, probably hoping I would see it and then shut up.

Peering forward, the passageway was probably twenty yards long, with a broken wooden box protruding out of the face of one of the walls just in front of us. It wasn't a coffin, it was like a tea chest, it's wood splintered open.

"Take a look," she said, "This is probably one of the condemned. Nothing grand and swanky about this guy. Hung from the gallows, most probably. This isn't the crypt, that's further down, this is where they dumped the shit, if you know what I mean."

I saw the skull and that was enough. I backed away, repulsed that I'd even looked inside. What was I thinking off? What had I become, snooping in to a dead man's last resting place?

Sergio pulled at the old matted jacket that lay damp and smelly, "A pauper with a death sentence, and a broken neck."

I turned away. What we were doing was just ridiculous.

"A murderer?" I asked.

"Not necessarily. It could have been one of Smelt's men. The Church did most of the hanging on this land after Smelt was put in his little cage. They cleaned out his Sadistic disciples by fair means or fowl. They weren't particular how they dealt with them."

We moved on, and all the time I kept pacing the way until I guessed we had reached fifty yards. I didn't say anything but I felt a little bit relieved when we did reach it.

"How far did you get the last time you were down here?" I asked.

"Not far. Another hundred yards or so."

"We aren't out of the woods, then?"

He didn't reply, he just kept plodding forward. Then we came to a junction of four tunnels. None showing any defining route to take.

"This is where the coal miners crossed the path of the crypt tunnels," said Sergio. "This is new territory to me. The walls are a coal seam drilled out by miners probably around William IV's time, 1830 or so. Hang on, there's even an inscription on the wall, carved with a knife."

"What's it say?" I asked. Sergio ran his fingers over the words, as though he was reading by brale.

"Something about the 'grace of God'. I cannot make out the beginning."

"A warning, then," I said.

"Probably," he answered.

I stepped back into a puddle about nine inches deep, and stumbled against the wall. Rats bolted everywhere, splashing and leaping about three foot into the air, before running away from our headlamps. I turned to try and grab something to break my fall ... when I saw a shadow of a figure scamper across into one of the tunnels ahead of me.

"Are you OK?" Sergio asked, leaning forward, holding out his hand to pick me up off the wet ground.

"Did you see that?" I asked.

"What?"

"A dark figure. Small, agile, moving across that passageway."

"No," he said, turning towards that particular direction. "Where?"

"Across there, down that tunnel," I said, pointing to the spot. "Honestly, it moved like grease lightening."

We looked at each other, then I fumbled in my belt to get hold of a weapon.

"It went down there, I promise you," I said, holding out a knife with a six inch blade. "It can't be far."

"You think someone else is down here?" he asked.

"Not so much 'someone' as 'something'."

I felt my hands physically shake. Then my arms. Then my legs. I had to drag some courage from somewhere, so I took a few steps forward to peep around the corner. I got to the mine shaft edge but froze to the spot. I put my arms onto the wall, thinking "I will count to five then move out and look into the shaft." But I stuck on four. I couldn't force five out of my mouth for 'love nor money.'

Then I began to feel sounds, not words. More a strange sensation, like a feeling. A shiver running down my spine. Trepidation and all of my senses switching to high alert. That was danger coming out of the unknown, and I wasn't ready for it. The sound came from right behind the corner. I'd take a guess and say no more than two yards away. It was a weird sensation, like a clicking sound whispered in a breath. The only sound I could remotely associate it with was like the clicking sound that a locust makes, combined with the deep nauseating breath of someone with asthma. It had a resonance that reverberated like … forever … a constant ticking.

I couldn't muster the courage to peep round the corner. I was petrified.

Then the sound suddenly stopped. Like stunned silence. I waited, but it was gone. Only then did I venture forward, but the passageway was clear.

"I promise you, it was right next to me. A couple of yards down this alley."

"Did you see it?"

"No," I said, probably relieved that I didn't. "It flashed past. But it must have seen my flash-light to know I was next to the wall. It wasn't frightened. It was ready to go face-to-face, and that is what worries me most."

We took our time, glancing down each tunnel to reassure ourselves. But I knew Sergio had come across this before.

"You know what it is, don't you?" I asked. "You've been here. You know what that 'thing' is."

He bypassed my words totally, saying: "We have a choice here, one tunnel was dug out by 'whoever' at the time of Henry VIII, while the other two look like coal-mines. The mines won't hold treasure, that's for sure."

"Sergio, what was that creature? I'm sure this isn't the time for a bonding session, but I'd like to get to the end of this tunnel having the same knowledge about it as you have. And that isn't the case at this moment."

"I don't know what they are, but they must have been here for centuries. Lord Wharton built a castle because he was petrified by them."

"He said they were gypsies that lived in the crypts around here," I replied.

"Yes, that is what Wharton said. Probably because nobody would believe what he was talking about when he described what he saw. What are they? They are human, to an extent. But not like the humans we know. I've seen them and I don't know what the hell they are! The only human trait they have is that they walk on their legs, but they run on all fours like a dog. What can they feed off in a tunnel? There's only rats down here. Perhaps there's some link into the sewage pipes, but what can they get from there?"

We wandered down the tunnel (rather than the coal-mine) and drifted down into the deep bowels of the damned. It was heavy going, and more than once we had to crawl through tight underpasses that were no more than 18 inches high, and a yard wide. But one thing struck me like a bolt of lightening – those subways had been used - often! They hadn't been hidden away for centuries. The entrances were not blocked off at any particular point, because they were like rabbit warrens. A sophisticated maze of holes that spread for miles in all directions. Never mind William's 'three level' map system, we were in an underground Metropolis.

"Have you noticed," I commented, "At no time have we had to dig. Every path; every hole; every mine-shaft leads somewhere. There must have been rock falls and mines collapsing over the centuries because of flooding and subsidence, but not here. If there has been a blockage, it has been shifted. I don't know what the system, or network is, but there is one. It's like the London underground."

Fay phoned for an update and we took a time-out, resting for a spell, time for food and drink.

"How far have you got?" she quizzed, asking the question we didn't really know the answer to.

"Just over a mile according to the steps on my wristband," I replied.

"Where would a mile have taken us to on your map?"

"Depends what direction you are heading in. Have you deviated at any point?"

"Not really, we have travelled due south virtually all of the way," I replied.

"Did you hear any traffic above you?" asked Fay.

"Yes, there was a rumble after about half a mile, we could feel a murmur rather than a sound. Vibrations but it was certainly traffic. Nothing since, for what must be, a couple of hours. But we are going deeper underground all of the time. I don't think we could hear anything that is above us at this level."

"The noise you heard will have been the A690 on Sutton Street. You passed under it. Due south puts you somewhere under Crossgate Bank at this moment. The Castle is almost directly east of you. But heading east you face the widest point of the river, then you have to consider the Castle is built on a hillside of pure rock. Nobody could have dug a tunnel in that direction without a JCB."

"Where is the narrowest point of the river?" I asked.

Fay replied: "Just below Prebends Bridge, which is about a mile south of your position. If there is an underpass, it has to be there. Then the Cathedral is only four hundred yards north."

That made a lot of sense, although options of tunnels were constantly being put in front of us. The coal-mines were easy enough to spot, but the deeper into the heart of the city we walked, the more links to the chain.

We maintained the due south for another fifty yards or so, and I looked at my watch, it was 9.18PM. Reaching yet another cross-section of shafts and passageways, we had multiple choices again. Each and every one could lead anywhere. But we heard a distant noise like a wailing or squealing. I shook my head to try to clear my mind of a constant chattering.

"Can you hear that?" I asked.

"Yeah, it's down this passageway. Do we go?"

"Why not, let's go."

I went first, cutting through a very narrow corridor, into a room with a deep depression like a Roman bath. It was filled with rats, frantically trying to escape.

"What the hell is this?" I shouted out.

"It's a rat trap!" said Sergio. "That's how they get their food. They trick the rats into this room and trap them. It's their larder."

"Boy do I hate rats," I replied, "Come on, let's get out of here."

No sooner had I said those words, then I tripped over the stone ledge and went hurtling into the water with immense force, cracking my head on the way down. I was bloody, concussed, and flapping about with hundreds of rabid rats. I tried to keep my head above water, and stop the vermin from eating me alive. They were three or four deep in the stinking, reeking water, biting any part of my body they could find. The blood was only encouraging them, making my face their prime target. The pain was everywhere about my head, as I tried to push them away. But then some started chewing my fingers, almost biting through to the bone, and I understood I wasn't going to last much longer.

Sergio threw down a rope, telling me to grab hold, and it tightened up as I grappled with it. I couldn't get it over my head, so we had to go with what we had, and it constricted around my wrist.

"Hang on," he shouted, "Grip the rope. Don't let go!"

He pulled me up the side of the pool wall, gradually lifting me out of the water, along with scores of rats sensing they had an escape route. They hung off my body, my head, my clothes. Jumping towards the top of the wall the very second they knew they had the spring in their legs to get to freedom. The rope was tight around my wrist and I knew I was going to be safe, but getting over that wall was a struggle. My clothes were soaking wet, and I was carrying my backpack and belt with tools and equipment, all adding extra pounds to that final push over the top. But I got there, as did a lot of rats, and I'm sure they were as grateful as me, to one particular Spaniard.

CHAPTER TWENTY

"I HAVE SEEN THE DARKNESS YAWNING"

I lay on the ground, my face a mask of blood, my lungs coughing up filthy dirty water laced with rat droppings. I must admit, I'd had better days. I wanted to reach inside my body and make everything right. Take away the pain and heal my fingers, my arms, my face. The guy from Spain, God bless him, did his best to put me right.

They say: "Your whole life flashes in front of you," but in my experience it was the opposite. It wasn't my past, I was done with that, it was my future. I thought about my daughter and Susan. It made me grateful, rather than sad. The idea of being eaten by rats started to freak me out. If only Susan knew. Well, she would eventually get to know, but thankfully not at that very moment. The experience was life changing. My new aim was to be someone's 'heart' … even if it meant breaking my own. The lesson I was learning was: perhaps I should be a better person.

Sergio mopped away the blood, and tried so hard to cheer me up. His expression was calm, almost entertaining: "You've taken a beating, my friend. Rats are evil creatures. I don't think you need stitches but there could be scars. But that could be good. If you have suffered it should bloody well show!"

That did me more good than any medicine or bandages. I laughed.

"I thought stepping outside of my comfort zone would be a challenge," I said. "We haven't even got half-way and I'm almost a hospital case. We have to find it now Sergio, we really do."

"I'm not so sure, my friend. Would it make your life any better? Is it really there? Thinking of something doesn't make it true. Wanting something doesn't make it real."

"I need encouragement, bud," I said, "We have to keep believing."

We moved out of one tunnel and down the next. I could feel the blood running down the back of my neck and the ache of the bites made to my fingers. We carried on regardless. Sergio wasn't convinced we were heading in the right direction so he checked the compass, saying: "We are still travelling south. We take the next tunnel heading east. OK?"

Personally I'd rather see the options, rather than make them before they appear. But I kept that to myself. Then we arrived in a cavern that was like no other. Tall, spacious, like a pot-hole cave. Transferring the scenery, from the coal walls we had seen everywhere, to limestone. The whole underground system was a labyrinth of winding passageways that all lead to that one giant chamber. There were waterfalls and sculptured stalactites formed over thousands of years.

"This is the final stop off before we go under the river!" said Sergio, convinced we were back on course. "This is why they chose this crossing. This is the gateway."

I looked around and the place frightened the life out of me. Nobody had pot-holed down there, for sure. That wasn't on the tourist trail. I heard a noise. A familiar noise. And all I felt was a dark Satanic link to an underworld I wanted no part of.

"Can you hear that, John?" said my fellow explorer.

"I can hear it alright," I replied, sinking into my wet, soggy boots. It was the sound of locusts clicking and heavy breathing. Whatever the creatures were … we had walked right into their living room.

I could feel eyes piecing me like needles. There I stood, the skeleton of an emaciated man, with clothes damp and grimy, and I had come to meet my destiny. Would they take pity on us? Because there was an "us", very much an "us", because my partner had experienced this before. I still hadn't seen them up to this point, but that was just seconds away.

"What do we do?" I asked.

"The options are simple. We either go forward or turn back."

"Can we walk straight through and hope they don't notice us?" I said, as though that was going to happen. When suddenly one of them leapt to ground level and cut off our exit backwards, walking backwards and then forwards, like a soldier on military parade.

"I guess we're going forward," said Sergio.

"I'm not sure we are going anywhere!" I stammered, trying to work-out what made up that weird creature.

My first impression was that it was of some human form, but that soon left my mind. It had a body shape that was incredibly athletic, balanced on two legs that seemed spring-loaded, constantly bouncing in a vigorous animated movement. It's legs were in perpetual motion. It's arms were thin, held forward motionless. It wasn't designed as a killing machine, as I couldn't imagine it doing much damage with its hands. It's fingers were long and scrawny, with nails sharp and pointed, almost manicured. That was not an animal that scratted like a rat, it was built for speed and stealth. Finally the head, which was human, to an extent, but looked part reptile. The first thing that struck me was its long flowing hair that party masked the face. Look beyond that and it had huge dead-looking eyes. I'm sure it could see, but not very well. The creature was developed for darkness. It's mouth was the most worrying part of its structure, because it had spiked teeth. They were shaped for killing and ripping. If it was going to attack, its head would do the damage, rather than its hands or arms.

They obviously could communicate in clicking noises, so they had a language, but nothing like our own. I imagine the clicking would travel further down the tunnels than human speech, so they had developed it over hundreds of years. More of them came down to investigate, moving in a manner that was more inquisitive, than threatening. We stood perfectly still. There was dried blood on my face and that interested one of them. It stretched out a long finger to touch my face, but I pulled away. That was not taken lightly. It opened its mouth to show its teeth, in an arrogant posture that meant business. It had no fear, but it pulled away when my lamp shone on it. I couldn't imagine it surviving in daylight.

I couldn't see how many they were in total, but there were five around us, and I saw the reflection of many more eyes up in the rocky face. Perhaps they had offspring peeping out of holes, looking down from their high vantage point, like birds in a nest. It was a little commune, and perhaps there were many more of them, spread out like little villages, underneath the big city.

All the while we hadn't spoken. Would the spoken word upset them? I had to find out. I didn't talk directly to them, but to Sergio.

"Which tunnel do we head for? Let's make a move, bud, this ugly mutation in front of me is spooking me out."

They didn't react any differently. I don't think they could pick up the frequency of our voices. Perhaps their hearing had evolved into something more complex over the years.

Sergio looked left then right: "If we are heading east, as we should be, the subway for the river has to be one of those on the left."

The creatures didn't seem alarmed.

"Can they hear? I'm not convinced they can," Sergio asked, just about answering my own question.

"They can hear themselves, for certain," I replied. "Let's watch what they do when I drop a coin."

I dropped a pound coin onto the stone floor and there was an immediate flurry of activity. The place was in total darkness, apart from our headgear, but they knew instinctively where the coin fell. One stooped down to pick it up, holding it in it's open hand, as curious as a child in a sweetshop.

"How do we get out of this? Do we just go, or offer them gifts?" I asked. "What have you got to offer? I've got half a sandwich and packet of mints. Do you think they will want more than that?" I almost laughed.

Before we had a chance to hand out presents, a larger 'being' appeared from up above, springing down from the rock face like a falcon coming out of the sky. It must have covered twenty yards in two seconds. Then all the other creatures backed away, leaving us with an all mighty brute of a beast that held the respect of all around it. Now I was terror-stricken!

"God forbid," I mumbled.

I thought I was about to pee my pants. My nerves tingled throughout my body. The creature stood two inches from me, breathing rancid breath into my face, just like Smelt did outside the Toll House. Smelt intimidated me for a reason, but I wasn't sure what that creature was up to. Probably the same, just I couldn't understand it's vocabulary. The clicks were like whispers. It was trying to communicate with a cacophony of strange babbling and gurgling sounds. It took exception to my head-light and it raised its hand to try to cover the front of the reflector. I went to switch off the light but the creature grabbed my arm, squeezing it in a threatening manner, trying to force my arm down: "Make your mind up … do you want the light on, or off?" I said, directly into its face.

It's companions surrounded me.

"Have these got something to do with Smelt?" I asked. "Didn't he have Satanic disciples?"

"Yeah, but they sent Smelt to gallows and then put him in a cage. It was thought he got retribution, and killed them all."

"Perhaps he missed a couple," I replied, "And they've developed into the Partridge Family here."

"We need a plan, John. Any suggestions? It's getting very claustrophobic around here."

"Walk through them, slowly," I replied.

Sergio, calmly and collectively, told me to head towards the tunnel: "The one on the far left. Let's see how far we get."

But our reflexes were no match for those creatures, and they stopped Sergio before he made two steps. Two of them stood in front of him, rocking and bobbing like boxers sparring in a ring.

"What I've learnt from the past," said Sergio, "If push comes to shove, think you are fighting a dog. These creatures don't use weapons and they aren't strong physically. One-on-one we can probably out-power them. They aren't much of a threat in any department apart from the head. But do not forget … the teeth are deadly. If they grab you, they lock, and they won't let go."

"I was hoping to talk our way out of this," I said.

"Go ahead," he replied. "If you're that optimistic. Please keep me informed."

"It's not one dog we are fighting, it's a pack of around twenty," I answered. "And God only knows how many are up there hiding in the darkness. We cannot take these on in a fight. We would be dead before we could throw the first punch. They move as quick as lightening."

We didn't have a multitude of options. The leader of the 'pack' wasn't doing anything other than swaying, like the rest of them. Bobbing away on his dog-like legs. So I took the initiative and tried to walk calmly past him. He pushed his face into mine, and I pushed it back, all the while conscious of those pointed teeth. I tried again, edging passed its rocking frame. It would have none of it and grabbed me. I needed back-up from somewhere, because all of them were getting mighty agitated. I took a cigarette lighter out of my body belt, and the large knife, and I had about ten seconds to decide which one to use first. Do I go with the flame or the knife? Sergio stood watching, then he did the same.

"Flame or knife, Sergio? Tell me what to do?"

The Spaniard walked over and showed the leader the full length of the blade right in his face.

"See this, Lassie," he smirked, changing his whole persona, "I will show you what it can do."

He held out his own left arm, then ran the blade about three inches down, creating a lengthy wound with blood seeping to the ground. He switched hands with the knife, and with his right hand he collected some of the blood, showed it to the creature, then rubbed it in its face. Immediately the animal backed away, horrified, flicking his long hair down his back then letting out a hideous whine. Sergio followed him, flicking more blood at his face. The rest of the pack were eager to jump forward to threaten us, but none made an outright attack.

"Come on," I shouted to my partner, "Let's go."

We walked to the tunnel, watching cautiously over our shoulder as they regrouped. The leader was frantic and that had the rest of them hyper, but I think they were as pleased to see the back of us as we were to see the back of them. We just had to hope and believe we were picking the right exit. Sergio had a last second change of heart: "That tunnel is heading upwards, so we won't get across the river. Let's go for the next one, that must be heading downward."

We switched direction, and within twenty yards we got the message, we were going in the right direction. Thankfully, Lassie and those 'freaks of nature' didn't follow. The show was over.

It was after midnight, officially a Saturday morning, and we were on our bellies crawling through, what I can only describe as, a subterranean rat hole somewhere underneath the River Wear. The stench was horrific, in a confined space that was so tight it meant it would have been impossible for us to turn round and go back. Not that we planned a retreat. Whoever designed and made that underpass, in whatever era that happened to be, deserves credit for the fact it was still water-tight hundreds of years later. However, it was a rat-infested death trap, and certainly not a quick exit to get from point A to B. So, if it was an escape tunnel, I would imagine it was a secret known only by the Cathedral's elite. An army couldn't possibly escape that way.

The entire stretch was a tomb of dark green moss, used as a playground for adventure-seeking rodents. I was pleased I was not the one doing the spade work at the front, brushing them aside and turning them back. Rats can get very territorial when they are cornered, and those 'scamps' had a big attitude problem.

We assumed we were at Prebend's Bridge, where the river is probably 70 yards wide. How handy it would have been to poke a periscope above the water to see exactly where we were. All the while we worked on the assumption that the river (or sea-level) is always the lowest point.

When we got to the end we didn't appear on the bank side or in the woods. There was a massive stone room, presumably built at the same time as the Cathedral, as a break-water. It was empty, but there were steps leading up to a big wooden door.

We had our own time to analysed what we had achieved.

"Nobody could get any big articles through that sunken tunnel," said the Spaniard, just confirming what we knew already. "Suggesting the treasure has always been on this side of the river. It could be in the room next to this one. If it is, it had an escape should things go wrong. Possibly the perfect place. Far enough away from the Cathedral, but still the right side of the river. The tunnel system is just a hoax."

"I don't think it's a hoax, Sergio. It's had a purpose in its day, I just don't think it involves the treasure."

Sergio had a theory: "The price the monks would have paid for being caught was an horrendous death. Henry VIII didn't mess about. So the top guy hiding the treasure was hardly going to announce where he was putting it … or that he was doing it at all. That was a secret meant to be kept. No more than three people would have known. Possibly only two."

"And anything could have happened to the pair of them," I added.

"Exactly!" he replied. "We are grasping at straws, but the fact remains … that treasure was never found. The gold could have been melted down and the jewels put into other relics, but not by the monks who hid it. Those were religious artefacts that meant more to the Church than the price of gold. I think we are yards away from it. Possibly beyond that door."

The door was about as solid as the one keeping the Bank of England secure. It was high up the wall with 12 steps leading to it. The River Wear isn't tidal, but it does rise and fall with the weather, as the moss on the stone wall showed.

The door was meant to stay shut, and it had done its duty over the centuries. Solid oak, meant to last. It was above the highest water mark, so the room behind it had never been flooded.

"There's no handle, no lock. It wasn't meant to be opened from this side. What do we do?" I asked, as I clambered up the stone steps to reach it.

"It hasn't got a key, but it's got hinges that are centuries old," came Sergio's reply. "That door is only as solid as the rotting, decayed metal that holds it in place."

The room was originally meant as a secret passageway down to the river. Accessible for those heading to a waiting boat. But time had taken its toll. The hinges were so rotten they weren't holding the door at all. It had dropped an inch or so and was just resting on its own weight.

We toiled trying to push it forward, but something was lodged against it from the rear.

"It's going to have to come this way," said Sergio, trying to fathom out a strategy … and finding one. "I've got just the thing. Mountaineering ice screws!"

He produced two of them from his rucksack.

"They are for ice but they will fit in wood," he said, holding them up to show me.

We screwed one on either side of the door, as near to the top as we could reach, then tied our climbing ropes. With a lot of effort, and a bit of rhythm in our style, the door came crashing down like the tumbling walls of Troy. A haze of grime and dust flew everywhere, covering us from head to foot. It got in our eyes and in our lungs, causing both of us to have coughing fits. But when the dust settled … there was a room full of things we never imagined. We found what we were looking for, but nothing in our lives would ever be the same again.

CHAPTER TWENTY ONE

"EVERYBODY HAS A SKELETON IN THE CLOSET"

Our lights flashed across the room that was stubbornly dark. No windows or peep holes, and the only door was the one we pulled from its hinges. There was a flash of brown as a couple of rats ran for safety, squealing as they jumped through the opening, then scurried into the water. Mould ate away at the walls and the floor, but to look beyond that was a sight to behold.

The tales handed down through the ages were true. Religious relics, brimming with silver and gold, lay in front of us. The long lost treasure of St Cuthbert, the gold cross of St Oswald, and the Cathedral's forgotten horde of Roman riches, all laid out in all its splendour. Guarded by a macabre collection of jewel-encrusted skeletons. The bodies of early Christian martyrs decked in lavish clothes and priceless jewellery. Some laid out on the stone floor, and some lying in make-shift coffins. There were jewels everywhere. Rubies, diamonds, sapphires and opals, hung around the necks of the dead. Crowns decorating the skulls of the long departed, and rings on boney fingers of skeletons that were promised eternal hope.

Many had name-tags and were renamed as saints, decorated with gold and affluent jewellery, and then packed away in coffins ready for the afterlife. A ritual not dis-similar to Egyptian mummies. A last act of Catholicism defiance and two fingers up to Henry, the King of England, and his Protestant church.

Although they had been re-named saints, probably by some high-ranking Catholic official, none of them qualified for the title. Under the strict rules of the Catholic church, saints had to have been canonised. Those lying before us, must have gone to their deaths believing they were saints in the eyes of the Lord. I can only guess the scene. What ritual took place, and how did they die? We came to the conclusion they must have been placed in there after death. It's very unlikely they were bricked in and starved. Religion was their life, and ultimately, their death.

Our first words were a mixture of profanities and disbelief, best not printed. The skeletons were difficult to comprehend. Lives lost for what? It's even more difficult to understand if they agreed to do it, and the signs suggest they did.

"Well, John, we've found it. William was right after all. We are looking at a king's ransom … in a graveyard."

"All together with a mass execution," I replied. "I wasn't expecting this."

Sergio picked up a ring that had fallen off a boney finger, and leant down to put it back in place: "They you go my friend. Have your ring back," he said rather tenderly. "Have you noticed, the thing about skulls is that you can never tell if they are smiling or sad."

"I don't think anyone smiles while giving their last breath," I remarked. "I wonder if they knew too much and became a liability? Were they poisoned to stop them talking? They were specifically laid out like this. That means they were killed, or killed themselves, elsewhere. It's just so bizarre."

"It's like the Last Supper. Did they dress up for the occasion, or were they clothed after?"

I could have asked questions all evening: "What do we learn from this?"

"We have learnt that we all die, and wither to dust, but jewels never fade or perish."

There were paintings, too, one depicting 'Christ the Redeemer' as well as 'The Destruction of the Temple of Jerusalem.' Five hundred years in a damp sandstone room, next to a swelling river, hadn't done them any favours, but I'm sure they could be saved.

Forgotten ornaments and relics of a period that had been written out of British history. All of it totally unique. Even if there was a door to walk out of (and there wasn't) we couldn't get away with stealing it. That would have been sacrilege.

"So what now?" I asked.

Sergio said it all: "I'm not going to rob graves, John. I draw the line right here."

I could almost feel the cold, perished grasp of skeletons grabbing my clothes and arms. The whispering of a dead man's lament. Were those whispers for real? Or was it my conscience pulling at my soul?

That was the end of the road. We had found our fortune and there was nowhere left to go … literally. The room was a bunker. A tomb underground, without doors or windows.

"We take nothing," said Sergio, "Leave it all to the dead. It is their payment into the after-world. Let them pay the piper."

We shook on it, and that was probably the closest 'spiritually' I have ever been to another person.

"You know," I said, looking around the dust and the dead bodies, "We could be anywhere."

"How do you mean?"

"We think we are the far side of the river, near Prebend's Bridge, but we can't prove it. We've crossed some water, somewhere, but let's be honest ... we don't really know where we are ... or how to get out?"

Sergio walked back down the stone steps: "This is the river," he said, pointing. "We swim under the brick wall and we are out into the open. We won't know where we are until we surface. Then we get our bearings and re-evaluate the situation."

"Do you know how dangerous it is swimming in the River Wear at night? Do you know how many students have fallen in and died in recent years?"

"We are not going to die, John," he remarked intensely. "We know what we are doing, we just don't know where the hell we are! We think St John's College is outside this building, but no pathway leads us right to it's front door. We are right on the river, possibly a purpose built building in the rock face of the Cathedral. There is that chance. Until we get into the water and rise to the surface, we don't have a clue."

We were in a dead man's tomb that had no exit, and we both agreed we would never again risk the 'subway of doom' under the river to face those creatures again. It had to be swim and see what happens. As simple as that.

"OK, let's go for it," I said, simply because we had no option.

But the silence that followed showed we both knew it wasn't going to be easy. It was not the kind of stillness that soothes and puts you at rest. It was the kind that was mind numbing. The silence was the blank page we could write our hereafter.

I could feel voices, rather than hear them. They echoed through to my heart, telling me that the Devil was pulling the stings.

———————————————

The water lay without a ripple. We were lucky – we thought – let's just get on with it. The plan was to stay hitched together with a mountaineering nylon rope, giving us a fair distance apart should we need it. But we weren't tied together as such, just a loop around our wrists that could easily be unhooked. Sergio took the plunge first and dipped under the wall, setting off at a fair rate of knots, expecting me to follow. But I misjudged the depth I had to swim down to, and I snagged my backpack on the wall, trapping myself under water. I splashed about in the otherwise silent night, but I couldn't free myself. I don't know if Sergio knew I was struggling, or whether he just ploughed ahead, but the rope was hindering us both. I was being pulled further along the wall, getting myself in major difficulties, and I was pulling the Spaniard back as I tugged and pulled at him. I had to let go of the rope, for his sake and mine.

The backpack was a hindrance at first, but it helped me float to the surface once I was free. I finally saw the sky as I gasped for breath, and I appreciated that more than anything. A moonlit night. Something to reach up to, to keep me afloat.

I could see bright lights in the distance, and that gave me my bearings. It was lights from the Durham Student's Union at Kingsgate Bridge I could see, and I knew I only had to swim against the swell a few yards to the wooden platform at the Old Boat House to stay afloat. I shouted for Sergio but he didn't reply. He must have drifted mid-stream and away from the river bank.

I grasped at the platform, but twice I drifted back, splashing and wallowing like a toddler in a big bath. But I made it 'third time lucky,' clinging on to the wood until I got my breath back. I dragged myself up to the top of the platform then collapsed on the pathway.

The walkie-talkie was dripping river water and would probably never work again, so I had no connection with Fay or Kimberley. I just had to find Sergio, who must have reached the opposite side of the river. I followed the course to Prebends Bridge, shouting and bawling, but I got no reply. I crossed the bridge and doubled back, but the pathway veered towards the church and away from the river, so I went back to the bridge. It was then I realised how difficult it would have been for him to get out of the water if he had swam that far. There is no pathway because there is a 30ft cliff face that stretches for half a mile.

That is the most treacherous place to be swimming in the whole or the River Wear.

Then I heard a number of students returning from a night out in the city, and I begged them to join the search. To their credit, they phoned the police and did everything that was humanly possible to try and find him. I felt the need to move my legs, no matter what direction. Run, and run some more. He had to be somewhere!

We searched everywhere. The dawn was breaking, and the wet evening disappeared with the slam of the police car door. It wasn't a screech around the city with blue flashing lights, simply the job of taking me in for questioning. No small talk from the PC who was driving, and I was pleased for that. The officer saved me the taxing job of thinking. Instead he made his delivery (of me) and left.

"You and your friend took a midnight dip, I hear," said the officer on duty.

"Sort of," I replied.

"How old are you? Don't you think you should have more sense? Students - yeah, we can expect it from them 'cos most of them are smacked up on drugs, or brain dead on beer. But what you did defies belief. What did you try and prove tonight?"

The questioning got no easier. I wanted to find my buddy but the paperwork got in the way. What could I possibly say to make sense of what we did? But I had to come up with something. Something pretty pathetic, but believable.

Here goes: "We did it for a bet. I bet him fifty pounds I could beat him across the river."

"And you hadn't been drinking or taking drugs?"

"No."

"We will check that out with the results of the drug test."

"I swear … we did not take drink or drugs, and the results will show that."

"You're just two bloody idiots who should know better!"

The paperwork took a lot of paper, and a lot of time, and I don't think a word I said was true. There must have been enough rubbish in there to put me away for a lengthy custodial sentence. But I didn't even care. They could have thrown me in a cell and switched off the lights. Sergio was going to turn up – eventually – in a body bag. He was probably at the morge before the i's were dotted and the t's were crossed on the sergeant's report.

Two hours later I caught a taxi to Fay's house, finding her (and my daughter) crashed out on the couch covered in a blanket. The conversation that followed was challenging, to say the least. No one loves the messenger.

It's very difficult to manipulate tragic truth round to something palatable. 'Sad' would do. But once you start with the strong possibility of 'death', the conversation never rises up the scale to 'sad', it sticks with 'catastrophic'.

Fay knew. She could tell with one look.

"What are his chances?" she asked.

"We looked everywhere. He may have got to the other side. I pray he did. But where would he go after that? The police say they have rescue teams there from Wearsdale and Teesdale, plus the Durham fire brigade. They will contact us if they find anything. That's it I'm afraid."

The reporters would have been to my house but I stayed with Fay and Kimberley, so I avoided the rat race.

Susan was furious that Kimberley and I "couldn't be bothered" to involve her, and we understood what she meant. It wasn't quite the way she said, but she got her point across well.

My daughter had issues of her own, which she told me about when Susan left the room. Smelt visited Fay's house that evening, and left them both traumatised.

"The lights flickered," she explained, "And cut out at times. Fay knew what was going to happen. She took me to the back of the room and told me not to be frightened because the ghost had no power in her house."

I stopped her there: "He only appears in that house when he is summoned, Did you play with the Ouija board?"

"Just a bit," she replied sheepishly.

"Just a bit? Why would you do that?"

"Fay thought if the ghost was in her house he wouldn't be bothering you down the tunnel. You wanted to get past the first 50 yards."

"What a ridiculous thing to do, girl. You don't understand what you are playing with!"

"We didn't want him to harm you, and Fay said you were in a very dangerous place."

"What happened? Did he talk?"

"We used the wooden board thing, and that triangle that you move about. I couldn't take it seriously. I kept laughing, which didn't go down too well with Fay. I've never seen a ghost before. My friend Linda has. She sees them all the time. She has one in her bathroom!"

The mind boggles.

"Anyway," she continued. "Nothing happened for a long long time. Then the light crackled, and lost a bit power, then went off. Fay told me just leave it because it would come back on. And it did. But there was a black shadow in the corner. A man in old clothes. His face covered by a hood. I tried to take a photo on my phone but he doesn't show up. Look."

Six or seven photographs showing nothing but the wallpaper.

"He was there," she insisted. "He really was."

"Did Fay talk to him?"

"She was trying to taunt him, but he didn't react. He sat and looked in our direction for about five or six minutes, sometimes bold, sometimes we could hardly see him at all. I couldn't see his eyes, but he was looking at us, I know."

"Were you frightened?"

"That's the strange thing about it, I wasn't that frightened. If he moved, or stood up, I'd probably have caked myself. But he didn't. He was just like a beggar that you see in the streets every day."

She then flooded me with questions. She asked about the treasure, what it looked like, and why did we leave it?

"Is there anything less immoral than stealing to be rich?" I asked her. "But that was our intention. We didn't take anything, but that doesn't make us better men."

"Will they find Sergio?" she asked.

"I don't know Kimberley, I really don't know. If I run into Sergio again, I promise, I will be a wiser man … and a better person. He came to help, and I sank us both."

"It's not ALWAYS your fault, Dad. People do make their own decisions. He knew the risks more than you did. Perhaps he sank himself. Think about that."

Four days later Fay was asked to formally identify Sergio's body. He was found by and ex-soldier and professional scuba diver called Joe Darlow. The guy ignored health and safety warnings from the police to go looking for our friend, and he found him within seconds of entering the water.

Police delayed the search because they felt the bad weather made it dangerous to conduct underwater exploration. The fast flow of the river convinced the police divers that the body could have been miles down stream, and forces were alerted at Chester-le-Street and Washington.

After hearing the news on TV, Darlow travelled to Durham from his home in Seaham to join the exploration. Having dived in that stretch of water for more than twenty years during training and archaeological exploration, he claimed nobody had a better knowledge of the hazards of the lie of the river than him and his brother.

He told newspaper reporters: "My brother and I learnt the ropes there, and we know that riverbed better than anyone. We both wanted to get involved because we wanted to do something to bring closure for the man's family. I dived in at 9am and I found him within a minute. The water wasn't that deep, probably only two meters, but I sensed where he would be. I was prepared to find a dead body, that was the aim I suppose. We had a moment together – I said 'I've come to take you home my friend' - and that is what I did. I got out of the water and my brother phoned the police. It was a very sad moment, but now I hope he is back with his family."

There was to be an inquest into Sergio's death, as expected, and I was the centre of media attention. Anyone who knew me … who REALLY knew me … knew I wouldn't have pulled any stunt to risk someone's life. The media were kind and didn't pack a punch, but the police did. The reporters made us out to be fools playing out a prank; the police didn't believe a word I said, and suspected foul play.

The Sergeant asked: "So you just decided to have bet on the spur of the moment, after midnight, down by the river? A night out, but neither of you had a drink, and you were both carrying caving equipment."

I was asked, straight out: "Did you murdered him?" and I'm sure he analysed my reaction.

The autopsy took a long time, but the result read: "Death by drowning due to mis-adventure." It was a weight off my shoulders, but it was a formality, really. It couldn't have been anything else.

I didn't do anything about the treasure. I didn't report it to anyone, or tip off the Cathedral. The poor souls in that room had gone to their deaths as genuine Saints, dolled up to the nines in the church's glorious finery. Who was I, a pauper from a building site, to strip them of their majesty?

I closed off the entrance to the Obelisk with reinforced concrete. The only way that would be opened ever again was if the tower was moved, brick by brick, somewhere else. Perhaps one day that will happen, and Pandora's box will be opened. When the lid comes off, they open the fortune cookie.

I only had one mystery left to solve, what to do about Smelt? And, having had her visitation from the monster himself ... Kimberley was hooked, too. She had finally seen a ghost, and that put her on par with her long-time school-friend Linda. The simple things in life can be so complicated.

William always believed the Toll House kept Smelt alive. His last notes suggested maybe there was a hidden room containing some religious artefact, or Smelt was guarding something. But his notes referred to a Tibetan term called 'Bardo', which is the state of existence intermediate between life and death. Or more precise, after death and before one's next birth.

William wrote: "Smelt had association with Tibetan Buddhists in Germany, and they moved with him to London, and then Durham. Bardo creates impulses from the previous life and offers a state of opportunity of liberation for a period of time. For some it can become a place of danger, as they move into a less than desirable rebirth."

Something was keeping Smelt in that state. I was determined to find out what it was, to allow him to move on and have his new rebirth. But, there was a down side, he was perfectly happy where he was!

CHAPTER TWENTY TWO

"I KILLED HIM ONCE … OR TWICE"

The final part of William's unpublished book centred on a religious cult that outstayed their welcome on Western Hill. Even though they hadn't been invited in the first place!
Although the last people to officially be on the electoral role at the Toll House were Martha and Reg Pascoe, they weren't the last to live there. In 1971 a gang of travelling hippies, looking for an abandoned building to stay the night, took it upon themselves to move in … and then they refused to leave. They claimed 'squatter's rights.'

Yasin Okaka and the 'Grateful Dead' - 'The Untold Story' by William J Woodhouse.
'Squatting' was an emotive subject in the 1970's, with many squatters claiming to be homeless people legally taking up residence in an empty property that has been abandoned. No-one has a right to simply move into a property that is not theirs, but as long as they didn't forcibly break in, they had legal rights.
The hippies moved into the Toll House, and the Catholic Church didn't know if evicting them was a civil or criminal matter. As it happens, the police didn't seem to know either. But it took over a year for them to pack their bags and disappear.
The band of marijuana-smoking 'flower children' were led by a Mormon called Yasin Okaka. He collected together a gang of doped-up freaks and called them the 'Grateful Dead' after the Californian rock band of the same name. He was a wild kid, originally from Turkey, with no proper grounding other than the Mormon commune his family were part of. He came to Britain on a one-way ticket, and toured the country spreading the word of Christ (his version), picking up converts along the way. Such cults were fashionable at the time, particularly in America, following on from Woodstock.

Yasin believed that Jesus paid for the sins of the world, and he (and his followers) tried to live a Christ-like lifestyle. They lived from hand-to-mouth with simple food, uncomplicated pleasures, and no electricity … because the church had disconnected it in their efforts to get them out.

Yasin ran a tight ship. He was the boss and that was the way he liked it. It was not a "one size fits all" commune were everyone had an equal say. There was no democracy under his rule. However, after a few months, some started to resent his supremacy. Fractions started to form. Drug use was rampant, but Yasin kept it in-house. Strict rules, meant to be obeyed, but his position was questioned by a guy called Josh Lewis. Not the brightest of men, and if you are going to kick authority in the teeth – why not use both boots?

Strange ghostly things were happening in the house, but with most of the Grateful Dead on LSD, (and other assorted stimulants), a blue dragon could walk across the living room ceiling and no-one would think it unusual. So when Smelt started playing his games, it just added to an evening's entertainment.

Sadly, it all went wrong for Josh when he invited local teenagers to the drug den. One of them, Kyle Butroid, was in his element. The local 'bad boy' with a distressing reputation. He terrorized the neighbourhood, and he had a catalogue of up-coming charges ranging from burglary to grievous bodily harm. That kid was more addicted to self destruction than narcotics, and he found a place to liberate himself.

Butroid was found in one of the bedrooms one evening with his face pushed through a plate glass window, a shard of glass having cut his jugular vein. His head held the weight of his entire body on the cut glass, leaving his legs dangling. The rain washed his face, as the blood drizzled down the wall. Anyone can kill, but Smelt made murder a revulsion. Nobody owns life, but never has a creature been so satisfied at owning death.

That was the end of the Grateful Dead, and the Toll House. The hippies disappeared into the wild blue yonder, never to be seen again. Leaving a vigilante group, formed by the late Kyle Butroid's gang mates, to pull the Toll House apart. They stole a massive truck from the local council depot and rammed it into the front of the living room of the building, taking out the wall and the roof with it. When they finished, the place was in ruin, never to be restored or renovated.

Of course the neighbours rejoiced, saying: "Nothing good ever came from that place," and there were calls for it to be flattened altogether. But that didn't happen. It was left as a gaunt shell of its dismal past, full of horror and fear.

Kimberley ran her hand over the living room wall where the paintings used to be in the Toll House, just as so many had done before. It was one of those things I couldn't resist, myself. I did it every time I visited.

"It's lush isn't it? Why is it a ruin and not been rebuilt?" she asked, taking out her phone to take photographs.

"What's the photograph's for?" I asked.

"Nothing particular. Facebook probably. I have to let my 'stalkers' know what I'm up to in daily life," she laughed.

"I bet you get a lot of 'hits' on Facebook for a building falling apart," I joked.

"You may be surprised. Take a photo of me please, Dad."

The workers had just clocked off and headed home, and I timed it that way to avoid the barrage of questions I was getting whenever I appeared on site. Everybody wanted to know about Sergio's swimming accident, and if I was up in court. McCracken was convinced I was up for murder! Well, there's a surprise. He didn't actually say those words to my face, but the rumour mill was working overtime.

I didn't have the keys to the site any more, and come to think of it, I didn't even have the key to the tea/coffee cabinet in the office, either. Where they giving me a hint?

Anyway, thanks to Len the security guard, I could get on-site. We walked over to see him, and his new co-worker, an Alsation dog.

"Nice dog, Len. Who gave you that? Is it on the pay-role?"

"It was McCracken's. He couldn't handle it, so it is the new guard dog. It gets paid with a big bag of Winalot a week," he laughed, "The same pay that I get!"

"McCracken dumped it on you?" I asked.

"Not really. He's only a pup. Good company."

We were soon joined by Fay, another 'virtual' private investigator for the day, all kitted out in overalls and headscarf. Ready for some graft.

"Let's all have a selfee," insisted Kimberley, and we even got Len in on the act, although his dog was having none of it.

"Yer dog's a bit flighty, isn't it?" I said.

"He won't go near the Toll House, John. There's something in there that spooks him. What are you guys up to?"

"Kimberley wants some photos for a university project on house design." Not the truth, but I was getting used to plucking a lie out of the air at short notice.

Much of the Toll House was crumbling to bits, and probably the safest section was the stable that our builders had repaired. The living room didn't have a roof, so that was safe enough. The bedrooms were still fully formed, with roofs, although two were hazardous. The plan was to look for hidden rooms under floorboards or false walls. Anywhere where something could be hidden. I didn't mind wandering around a 'death trap' on my own, but I had second thoughts about having inviting the ladies.

"You two stay on the outside of the building, look around the garden and woods for hatches or doors, and I'll cover the inside," I said. "And try the stables."

I was drawn to a wooden cross I saw in the woods, something I had not noticed before.

"Have you seen that cross before, Fay?" I asked.

"I can't say I have. But the shrubs have been recently trimmed back. Perhaps it was hidden."

The cross had lost most of its varnish, so it had been there for some time. The inscription read: "The Unknown Child – Durham Police".

Was that the spot where the unknown child was found by police in the 1950's? William wrote about it in his final notes when explaining the story about Martha Pascoe and Dumitru the Romanian gypsy.

It was not Reg's son, because Matha's story was confirmed by neighbours. She did tell the truth to the police, she was never pregnant. No-one ever got to know who the dead child was, or how he came to be buried in the garden. But forensics proved he had been sacrificed, before his body was burnt. A tale commonly associated with the building over its history. Sacrificial 'gifts' were Smelt's calling card.

Martha and Dumitru always insisted they had nothing to do with that child, and most likely they were telling the truth. But they both served a couple of months in prison during the investigation. They were freed on appeal.

The police marked the spot with the wooden cross, which they paid for themselves.

It was hard to prove right or wrong, but the death and burning had all the hall-marks of another Smelt slaughter. Is there a greater evil than someone who treats a child as a commodity? Who was he trying to appease?

"Dad, come and see this!" shouted my young daughter, holding high her phone. She was really getting into this 'searching for the truth' malarkey. I walked over and she showed me her phone.

"The photos we have just had taken … take a look at them."

Each of the five photos had the shadow of a man standing by the back door of the Toll House. They weren't exactly crystal clear, and it took a bit of imagination to make out his shape, but they were taken at a time when nobody was stood there. It was something, at a time when Len's dog was fighting to get off his lead.

"That's not all," she said, switching her phone to 'on-line'. "I put those photos on Facebook. The shadows are not there. Look!"

She flicked back through her photo library: "Look at the photos I took at Fay's house. There was no sign Smelt was on them yesterday, but he's there today, crouched in the corner."

Faint and nothing more than a grey silhouette, but it was him.

"He is playing with my phone, Dad. Don't you see. He can't alter Facebook but he can alter my phone. How can he do that?"

"Go back to the photo of the Toll House," I said, as she backtracked through the library once again. "Look where he is standing," I pointed out. "See! That is where the cellar is. That is where we should be looking. William said the bones could be the key. Why, after decades upon decades of people living there, have they not been moved? Everybody who has lived there must have seen them. They must have. And who would want a cemetery under their feet?"

"Do we take them?" asked Fay. "Oh boy, there is going to be blood and snot over this. We are going to upset him."

I summoned Len to bring his dog to where we were standing.

"Len, take the dog to the back of the Toll House. Just see what he does."

The dog acted frantic at first, barking and pulling at the lead. Sometimes wanting to attack, sometimes wanting to pull away in fear. Then the barking stopped, as though the dog was confused, looking and listening. I seized the moment.

"Right, I'm going down the cellar. You all stay here, but when I call you Kimberley, come down the stairs."

"Why me?"

"Please, do it, and bring your phone."

I was prepared for this. I had a bag with a number of tools and plastic bags, and I walked into the house and then down the stone steps into the cellar. The door was locked, as it always was, so I unscrewed the latch and forced it open with a crowbar. I was in, but as soon as I entered I heard Len's dog starting to bark.

It was daylight outside, but pitch-black inside the damp, foisty chamber. I had a torch and scanned around, seeing old rusty pots and pans that had been thrown down there randomly. The room was a dumping ground for all manner of implements that would never be used again. An old anvil stood in the corner, and I assume it hadn't been used since the motor car took over from the horse. Next to it was a rusted up 'reel mower' used for grass cutting before electricity or the petrol mower. The hatch to the bones of 'whoever' was right by the wall, and there was nothing stopping me from opening it. But I walked back up to the house and called Kimberley.

"It's OK, girl. Steady as you walk down the steps."

I shone the light and I told her to stay by the door.

"I want you to take photographs of this room and let's see what it shows."

The flash clicked, the photos were taken. But nothing unusual showed up, just what we could see ourselves. The anvil; the reel mower; old horse brasses and horse shoes hung from the wall; but no shadows or images of spooks.

"Right, I'm going to open this hatch and I'd like you to take a video of me collecting the bones ... if the bones are still here. OK? Nothing is going to happen, I just want evidence that I've done this."

There was a latch, and a bolt that I slid along, and I could feel the wooden hatch was free to pull up. I tugged on the rope and it lifted, unearthing a skeleton in a pit wearing old ragged clothes. It had been disturbed, none of it was in it's natural shape. The head was separated from the rest of the bones, a good 2ft from the rest. It's coal-black eye sockets seemed to survey whatever we did, and I'd swear it moved as I scanned the chamber with the torch. It was just my imagination, the shadows playing tricks, but I didn't know what to expect next. I felt we were entirely dependent on Smelt's wishes, held hostage to a force we couldn't control. It was as though he was saying: "Don't turn round because you won't see me." I sensed that a lot. Those very words. And then he would answer himself: "You turned round, didn't you? But you didn't see me."

My mind was scrambled. There was no-one talking – get a grip!

William knew the bones were there, even though he had never seen them, so they were documented. But he didn't know for certain if it was the body of Smelt. However, he believed they were, and William was never wrong.

The skull was intact, no holes or indentations, no evidence there had been a head injury. But the hands and feet seemed to have had some kind of bone disease. They seemed brittle and easily broken, I would imagine. Then I noticed a chalk white patch in the soil as though someone had tried to treat the skeleton at some stage. I didn't know if the liquid, whatever it maybe, was to preserve or break down the bone.

"Take a couple of photos, Kimberley. Show the shape the skeleton is lying."

She leant forward and did as I asked, then backed away. I jumped into the pit to collect the bones and bag them. I picked up the skull first, noticing it was remarkably large for a human head. It looked Neanderthal. A very pronounced forehead and wide jaw with a couple of teeth missing. That was not the head of a modern human. Were Neanderthals human?

Once again, I felt a presence, but knocked the thought back. I sure as hell scare myself. I turned to look for Kimberley, who had been remarkably quiet for sometime, then I suffered the horror of horrors. She was 2ft off the floor, her body pinned against the wall by pressure being put on her throat. I'd heard all the tales from the past.

About Smelt's power and his mystifying ritual of hanging his victims like a crucifix on the wall. I'd read the stories about the damage he could do when the mood took him. But, this was different – it was not a story - it was for real! Fully formed, powerful, and grotesque. Pound for pound there was nothing I could do to stop him, but in that form … was he vulnerable? Could he bleed?

The main concern was getting his hand off Kimberley's throat, so as he had his back to me, I picked up a claw hammer and tried to wedged it into the back of his skull. His dirty stinking red hood stopped it penetrating the skull itself, but he rocked forward and loosened his grip on my daughter. I realised then, in that human form it was possible to hurt him physically. Kimberley fell to the floor, unconscious, and I tried to drag her clear by her arms. She was breathing but in ragged, shallow gasps. I had to get her away. But that meant carrying her up the stairs, and although Smelt was down – he was not out. I swung the hammer to hit him in the face but he parried the blow. I swung again and this time I beat his defence and caught him in the cheekbone. The bone shattered with a loud crunch. But he grabbed my hand and the hammer spun away under an old wooden workshop table. Once he had me in his clutches I knew I would never beat him for strength. I had to break away from his grasp, and quickly. He swung me round and threw me into a corner full of rusted metal junk. Old metal garden chairs and garden furniture. I clashed my head and split open my forehead, a gash two inches long. Blood ran and I lost my composure for a few seconds, but all I could think of was: "Don't let him get hold of you!"

He reached out and I pushed his hand away with a wooden pole that I found on the floor. But he had me trapped in the corner, and I had to fight my ground somehow. Then Fay appeared down the stairs, frantic and excitable, screaming and shouting. But it distracted Smelt for a moment, giving me just enough time to thrust one of the metal chairs in his face, adding to the pain of his smashed cheekbone. It rocked him, and I struck him again, trying to get myself out of that corner. But he grabbed my leg as I attempted to squeeze past him, pulling me to the dusty floor, getting the grip he wanted. I just knew he would try and break my leg and he had the strength to do it. I was exposed but I kicked out with the other leg, smacking him full in the mouth. I was giving as much as I was taking, but it wouldn't last for long.

Kimberley was not making a move, and I was desperate to get to her. That guy had ruined the lives of so many people and I wanted to rip him apart. I kicked and kicked but he squeezed my other leg, twisting me over with strength I have never known before, popping my knee-cap out of joint. The pain shot through my body right up to my brain. He had me where he wanted me. I believed I was finished. He let go, stood back knowing the fight was over and he could do whatever he wanted, He came at me, aiming for my throat. His trade-mark, 'pin them against the wall and squeeze the living daylights out of them, as you hang them up on a make-believe picture hook.' It was going to happen – and it would have happened – but Fay thrust a rusty old screwdriver into Smelt's left eye. She pulled away, leaving it embedded. He sent out an ear-piecing roar that rocked the building, and gave us some hope of a getaway.

"We can't kill him John," shouted Fay, "He won't die!"

"Get that hammer from under the table," I said pointing to the spot. "Get it Fay."

Smelt removed the screwdriver and we could see his legs begin to weaken. But he wouldn't go down. My leg was in agony, but I managed to edge nearer to Kimberley, while Fay recovered the hammer.

"Drop into the pit and smash up the bones, Fay. Every last one, starting with the skull."

Smelt made a lunge at her, throwing a fist at her face, but miraculously she ducked it. She was in the pit before he could launch another one. Smelt stood above her, looking on as she raised the hammer, then she crushed the skull with an almighty blow. She knew she had only one crack at swinging that hammer, and she wasn't going to fail. The skull crumbled into pieces as she pulverized it.

A sudden gust of pain jolted through Smelt's head as his face began to disfigure and crumble. At last we had found a way of damaging him. He had rebuilt and remodelled himself in the past, so there were no guarantees it would be permanent. He put his hands over his face in a futile effort to put it all back together again, but every feature was disfigured. The more bones Fay crushed, the more he suffered. He fell to his knees and his ribcage cracked like brittle twigs. He inhaled a trembling breath from lungs that were devoid of oxygen, pumped by a heart that was running out of time. Even if we were to end his life, I just knew, death would just be his next great adventure. I wanted him to say: "I've had enough, I want it to end," but not only was he unable to talk, he wouldn't give us that satisfaction. Even dying … he was prepared to do it one step at a time.

I wanted his final collapse to be spectacular and brutal. But he fell face-first and somehow melted away into an eerie grey/black shadow. He disappeared right in front of our eyes.

Kimberley was still unconscious, but her breathing seemed to be improving. I phoned for an ambulance, giving the Emergency Services a bullshit story about an accident involving a fall down some steps into a cellar.

"You BOTH fell down together?" asked the lady at the other end of the phone, seemingly doubting the story even before I got into full flow.

"Yes, the light went out and we lost our footing. I've broke my leg and my daughter is unconscious."

The greyness in her face had, all but, disappeared. All we needed was her to wake up. My leg was broken, my knee-cap was shattered, and muscle tissue was ripped. No way could I walk. Len brought us blankets and pillows and he made Kimberley as comfortable as he possibly could.

"What the hell happened here?" he asked, shining his torch in my face.

"We fell."

"What do we do now?" asked Fay.

"Could you do this for us? Put all of the bones in a bag and take them to the Wear and dump them in the river," I asked. "As quick as you can, before the police arrive. We have to get his presence away from here, Fay. I'm not convinced we have killed him, but if we haven't, let's make him someone else's problem."

She ran home across the building site to get her car, carrying the fragmented skeleton bones of a psychopath in a supermarket shopping carrier. That's something you don't see every day.

Len was persistent: "What REALLY happened, John?"

I had to give him something: "Once upon a time, in a place filled with evil, there a very nasty man who did horrific things to people. So those people opened the gate and sent him to Hell!"

He didn't answer, and I didn't expect him to.

"Don't worry Len, the innocent have nothing to fear. The ghost won't get you."

"The ghost? Is it dead?" he asked.

"I killed him once ... or twice … in a manner of speaking."

The sirens wailed and the blue light flickered. The cavalry had arrived.

In hospital the doctor didn't believe my account of events that Kimberley "caught her throat on a step as she fell." So the police got involved, as you would expect, suggesting there had been physical abuse. He wasn't wrong, but as was so often the case with Smelt, others got the blame. But I would rather DIE than be accused of abusing my own daughter.

The doctor explained the after affects of strangulation: "It can take less than ten seconds for a person to lose consciousness as a result of strangulation. However, if that happens – as it did in this case – it can cause psychological injury such as depression, severe stress or amnesia. There can be neurological injury such as loss of memory, facial paralysis and weakness down one side of the body."

"How is my daughter, at this moment?"

"She is awake," he replied.

"Are there any of the side effects you have spoken of?" I asked.

"Only time will tell."

The policeman interrupted: "She said someone tried to strangle her."

"Did she say it was her father? Because that is what has been suggested!" I asked.

"She wouldn't say who it was, but you were there Mr Hampson, you must know more about it than she does. She passed out."

"OK, I will tell you. The same person who tried to strangle my daughter had the strength to twist my knee-cap out of the socket and break my leg. I know you won't believe a single word of the description I would give you. Does my daughter or Mrs Jones have the strength to do that? Because, somebody did."

"We have some bad news about Mrs Jones, I'm afraid," said the policeman. "She won't be able to give her own account of the story."
I just knew ... the officer of the law didn't need to fill in the details. It hit me right between the eyes.

"My mother wanted a cremation," said Sarah. "She told me - 'Don't bother with a church I don't believe in, just take me straight to the oven.'"
Straight talking, but Fay (in the short time I knew her) was always the same. Selective in what she heard; but never selective in what she said. But I agreed with her choice of venue for the funeral. No matter what you choose to do with your body after death, it won't be very endearing
The police said she was involved in a "head-on car crash, and died at the scene of the accident." It happened less than 300yds from the Toll House, just minutes after she had left us.
Her death was the 'straw that broke the camel's back.' I will never recover from it. Do I blame myself because I sent her on that journey? Or was it wrong-place-wrong-time? It doesn't really matter. It was MY fault! And I was to blame for Sergio's death, too.
Of all the words spoken in sadness, the cruellest must surely be, "If only!"
Police forensics claim she was travelling too fast, and spotted a broken-down car just a little too late. She manoeuvred right, catching the back end of the parked car, then spun head-first into an on-coming van. She barely had time to scream before ploughing into the vehicle, killing herself and badly injuring the driver of the van.
She went through the delicate procedure of the break-up with Sergio, getting to un-know each other, then going through the reverse process when he returned. I don't think they ever fell out of love, they just fell out as friends, and that was the catastrophe.
I managed to get to Fay's funeral, released from hospital in a wheelchair for the day, pushed by Kimberley. Thanks to the grace of God, my daughter recovered fully and was out of hospital within three days. I wasn't so lucky. I had several operations, and treatment is still on-going. I will never walk properly again. But ... the bruising

on my leg showed large finger prints, proving it took a large person with enormous strength to do the damage it did.

When I was finally released from hospital, Kimberley and I went to the police compound and checked Fay's car, or what was left of it after the fire brigade had cut it open. There was no mention of a bag of bones in the police report, and we couldn't find them when we looked in the boot and back seat. She hadn't got to the river because the car was heading towards the city when it crashed.

———————————————————

In a world of diminishing mystery – the unknown is still out there. Trust me – it is. But be very careful. It's like the menu in a posh restaurant that doesn't show the prices. You know the secret is going to cost.

Smelt was guided by something, but whatever it was, it didn't want to take him.

Maybe ... the greatest trick Satin ever pulled on the living world ... was convincing us all there was only one of him!

The Toll House still remains, and just like Kimberley ... Len's dog still won't go anywhere near it.

ALSO FROM THIS AUTHOR:-

Kev Fletcher started writing professionally in the 1980's as a sports reporter, covering football for local newspapers and publications in the north-east of England.
It wasn't until 2016 that he ventured into the world of fiction, with his highly acclaimed novel *Visitor From The Somme*. A book portraying the life of a soldier in WW1 from a very unusual perspective.

That was followed by *Secret Gospel Of Holy Island*, a story with more twists and turns than a Sherlock Holmes mystery. It holds the reader from beginning to the end, culminating with a magical ending that took my breath away.

Kev can be contacted by e-mail: kevfootymad@gmail.com

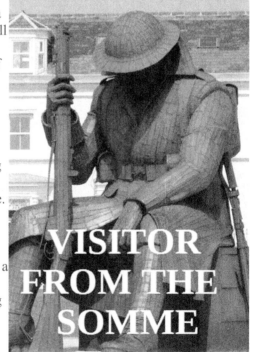

VISITOR FROM THE SOMME

"VISITOR FROM THE SOMME"

A six year old girl is visited periodically by the ghost of a soldier who fought and died in World War 1.
This action packed novel sees the young Private try, with the help of the child, to return to his past. But all is not as it seems.
There are many twists and turns in a tale that is both captivating and moving.

THE MAIL: *"The story is based on a real life situation. The soldier and the child did meet, and many of the war situations actually happened. Full of sympathetic characters, wild high-stakes adventures, and countless exciting details of life in the trenches. Hopefully the first instalment of this tale. There has to be a follow up."*

"THE SECRET GOSPEL OF HOLY ISLAND"

Holy Island. The jewel in Northumberland's historic and righteous crown. I'm sure it is, but a crown of gold or a crown of thorns?

34-year old Linda Wilson travels to Holy Island to walk in the footsteps of the past. To relive the memory of days she spent on the island with her husband, who recently passed away.

She comes across a 'stranger' who gradually transforms her life, not always for the good, in a tale that grips the reader from the first chapter.

The book is more fact than fiction, and all dates and historical references are true. The question is … what do they REALLY have hidden away on Lindisfarne?

THE MAIL: *"This is most possibly the WORST (or BEST depending what you go on) cliffhanger I have encountered in a long time. It leaves you more than just hanging, you are grasping for your life on a thread that is fraying and there is nothing to do but hold on. Brilliant ending."*

AVAILABLE FROM AMAZON AND LULU.COM

Printed in Great Britain
by Amazon

25675268R00116